C90 2205551

Kelly Elliott is a *New York Times* and *USA Today* bestselling contemporary romance author. Since finishing her bestselling Wanted series, Kelly continues to spread her wings while remaining true to her roots and giving readers stories rich with hot protective men, strong women and beautiful surroundings.

Kelly has been passionate about writing since she was fifteen. After years of filling journals with stories, she finally followed her dream and published her first novel, *Wanted*, in November of 2012.

Kelly lives in central Texas with her husband, daughter, and two pups. When she's not writing, Kelly enjoys reading and spending time with her family. She is down to earth and very in touch with her readers, both on social media and at signings.

Visit Kelly Elliott online:

www.kellyelliottauthor.com
www.twitter.com/author_kelly
www.facebook.com/KellyElliottAuthor/

D0865635

WITHDR
LI

THE LOVE WANTED IN TEXAS SERIES

Without You
Saving You
Holding You
Finding You
Chasing You
Loving You

WITHDRAWN FROM STOCK
IN LIBRARIES

Loving You

Love Wanted in Texas
Book Six

Kelly Elliott

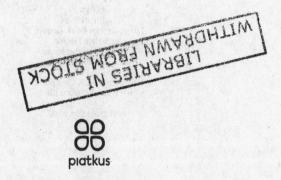

WITHDRAWN FROM STOCK
LIBRARIES IN

piatkus

PIATKUS

First published in Great Britain in 2016 by Piatkus
This paperback edition published in 2016 by Piatkus

1 3 5 7 9 10 8 6 4 2

Copyright © Kelly Elliott 2016

The moral right of the author has been asserted.

*All characters and events in this publication, other than those
clearly in the public domain, are fictitious and any resemblance
to real persons, living or dead, is purely coincidental.*

All rights reserved.
No part of this publication may be reproduced, stored in a
retrieval system, or transmitted in any form or by any means, without
the prior permission in writing of the publisher, nor be otherwise circulated
in any form of binding or cover other than that in which it is published
and without a similar condition including this condition
being imposed on the subsequent purchaser.

A CIP catalogue record for this book
is available from the British Library.

ISBN 978-0-349-41352-5

Printed and bound in Great Britain by
Clays Ltd, St Ives plc

Papers used by Piatkus are from well-managed forests
and other responsible sources.

MIX
Paper from
responsible sources
FSC
www.fsc.org   FSC® C104740

Piatkus
An imprint of
Little, Brown Book Group
Carmelite House
50 Victoria Embankment
London EC4Y 0DZ

An Hachette UK Company
www.hachette.co.uk

www.piatkus.co.uk

Dedication

THIS BOOK IS dedicated to everyone who has ever picked up and read *Wanted* or *Broken* and fell in love with these amazing families. Thank you for being a part of this journey with me.

"Family is like music. Some high notes, some low notes, but always a beautiful song."

WANTED
family tree

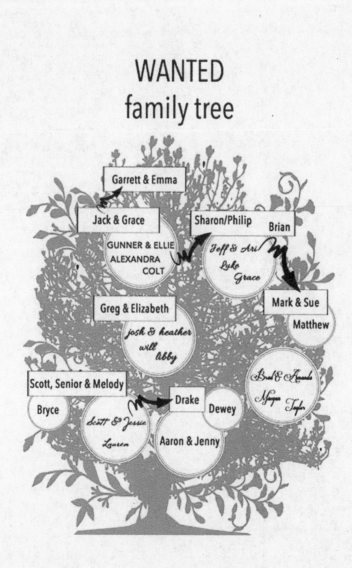

One

Taylor

July—Paris, France

I STOOD FROZEN as I stared at the Mona Lisa while everyone around me went on about some café we were headed to after this. Doing my best, I tried to ignore the fact that Jase kept staring at me. It was our sixth and final day in France and I had somehow avoided him successfully the entire trip. Of course, the fact that Cammie never left his side was another reason I had successfully kept my distance.

"Qu'en pensez-vous? Elle est belle, est-elle pas?"

With a quick look to my left, I saw my French professor standing next to me.

"I think it's amazing and yes she is beautiful," I beamed.

"As is your French, Taylor. Please don't lose it."

Glancing down, I nodded my head. I'd been taking French since high school and loved it. At one point I thought I wanted to move to France, until my father told me I'd break my mother's heart and put him in an early grave if I followed such a dream.

"We're going to be headed out for lunch after this."

With a weak smile, I nodded my head and replied, "I'm not feeling that great, Professor Beaumont. I'm going to head back to the hotel and rest."

Her hand immediately touched my forehead as she frowned. "You don't feel hot."

"No, I think I'm tired and in need of some alone time. I have a book I'm ready to crawl into bed with."

She frowned as she said, "I know you're staying on a few extra days along with a few other students, but this is our last day out as a group. Are you sure you're not feeling up to it?"

My eyes shot over to where Jase was. He was standing in a small group of people, but his stare caught mine. His angelic blue eyes stood out even more against his dark hair.

Professor Beaumont's voice pulled my attention away from Jase. I gave her a pleasant smile and replied, "I'm positive. With me staying on a few extra days, I think it's best if I rest up a bit."

With a sad expression, she nodded her head, turned, and headed over to the group.

"Okay, listen up. I know you're all adults and some of you have opted to stay on a few days after the tour ends this evening. Taylor is not feeling well and will be heading back to the hotel, so if you're not staying the extra days or going to dinner tonight, and you want to say goodbye to her . . . now is the time."

My mouth dropped open as all eyes were now pinned on me.

"You're going back to your hotel?" Jase asked as I shot Professor Beaumont a dirty look.

Clearing my throat, I gave my best smile and said, "I am. I'll see y'all for dinner though; I wouldn't miss it for the world."

Ugh. The last thing I wanted to do was sit through dinner and have to listen to some of the pompous classmates I'd been forced to deal with the last few years. Especially Cammie North, who currently wore a smile so big she could light up the entire Paris skyline at night. She had been trying like hell to get Jase to spend time with her the entire trip.

After the tour, everyone decided to head back to the hotel to change before heading to lunch. Sitting down on the bed, I dropped back and let out a moan. Every time I stole a peek at Jase he was watching me. I loved it and hated it at the same time. With him I didn't know whether I was coming or going. Did he like me? Did he not like me?

Sighing, I tried to wipe all things Jase Morris from my mind.

The knock on the door had me sitting up quickly. "Damn it," I whispered as I got up and headed to the door.

Throwing it open, I started talking. "Professor Beaumont, I really don't—"

Jase stood in front of me with a grin that showcased both dimples, and eyes that sparkled like diamonds.

"Jase? Wh-what are you doing here?"

"I wasn't hungry."

My eyes narrowed as I gave him an uncertain look. "So you thought you'd come to my room? Why?"

He took a few steps closer to me, causing me to back into the room. "Because I can't stop thinking about you."

With a heavy heartbeat, I stood tall and in my place. I was not going to let him see how his words affected me. "Jase, I'm not going to play games with you. This push and pull thing has gotten old and honestly, I'm done playing it."

His eyes fell to the floor as he took in a slow deep breath. My breathing was so labored I was sure he noticed.

"I've been an asshole and I know it." He pierced me with his blue eyes. "I want so badly to be the perfect guy for you because perfect is what you deserve, Taylor. If I was half the man my father raised me to be, I'd walk away from you forever."

I slowly shook my head. "Why do you think you're not good enough for me? You've never even given us a chance."

A wicked smile spread over his face while his eyes turned dark. "When I think about you all I can think about is taking your innocence. I want to bury myself so deep inside of you I forget everything and everyone around me until I'm consumed by only you."

My breath hitched as I reached out for something to hold on to. "I thought you weren't interested in me and that's why you moved on."

His gruff laugh felt like a slap. "Moved on? You think I've moved on?"

Anger quickly engulfed my body. "Yes, I think you've moved on.

You act like you want me, Jase. Then the next thing I know you're out with different women and not even looking twice at me. It's as if I don't even exist to you. And I'm sorry, but I think I deserve someone who wants me."

His brows pinched together. "You think I don't want you?"

I knew the moment I spoke my voice would tremble. Admitting what had been swirling around in my head for months proved to be harder than I thought. It needed to be said, and even though I was scared to death it might push him away, I forced it out.

"I'm a virgin and that scares you. Admit it. I'm not experienced enough for you, so you take up with women who know what they're doing."

Jase slowly shook his head. "I want you more than the air I breathe. I've woken up countless nights because I can't get you out of my head. My dreams and thoughts are consumed by you. You make it seem like I'm sleeping around with a million different girls. I've made a few mistakes, Taylor, and I've done some things I'm ashamed of and the last thing I'd ever want to do is hurt you."

My mouth parted open to talk, but I quickly lost my words.

"Taylor, I've never been so attracted to a woman before like I am you. From the first moment I saw you I knew you were different. *That* is what scares me. *That* is why I'm so confused. You have the power to bring me to my knees and destroy my entire world."

A single tear rolled down my cheek. "I don't want to destroy your world, Jase. I want to be a part of it. Why won't you make love to me? Why am I not even worth the chance to try?"

Walking all the way into the room, he shut the door behind him. Cupping my face with his hands, he leaned down and brushed his lips against mine. "Taylor, why aren't you listening to what I'm saying? Please listen to me when I say I'm the one not good enough for you."

It was time to speak from my heart. I wanted Jase to be the one to take my virginity. I wanted to look into his eyes as he made love to me. I wanted him more than I wanted anything in my life.

"Make love to me, Jase. *Please* want me."

His eyes looked lost for a moment, as if he was battling an internal struggle. "Sweetness, I want you more than anything. Are you sure you want to do this? Once it's done, there is no taking it back," he whispered as he gazed into my eyes.

"I've never been so sure of anything in my entire life."

The smile that spread across his face caused me to do the same. "Taylor," he whispered before pressing his lips to mine. I'd never experienced such a kiss before, and I knew no other man would ever be able to make me feel that way again.

He frowned and his eyes looked so confused. "I don't want to hurt you, Taylor."

Taking a step back, I lifted my shirt over my head and tossed it to the floor. "Then go slow," I spoke in a quiet voice as I stepped out of my shorts and stood before Jase in nothing but a lace push-up bra and matching panties.

My stomach felt as if it was flipping from a thrill ride when Jase licked his lips and let his eyes move over my body. "My God, you're absolutely perfect. So damn beautiful."

The way he looked at me did weird things to not only my stomach, but my heart as well. "Are you just going to stand there and look at me?"

Shaking his head, he took a few steps closer and pulled the T-shirt he had on off. Trying not to react to his perfect body, I suppressed the moan I wanted to let out.

He had the most amazing body with abs to die for. Good lord he had that ever-loving V that was plunging into his jeans. "Sweet Jesus," I mumbled as he smiled and unbuttoned his jeans.

"I want to kiss every inch of your body. Touch you until you beg me for more."

My eyes snapped up to his as I took a few steps back and hit the bed. "I've never . . . I mean . . . I haven't ever . . ."

Swallowing hard, I watched as he pushed his jeans down and his dick sprung out.

Oh no. He's huge!

Panic filled my body as I continued to stare at him.

It's never going to fit.

When his hands touched my arms, I jumped. "Hey. If you're not ready for this, we don't have to do anything."

Slowly shaking my head, I looked up as I clamped down on my lip.

"No. It's just I've never seen a man naked before and I need a second to . . . to um . . ."

The thoughtful smile that spread over his face made me blush. "You are so innocent; it makes me want you more."

Taking a deep breath, I closed my eyes as I felt his hand on my cheek. "Talk to me, sweetness."

My breath hitched as I looked into his beautiful blue eyes. "I'm scared."

"Of me?"

My eyes drifted away before locking back onto his. "In part. You have invaded my thoughts and dreams for so long. I can't tell you the countless nights I've dreamt of this moment."

His eyes burned with something I'd never seen before. "It's the same for me. I've pushed you away for so long because I'm afraid."

My brows lifted. "Of?"

"Hurting you. Not being good enough for you. I could keep going on."

"That's nothing but nonsense."

He shook his head. "Not to me. I look at you and all I can think of is if you married me you'd be stuck in Llano being a rancher's wife and that's not what you deserve."

My heart pounded in my chest. *Married?*

"Aren't you jumping a little ahead?" I asked with a giggle.

Jase attempted to hold back a smile. "I guess so, but those are the things that have invaded my thoughts."

This was the moment I had been longing for. Waiting for. There was no way I was going to let our stupid fears get in the way.

"Make love to me, Jase. I don't want to think about anything else but you and me together."

Two

Taylor

MY CHEST HEAVED as he reached behind me and unclasped my bra, letting it slowly slip down my arms until it fell to the floor. When his hand cupped my breast and his mouth sucked on a nipple, my head dropped back as the pleasure rushed through my body.

"Oh God," I whimpered.

I'd never felt like this before and I wasn't sure what I was supposed to do.

Whispering his name seemed the logical thing to do . . . that and take his dick in my hand, causing him to moan while he gently bit down on my nipple. It felt so soft, yet so hard.

Sucking in a breath, my body shuddered as his lips moved across my neck while I continued to stroke him.

Once my other nipple was in his mouth, I was sure I had died and gone to heaven.

What would the rest of it feel like? Would it hurt? Surely it would.

I'd listened to my sister and the girls talk about how the first time was not so great. If anything, they had wished for it to be over quickly.

I couldn't imagine wanting this to end. Ever.

"I want to taste you, sweetness." Jase spoke against my skin as he peppered kisses down my body until he was on his knees. I missed the feel of him in my hand the moment he was gone.

"Yes," I mumbled as I reached up and touched my sensitive nipples.

"Fuck that is hot as hell."

My mind was spinning. *What was hot as hell?* Lifting my head, I stared down at him looking up at me. "Wh-what?"

"You touching yourself. It's driving me crazy."

It was then I really noticed what I was doing and I dropped my hands. Jase smiled as he slowly peeled my lace panties off.

My breathing grew heavier as I fought to drag in one breath after another.

"So beautiful," he whispered as I stepped out of my panties and he ran his hand up the inside of my leg. "Sit down on the bed."

Before I had a moment to think, I did as he said. He was still on his knees as he moved forward a bit more and ran both hands over my legs, causing a shiver to run over my body.

"I want to memorize every inch of your body."

Slowly pushing my legs apart, he kissed the inside of my thigh.

Oh God. I've never felt so amazing.

"Lay back, sweetness, while I taste you."

My eyes widened in horror. "You're going to . . . down there?"

With a wicked smile, he winked at me before he buried his face between my legs.

"Ohmygod!" I cried out as I felt his tongue slip inside of me. Something raced through my veins as I dropped back and grabbed the bedding with my hands. My back arched while I took in the sheer pleasure of his mouth on me.

This. Is. Freaking. Amazing.

"Jesus, you're so wet."

I hissed as I felt his finger push into me. It wasn't like the feeling was new. I had given myself plenty of orgasms, but *his* finger in me. *That* did something to me.

"So tight. So perfect."

His mouth was on me again, licking and sucking as my body shook with anticipation.

"Yes . . . oh God!" I cried out, not caring how loud I was or who might hear.

I felt him push another finger in. Pleasure and pain hit me at the same time.

"Jase!" I cried out as my orgasm started from the tip of my toes and moved up. Angling my body to just the right position, he took me to a place I'd never been before.

I slammed my hand over my mouth to hide the screams of absolute pleasure in case anyone was still here at the hotel and had not left for lunch yet.

When I finally felt myself coming back to earth, I felt Jase's body over mine. He was kissing along my neck as I wrapped my legs around him, pulling him closer to me.

"I want to kiss you," he panted in my ear.

"Kiss me! God Jase, I want more of you!"

The desperation in my voice shocked me as I begged him for more. When his lips pressed to mine, I swore I tasted blood before I tasted myself. Never in a million years would I ever think I'd let a guy go down on me and then kiss him.

Jase was no ordinary guy. He was so much more.

When we finally needed air, he pulled away and stared into my eyes for what seemed like forever.

"Condom, Taylor, I need a condom."

My chest tightened. "Please tell me you have one."

With a smile that caused my stomach to flip, he said, "I'd have never come to your room without one." I lifted a brow as he pushed off me and laughed. "Hopeful, I was very hopeful."

He reached into his jeans and pulled out his wallet. Ripping the condom open, I watched him put it on.

"I wish you would have let me do that."

He let out a huff and shook his head. "If I had let you put that on I'd have embarrassed myself."

"Oh," was all I managed to say.

With his eyes sparkling like I'd never seen them before, he crawled over me again and pushed himself against my already sensitive clit.

"Promise me you'll tell me if I'm hurting you."

I nodded. "I promise."

His hand moved between my legs as he pushed his fingers inside of me. I moaned in pleasure as he moved faster. I could feel the build up again.

"Jase! I want you inside of me," I cried out as he pressed his thumb on my clit, causing my orgasm to erupt like a volcano. His mouth captured my moans as I felt his hand retreat and he positioned himself and slowly pushed in as my body was still riding from my high.

"Fucking hell," he hissed against my mouth. "Oh God, you feel amazing."

Pressing my lips together, I held my breath as he slowly pushed in more and pulled out. Each movement was laced in both pleasure and pain, but more the later.

"Relax, sweetness, you've got to relax."

With a deep breath in, I relaxed my body as I released the air, letting Jase take me.

"Jase," I whispered as he stopped. "No, don't stop!"

"Are you okay?"

"Please don't stop."

His lips softly kissed mine as he pushed in further. I'd never felt so full and complete in my entire life. The burning would have been worse had it not been for him kissing me. I fought to keep my tears back. The pain was more than I thought it would have been.

His lips pulled back and he stopped moving. "I'm all the way in, baby."

My eyes closed as he kissed the tip of my nose, then my lips and along my jaw.

"Jase," I whispered as I wrapped my arms around him. I loved that he had little nicknames for me. Each time he called me sweetness or baby, my heart melted.

He slowly moved in and out. It was like nothing I would ever be able to describe.

Pulling his head back, his blue eyes captured my gaze. "It's probably way too early to say this, but I love you, Taylor. I've loved you from the first moment I saw you."

A single tear slowly made its way down my cheek as I replied, "I love you too. I'll always love you."

Something moved across his face, but was gone as quickly as it came.

He moved again, this time he was not so in control as he moved faster. My body fought between it hurting like hell and feeling amazing. My hips found a rhythm as I kept up with him. I'd heard friends talk about never being able to have orgasms during sex, and some had them all the time. I knew I was going to be keeping company with the ones who did as my entire body became enflamed.

"Jase," I panted out. "I'm going to come again. Oh God! Oh God!"

"Fuck!" he called out as he pushed in hard and fast and called out my name.

We had come together. It was the perfect ending to a beautiful moment.

Nothing would ever be the same again.

Nothing.

Three

Jase

"WHEN CAN WE do that again?" Taylor asked with a giggle.

We laid on the bed as I held her in my arms, still relishing in the high from making love to her.

"I think I need lunch, then maybe we can sneak back up here."

Resting her chin on my chest, she flashed me a smile that caused my stomach to drop. "Lunch? I am kind of hungry."

I nodded my head. "Let me go back to my room and change. I'll meet you down at the hotel restaurant in fifteen minutes."

Her eyes lit up as I pulled her up and kissed her. The soft moan that escaped from her lips made my body instantly warm.

When our lips parted, we held each other's gaze. "Finally," she whispered with the sweetest smile.

A lump formed in my throat. I felt like a dick for all the times I led her on, only to push her way. My own stupid insecurities played a role in that and I still wasn't sure if I was the guy she needed. That first night alone in her apartment when she told me her dreams of wanting to become a financial analyst for her grandfather's company in Austin,

I knew she would never be happy being a rancher's wife. It was my dream. Not hers.

I made it down to the restaurant with a few minutes to spare when I saw Cammie North walking up to me.

"Fuck," I mumbled under my breath.

"Where were you?" she asked with a fake smile.

We had messed around a few times and had one crazy night I wanted to forget and put behind me. The best thing for me to do was nip this shit in the bud. "I was with Taylor."

Her eyes turned dark. "Taylor?"

"Yes, Cammie, Taylor. We're together now, so whatever fun you and I had in the past, it's in the past."

Something moved over her face. "What would Taylor think if she knew you got drunk and fucked me and then my best friend?"

I grabbed onto her arm and pulled her closer to me. "Are you trying to threaten me?"

Her eyes searched my face before letting out a curt laugh. "With that little bit of information? No. I highly doubt she'd care she is so fucking infatuated with you."

With a glance over my shoulder, she looked back and kissed me before I could stop her. Grabbing onto her, I pushed her away while she let out a chuckle.

"Listen, I don't know what game you're playing here, Cammie, but I'm not interested in you."

Something evil moved over her face. "You'll never make her happy, you know that right?"

My hand pushed through my hair as I sighed. "So you've told me before."

"Your little princess would never be happy playing farm girl after she lands her dream job."

My heart felt as if someone was squeezing it. "And you would?" I asked.

Taking a step closer to me, she nodded her head and went to grab my dick. Pushing her away again, she softly said, "To have you every day for the rest of my life. Yes, I would be very happy. But I'm warning you, if you walk away from me Jase Morris, it will be the biggest mistake of your life."

Letting out a laugh, I replied, "I'll take my chances."

Turning, I saw Taylor standing there. She looked over my shoulder at Cammie.

"Think she saw the kiss?" Cammie whispered as she walked past me. "Hey, Taylor. Hope you're feeling better. You look awful."

Taylor shot daggers at Cammie as she walked by.

"Don't listen to her, Taylor. She's a bitch."

When she looked back at me, she asked, "What happened?"

I knew it was best to be honest with Taylor. For all I knew she had seen Cammie kiss me.

"She kissed me, but I pushed her away immediately. She was just trying to cause trouble like always."

Glancing down, she pressed her lips together before looking back up at me. "Is she one of the girls you've slept with before?"

I wanted to tell her no, but I would never lie to her. "Yes."

"I see."

Taking her by the arms, I pulled her closer to me. "It's my past, Taylor, and it has nothing to do with us right now. I swear to you, nothing has happened between us in over a year."

"Okay," she barely spoke.

Placing my finger on her chin, I lifted her eyes to mine. "I swear to you. Please say you believe me."

She paused for longer than I wanted her to before she offered a weak smile and said, "I believe you."

"Let's eat okay, sweetness?"

She nodded as I slipped my hand around her waist and led her to the restaurant.

After we ordered drinks, Taylor and I quickly forgot about Cammie.

"So, what are your plans once we get back to Texas?" I asked as I took a bite of food.

Her smile lit up as she said, "I'm starting work for my grandfather. He's offered me an analyst position within his company."

My stomach twisted and Cammie's words rushed through my head. *How would this work between us if she worked in Austin and I worked in Llano?*

"That's awesome," I said with a forced smile.

"What about you?" she asked.

With a hard swallow, I reached for my beer and took a drink. "I'll be heading to Llano to work on my father's ranch full time."

Her smile faded as she looked down at her food and pushed it around. "How often will I get to see you?" Glancing up, she continued to talk. "I mean, with you living in Llano and me in Austin, how are we . . . I mean . . . I could always go part-time at my grandfather's company."

It was then I realized I could never let Taylor walk away from her dream . . . no matter how much I loved her. I knew what I had to do and it was going to destroy both of us in the process, but it was the only thing I could think of.

Taking in a deep breath, I slowly blew it out. "This isn't going to work."

Her eyes widened in shock. "Wh-what isn't going to work?"

"This. Us. I mean, if you're going to be starting a new position within your family's business, you'll be working long hours. I'll be working long hours and we'll be almost three hours away from each other."

Slowly shaking her head, her mouth parted open. "What are you doing, Jase? Do you regret what happened between us?"

"What? No!" I gasped. "What happened between us earlier was the best thing that has ever happened to me."

Tears filled her eyes. "Why do you keep doing this?"

"I . . . I'm just not sure I deserve you and I would never want you to leave your job because of me."

"Why do you think you don't deserve you?"

My eyes looked over at Cammie who was sitting at the bar watching everything. I knew if given the chance she would tell Taylor about the night I spent with her and her friend.

Pushing my hand through my hair, I lowered my voice. "I've done something in my past I'm not proud of and if you ever found out about it . . . you might think differently of me."

Her eyes widened in shock. "You think that little of me? So you have a past? I don't care about that."

My head was spinning. "I want to feel like I deserve you, Taylor.

I've never felt this way about anyone before."

Taylor stood, pushing her chair back. "But yet you sit here and tell me it won't work. I should have known you would do this. You got what you wanted and you're casting me to the side . . . again. My sister was right about you."

Pinching my eyebrows together, I stood up. "What? That's not what I'm doing at all. I love you, Taylor, and I only want to do what is best for you."

"So, fucking me and then telling me it won't work is best for me?"

I quickly glanced around before turning back to her. "No, wait, that's not what I meant."

She held up her hand. "Are you with Cammie also?"

My head jerked back. "You're seriously going to ask me that after what happened between us today?"

With a shrug, she stared at me. "Well, I don't know, Jase. Maybe there is more to you I don't know about." She folded her arms across her chest while waiting for an answer. *How could she think I would do that to her?* "No, I'm not with Cammie. I'm not with anyone."

Hurt instantly washed over her face as I pushed the chair back and walked away. Before I was even out the door, Cammie was walking up to me and following me out.

"It would have never worked, Jase. You have to know that."

Once I stepped outside, the humid air hit me and took my breath. I turned to the left and walked. I had no idea where I was even going. Cammie followed me for a bit before I stopped and looked at her. "Leave me alone for fucks sake, Cammie."

Her jaw tightened as she narrowed her eyes in anger. "Are you dismissing me?"

With a roll of my eyes, I shook my head. "Fucking hell yes! I don't want to have anything to do with you."

She shook her head. "You just made the biggest mistake of your life, Jase Morris."

"Somehow I think the biggest mistake of my life was walking away from Taylor just now."

Four

Jase

October—Llano Texas

I SAT AND stared out over the pasture as my father went on and on about Ava breaking her leg and staying back in Montana.

"I'm sure she's gonna be fine, Dad. Stop worrying."

"Did you even hear a damn word I just said?"

Turning to face him, I gave him a blank expression. I'd spent the last few minutes dreaming of my lips on Taylor. Hearing her soft moans as I made love to her. "Yeah, you're going on and on about Ava."

He pinched his eyebrows and shook his head. "Son, I haven't said a damn thing about Ava in at least ten minutes. Don't tell me you've been sitting there nodding your head and mindlessly answering me."

"Um . . ."

He shook his head and walked over to the fence we had just finished repairing. "Do you see this fence?"

Okay, where is he going with this?

"Yes. I see the fence."

"I might as well have been talking to it for the last hour. What in the world is weighing on your mind, son? You haven't been yourself ever since you got back from Europe, and I swear if I didn't know any better I'd say your favorite horse died this morning with the way you're sulking."

Jumping off the tailgate, I smiled. "I'm not sulking and nothing is wrong. I'm just tired I guess. Went out last night with a few friends."

He lifted his brow and gave me that look when he doesn't believe that line I'm feeding him. "Tired? Well you better snap the hell out of it."

I gathered up the tools and put them in the bed of the truck before facing him and asking, "How did you know Mom was the one?"

He stopped and looked at me. It never failed, any time he talked about or thought of my mother his eyes lit up. With a chuckle, he shook his head as if lost in a memory.

"The first time I met your mother I wasn't sure if I wanted to kiss her or strangle her."

"That's funny, Mom says the same thing about you."

A roar of laughter escaped from his lips. "Yeah well, there was an attraction there from the very beginning. One I'd never felt before, so that was probably my first clue. Then my desire to protect her from everything and everyone was most likely the second clue."

"You never felt that with any other girl besides Mom?"

He shrugged and replied, "I'm sure to some point, but with your mother everything was different. She consumed my every thought. One day it hit me how much I cared for her, but I was stupid."

"What do you mean?"

"I pushed her away because I didn't think I was good enough for her."

My heart dropped as I listened to my father.

"She walked away from me and it felt like I couldn't breathe. I knew in that moment, I wouldn't ever be able to live without her. Life just wouldn't be the same if she wasn't by my side, so I went after her and told her how I felt."

I reached for the fence pulls and sighed. "What if you feel all of that, but if you follow your heart, you risk making her unhappy?"

"How would you make her unhappy if you follow your heart and it leads you to love?"

"I don't know, say she isn't a country girl. She wants a life in the city, working and doing the whole corporate world thing. I mean, Mom already lived here."

He leaned against the truck and studied me. "Talk to me, Jase."

I dropped my head. "Shit," I mumbled under my breath. "I messed up, Dad."

"You messed up how?"

"Taylor. The first time I saw her it felt like the air around me changed. She smiled and I was lost in her eyes. I hadn't ever seen a girl so beautiful before. Everything about her was perfect, especially the little dimple that only comes out when you really make her laugh. Every time I saw it I had to fight the urge to kiss her."

Glancing over to my father, he smiled and motioned with his head for me to keep talking.

"I tried like hell to stay away from her." With a chuckle, I looked at him and asked, "Do you remember when I went to Durango that summer?"

He nodded.

"She was there. I couldn't believe it when she walked up to me and told me about some stupid bet she was in with her sister and friends. It was almost like a sign or something. Anyway, I ran into her one day back at school and ended up going back to her apartment. Things started to get a bit . . . heavy . . . but she stopped it and dropped the news on me that she was a virgin."

"Oh God," my father whispered. "Please tell me you didn't?"

My father and I had always had such a close relationship. Finally being able to allow myself to talk to him about what was going on was somewhat of a relief. I knew he would listen and not judge me.

"As much as I wanted to, nothing happened. She wanted to stop, so we did. I respected her too much. But then she started talking about her plans after school and how she wanted to be some financial analyst for her grandfather and it hit me. Our lives would never go down the same path."

With a huff, he shook his head. "Why?"

"Dad, for one, she's way too good for me. Beautiful, smart as hell, and wants a life in the city. I'm a rancher. My life consists of mending fences, raising cows, and coming home smelling like fucking hell."

He lifted a brow. "Do you wish you had gone a different route?"

I sighed heavily. "No. I mean at one point I wasn't sure, but I know this is the life for me. This is the life I want and I would never ask her to give up her dreams to be with me."

"So instead you told her how you felt?"

"Um . . . not exactly. I ignored her mostly."

His hands slapped against his face as he made some horrible sounds and dragged them down before dropping them to his sides. "You ignored the girl?"

"Mostly. When I couldn't take it, I'd send her a text or talk to her just to hear her voice. Dad, I'm no good for her. I fucking woke up with a girl in my bed one night after seeing Taylor at a party. I got so drunk I screwed around with two different women. Who does that kind of shit if they care about someone else? The guilt about tore me in two. I had to tell her about it just to get it off my chest."

His mouth fell open. "You . . . you didn't. You told her that?"

I slowly nodded my head. "Well, I kind of left out the fact I had slept with two girls on the same night and mentioned just the one." He pushed off from the truck and walked up to me and slapped the living shit out of the back of my head. "What kind of idiot did I raise? First off, don't ever mention the other girl to her. She doesn't need to know what one stupid drunk night led you to do." Shaking his head, he asked, "Why in the world would you tell a girl about sleeping with another girl?"

"I-I don't know! She confuses me!"

He shook his head. "She confuses you? Tell me you didn't do anything else to hurt this poor girl."

I swallowed hard. "I um . . . I tried to stay away from her, Dad. I honestly did, but every time I would look at her, she would be looking at me. I thought we could make it work."

His face fell. "What. Did. You. Do?"

I dropped my hands to my knees as I tried to bring air into my lungs. "It was in Paris. I couldn't take it any longer. I needed to tell her how much I wanted her and loved her."

"Loved her?"

"She skipped lunch and I went to her hotel room."

"Oh mother of God, I'm not liking where this is going. Did you say you loved her?"

I dragged in a deep breath. "Yes, Dad. I said I love her."

He swallowed hard and motioned for me to keep talking. "I told her I didn't think I was good enough for her and she said it was nonsense. She asked me to make love to her and . . . and . . . I did. I made her mine."

Standing up, I turned to him. "I told her I loved her and she told me she loved me and always would. That freaked the hell out of me. Afterwards, I ran into Cammie who told me Taylor would never be happy with me and I freaked out."

"Who is Cammie and define you freaked out?"

"Cammie is the girl I slept with that I told Taylor about."

He nodded his head. "The freaking out? What did you do?"

"I told Taylor things between us wouldn't work and she got upset."

He let out a curt laugh and walked away from me as he said, "I would imagine she would be upset seeing as you just had sex with her. Tell me, was she still a virgin, and please for the love of all that is good in this world say no."

I frowned and shook my head. "I did what I thought was best. If I kept acting like everything was okay, we would have grown apart and you know I'm right. She would have been in Austin and me here. How would that have worked, Dad? I mean, when I talk to her I can still feel—"

He opened the door to the truck, grabbed something and then slammed it shut before walking over to me.

"When you talk to her? You still talk to this girl?"

"Of course I do. I love and care about her."

His mouth fell open. "Listen to what you just said. You have toyed with this girl's heart, Jase. You took her virginity, told her you loved her and then five minutes later told her things wouldn't work out, yet you still talk to her?"

"I love her, Dad! I can't help the way I feel."

My father scrubbed his hands down his face and moaned. "That poor girl. If I was her father I'd hunt you down and shoot you in the balls."

I moved my hand and adjusted myself. The very thought of being shot in the balls made my stomach turn.

"I said I messed up!"

He shook his head and pointed his finger at me. I'd never seen my dad so mad before. "No, Jase, you didn't mess up. You fucked up. You royally fucked up."

I closed my eyes and silently cursed myself. "I know and I feel like I can't function right. My sleeping is off, I never feel like eating, and yesterday she said she had a date."

"Good. I'm glad she had a date. You can't take something like that from someone and then change your mind. You deserve whatever punishment she gives you."

My mouth snapped shut as I stared at him.

"She is moving on. Jase, if you have no intention of making a future with this girl, you have to let her go."

I'd never in my life felt the urge to cry. Except for when my mother accidentally dumped my fish into the garbage disposal. I actually cried then. Poor, Shark. He didn't stand a chance.

"I can't let her go." Turning away before the threat of tears turned into a water show, I shook my head. "I can't let her go, Dad."

His hand gripped my shoulder as he squeezed it. "Jase, you either love this girl enough to let her go, or you go after her and drop down on your knees and beg her to forgive the stupid ass way you handled things. If it's meant to be, love will figure out a way."

With a slight push, he mumbled something about the apple not falling far. "Come on, let's get this stuff put in the truck and get back to the house. Your mother will have dinner ready soon."

The entire ride back to the house I stared out the window. My heart told me what I should do, if only my head had the same plan.

Five

Taylor

"HOW WAS THE date?"

Gazing down at my beautiful niece, Charlotte, I smiled and said, "It was okay."

"Okay? That's it?"

With a shrug, I made baby sounds while Charlotte stared off into space. "Yep. That's it."

"Huh."

Glancing over my shoulder, I stared at my sister. "What's that supposed to mean?"

With a shrug of her shoulders and a smirk, she replied, "Nothing. It's just you haven't really been the same since your little encounter with Jase in Paris."

The mention of his name had my body reacting. "I don't want to talk about him."

"Huh."

"Ugh. Stop saying that, Meg!"

"I'm not saying anything."

I placed Charlotte in her bassinet and sighed as I fell back onto the couch. "You're implying something."

"I'm doing no such thing."

Peeking over to Grace, I couldn't help but notice her holding back a smile as she held her son, Trey, in her lap. "What are you smiling about?" I snapped.

"Damn girl, settle your tits. I'm not smiling about anything."

Turning to look at Meagan, Grace frowned as Meagan said, "Told you."

Standing, I shook my head. "So, I hardly ever get to come to town and hang out with y'all and this is how it's going to be?"

"Sorry, Tay, it's not fair of us. We'll stop," Meagan said as Grace laughed.

"The hell we will. I'm guessing by your bitch mood you're in, the date didn't go like you planned and you most likely thought about Jase the entire night."

"I did not."

Grace lifted her eyes and gave me a *really* look.

"As much as I love hanging out here, I think I'm going to go visit Lauren. *She* won't mention Jase."

Grace made a huff sound as my sister laughed.

Twenty minutes later I was knocking on my best friend Lauren's door.

"Oh my glitter! Tay, what are you doing here?"

I couldn't help but smile as I took in Lauren. Something was different about her. Her face seemed to be glowing.

"Just wanted to come visit everyone. I was missing home."

Pulling me in, Lauren engulfed me in a hug and started crying.

"It's . . . so . . . good . . . to . . . see . . . you!"

I patted her back as I replied, "It's good seeing you too, sweetie." Pulling back, I looked at her cautiously. "Lauren, is everything okay?"

With a wave of her hand, she nodded. "Yep. I'm just so happy to see you."

I had known Lauren my whole life and I knew something was not right. She was never this emotional. "Did you and Colt have a fight?"

Her head pulled back in surprise. "What? God no! Everything with

Colt is amazing. It's beyond amazing."

Breaking down into tears again, I wrapped my arms around her and led her over to the couch. "Please tell me what's wrong, Lauren."

She wiped her tears away and smiled. "Oh, Tay, nothing is wrong. Everything is perfect. It's amazing. It's beyond amazing."

Her eyes were a beacon of happiness. "Yes. You've already said that. Dang, you must have had some good sex this morning to be in this good of a mood."

With a slight push, she shook her head. "I'm about to burst!"

"With?"

Placing her hand over her mouth, her eyes teared up again.

"Okay, you're freaking me out. Are you about to burst because something happy has happened?"

She nodded.

"With you?"

She nodded again.

I laughed and said in a kidding tone, "You're pregnant."

Lauren stared at me with the biggest smile on her face I'd ever seen.

"Oh. My. Lauren! You're pregnant?"

We both jumped up at once and wrapped each other up in a hug while jumping like fools.

"I'm pregnant!"

"You're pregnant!"

When we finally settled down, I held her out at arm's length. "No wonder you're glowing. I noticed it the moment you opened the door. When did you find out?"

"Ten minutes ago!"

"Oh wow . . . wait. What? You *just* found out?"

She jumped up and down as she screamed out, "Yes!"

"Holy . . ."

"Shit! Holy shit!" Lauren said as she grabbed my hand and pulled me to the master bathroom. When she picked up the pregnancy test, she squealed and shoved it in my face.

Jumping back, I yelled out, "Gross! You peed on that thing!"

"Look! Look! Look!"

Laughing, I shook my head and said, "I can see it from here. It for sure says you're pregnant."

For one brief moment, jealousy raced through my veins before I quickly got it under control. "Does Colt know?"

She wrapped her arms around her body and shook her head. "No. I didn't even tell him I was suspecting it."

"Have you been trying?"

"No. I started feeling kind of tired lately and when I didn't get my period, I got curious."

I took her hand in mine. "I take it this news makes you happy, then?"

Pressing her lips together, she nodded as more tears rolled down her face. "Colt?"

"I . . . I think he's going to be happy. We hadn't planned on kids this soon, but I swear to God there is something in the water here!"

Laughing, I pulled my best friend into my arms. "Remind me to drink bottled water."

Lauren gasped and pulled back. "What? Are you having sex? With who? Why haven't you told me?"

I held up my hands. "Whoa. Settle down, girl. I'm not having sex."

Lauren frowned. "Well, that sucks."

"Yeah, I kind of liked it the one and only time I tried it. It would be nice to experience it again."

Lauren hooked her arm in mine as we made our way to her kitchen. As we walked through the house, I couldn't help but smile. Everything about the house screamed Lauren. It was decorated in a French country theme, like something straight out of a home and garden book.

Walking into the kitchen, I looked around. "Did you paint your cabinets?"

Lauren glanced over her shoulder and stared at me. "No. They've always been this color."

"Huh. Well did you do something different in here?"

She placed two glasses on the counter and pulled out the orange juice as she looked around the kitchen. "Nope. Nothing's changed."

With a frown, I brushed it off.

"Okay, so talk to me. I thought you had a date last night. No go?"

"Oh, it was a go. I mean he certainly thought it was a full on green light."

With a giggle, Lauren took a sip of the orange juice and then sat on a stool at the kitchen island. "Do tell."

Chewing on the corner of my lip, I replied, "There's really nothing to tell. David is a nice guy, cute, a good sense of humor, kisses okay."

"But . . ."

"But nothing. He's just not . . . he's not . . ."

"Jase?"

With a frustrated sigh, I mumbled. "Oh, not you too."

"Okay, well help me understand why you didn't have sex with this nice, cute, good sense of humor, good kisser."

"Because I'm not about to jump into bed with every guy I date."

Lauren grinned. "And . . ."

With a roll of my eyes, I huffed. "And he moved too fast. I mean, he had his hand up my dress before they served dessert."

With a snicker, Lauren shook her head. "Damn . . . well, you can't blame him. Look at you. What guy wouldn't want to stick his hand up your dress?"

With a weak smile, I looked away.

Jase.

"Change of subject. How's work?"

Ugh. That subject isn't any better. "It's okay. My grandfather is driving me crazy, and if my grandmother tries to set me up with one more guy, I may have to leave my job."

Lauren perked up. "Seriously? Because if you're serious, I could really use your help here."

I chuckled. "Oh, right. Like you could use a financial analyst on the payroll of your breeding business."

The smile that spread across Lauren's face caused my breathing to hitch. "You're serious?"

Lifting the glass to her lips, she finished off her juice and set it down on the counter. "I've never been more serious in my entire life."

Six

Jase

"DAMN, DUDE, YOU never want to do anything anymore. What happened to you?"

Pulling the hay bale off the trailer, I wiped the sweat off my face. "What do you mean what happened to me?"

Rick lifted his hat and wiped his forehead. "I'm just saying, before you went off to Paris last summer you were fun. Now you're a stick in the mud."

"I'm not a stick in the mud."

The smell of the hay caused me to take in a deep breath. Something about that smell brought back memories of following my father and Reed around the ranch, trying to be just like them.

"You never want to go out. You never want to hook up with anyone either. When was the last time you got some pussy?"

With a roll of my eyes, I shook my head. "Nice, Rick."

He pointed his finger at me and shouted, "See! Like that. The old Jase wouldn't have cared less if I had said the word pussy or not."

"I don't care if you say pussy." I shrugged and grabbed another bale. "I'm not in the mood to date any of these girls we grew up with. All the good ones left and moved on with their lives."

"Damn. The good ones?"

"You know what I mean."

We worked for a few minutes in silence and I enjoyed every second of it, until he started talking again.

"You remember Jill Gates?"

"I should hope so. I dated her senior year and took her to prom."

Rick laughed as he unloaded another bale of hay and stacked it in the barn. "Yeah well, she's back in Llano."

"I thought she moved to Oregon or something."

"Washington."

"She didn't like the rain?" I asked with a smirk.

Rick shook his head. "She didn't like that her fiancé was sleeping around. My mom said she decided to come back and work for the elementary school. She's a teacher."

"Huh. I bet she hates that. All she ever talked about was leaving Llano."

"Well, she's back and rumor has it . . . she was asking about you."

I stopped and looked at him. "Me, huh?"

With an evil smile, he nodded and said, "Yep. I bet I'd be right in saying she'll probably be at Joe's tonight."

Thinking back to what my dad had said to me last week, I knew I needed to decide what I was going to do. It was time to either move on and let Taylor go, or go after her. Going after her meant trying to work a relationship living apart from each other and I wasn't sure how easy that would be.

"So? You in or out?"

Blowing out a frustrated breath, I looked out over the field. As much as I didn't want to let Taylor go . . . I knew what had to be done.

"I'm in."

Rick slapped me on the back and practically shouted for joy. "Yes! Tonight is going to be awesome. There's a new band playing there tonight also."

I pulled my head back in surprise. "At Joe's?"

Rick looked at me like I was saying something wrong. "When was the last time you were there, dude?"

With a shrug, I replied, "I don't know . . . about a year or so."

His smile grew bigger. "You're in for a few surprises tonight."

❧

WALKING DOWN THE stairs, I stopped in the living room and smiled when I saw my parents sitting on the couch together. They were both engrossed in a movie while holding hands.

"Hey, I guess I'm going to go out for a bit. I won't be home late."

They both turned and smiled. "Where ya going?"

"Joe's."

"Joe's . . . what memories we have of Joe's," my mother said as she looked at my father who smiled lovingly at her.

"Yeah, I don't need to hear about them, but thanks."

I started for the door, but stopped and decided now was a good time as any to let them know my plan.

"So, I was thinking . . . the old hunting cottage is just sitting empty. I could fix it up and move in, if that's all right with y'all. I've contacted an architect in Mason who I've spoken with a few times. When the time comes, I'd like to build a place on the property y'all gave me."

My parents, as well and Reed and Courtney, bought out our neighbor's ranch and spilt it between me, Liza, Walker, and Ava. We each received a little over twelve hundred acres.

"Jase, this house is plenty big enough for you to stay here. There's no rush in moving out."

My father shook his head as he pulled my mother closer and kissed her on the head. "I'm going to guess our son would like a little privacy."

"Well, you have privacy here!" my mother said sitting up and giving me a serious look.

All I could manage to say as I looked at my father was, "Um."

It wasn't like I was planning on bringing a girl home anytime soon, but if I was moving on with my life and letting Taylor go . . . I needed to have my own place.

It must have clicked with her because she blushed and said, "Oh, I see. Well we'll do whatever you want to the cabin to get it fixed up for you."

With a nod to my parents, I grinned and said, "Thanks. I should probably be heading out. Rick will be waiting for me."

"Have fun, sweetheart. Don't drink and drive."

"I will and don't worry, Mom. I have no intentions of drinking."

Drinking only ever led me to trouble. The last thing I wanted to do was get hammered and end up with Jill in the backseat of my truck.

My phone buzzed in my pocket as I got to my truck. Pulling it out, it was a text from Rick.

> *Rick: Dude where are you? The band has brought fresh pussy in. The girls in this bar are beyond beautiful. I'm in absolute heaven right now.*

Sighing, I got in the truck and shut the door. I sent him a quick reply and prayed I made it through this night.

> *Me: I'm leaving now. I'll be there soon.*

By the time I got to Joe's, Rick had called three times. Each time I ignored it. Walking into the bar, my eyes widened in surprise. What once was a small country bar looked like a full-on club. The dance floor was huge with the stage straight ahead. The band was covering "Moonlight Crush" as half the bar seemed to be dancing.

"I was really hoping I'd run into you tonight."

Turning on my heels, I came face to face with Jill Gates. "Hey, Jill. How are you?"

Her eyes moved over my body with desire. Looks like she hadn't changed much.

"I'm doing much better now that I see you. I was hoping you hadn't decided to become a city boy."

With a light laugh, I pushed my hand through my hair. "Yeah, well at one time I thought I wanted something different, turns out ranching is in my blood. Besides, I really enjoy working with Walker and my dad."

With a polite grin, she tilted her head. "So . . . are you going to offer to buy me a drink?"

And so it begins. "Sure. Sorry about that."

She waved off my rudeness and walked past me and up to the bar.

The band was taking a break and a DJ was taking over as I ordered myself a Coke and Jill ordered some fancy-ass drink that caused the bartender to shake his head as he walked away.

"What have you been up to since you graduated?" she asked, taking a sip of her fruity looking concoction.

Glancing around the bar, I took in the new place. Rick was right; it was bigger and for sure catered to the young crowd. I took a drink and looked back at her.

"Went to Paris, then pretty much started working full time for my father. Went to Montana for a bit, other than that, haven't been up to much. You?"

"Well, I met someone in college. We got engaged and he decided he liked sticking his dick in other girls. By the time I found out, I'd already moved to Seattle with him and we had rented a house. I had a great job at a great school district that I had to walk away from."

"Why did you have to walk away from it?"

Her lips parted as she stared at me like I had just grown two heads. "Well, I couldn't very well move out and get my own place on my salary. New teachers don't make that much, ya know. Daddy said I could come home and stay with them until I could afford to buy myself a nice little house. That's my plan."

Bringing the Coke bottle up to my lips, I nodded and said, "Good plan."

"I think so," she said as she squared off her shoulders. "What about you? You still a partying guy or are you ready to settle down? Rick mentioned you had some land that you got from your daddy."

Good lord. This girl was on the hunt for her next keeper. "Nah, I've got a few years before I want to settle down with anyone."

Her hand came up and landed on my chest as she laughed and shook her head. "Jase, you always did know how to make me smile."

I lifted my eyebrows and finished off my Coke, motioning to the bartender for another. "Not sure what I said to warrant a smile on your face, but glad to be of help."

We sat there and talked for a few more minutes before Jill busted out and said, "So are you going to ask me to dance or not?"

Setting my drink down, I held my hand out for hers. As we walked out to the dance floor, Rick smiled and slapped my back.

"She's in a dress . . . easy access."

I gave him a push and said, "Shut the fuck up, asshole. It's nothing like that." The last thing I wanted to do was hook up with Jill. Especially when every waking moment was consumed by thoughts of Taylor.

With a smirk, he replied, "If you say so, Morris. If you say so."

Pulling Jill into my arms, I cursed under my breath when the song changed to a slow one.

"Great," I mumbled.

Jill looked up at me and smiled. "I know. Perfect timing."

Forcing a smile, I pulled her closer to me so I didn't have to talk to her. *The sooner this night was over the better.*

Seven

Taylor

"IT'S PACKED IN here!" Lauren shouted as Colt held her close to him. The moment Lauren told Colt she was pregnant, I thought he was going to jump through the roof he was so happy. I had been sworn to secrecy until she got further along. I don't think I have ever seen them both so happy.

"Wow, this place is huge. It's deceiving from the outside," I said looking around.

"Come on, let's get some drinks," Lauren said pulling Colt and me toward the bar. She looked over her shoulder and smiled. "Well, I'll take water, y'all can drink."

Colt ordered a Coke since he was driving. I went ahead and ordered a beer. I hardly ever drank and couldn't really hold my alcohol, so I always played it safe by ordering a beer and sipping on it all night.

Lauren took a drink of her water and turned to Colt. "Let's dance!"

Jumping up, she pulled him out to the dance floor as I chuckled and continued my people watching.

The song changed from a fast song to a slower one. *Oh, it's Dan and*

Shay. I love that group. Scanning the dance floor, my eyes came to a halt.

"Jase," I whispered as I watched him dancing with some girl. All of sudden the lyrics to the song played loudly in my ears.

He wasn't talking at all to her, but he held her close to him. "Bastard," I said out loud as the guy standing next to me at the bar looked at me shocked.

"Oh shit, did I cut in front of you?"

Pulling my eyes off of Jase and the girl, I took in the sight in front of me.

Cowboy. Tight jeans, nice body, boots, and a smile that would knock any girl off her feet. Any girl . . . but me.

"Nope, sorry that wasn't directed at you. The guy who asked me to dance is dancing with someone else."

I pouted as he smiled bigger. *Good lord . . . when did I learn how to flirt?*

Reaching his hand out for mine, he winked and said, "His mistake just became my gain."

With a flirty grin, I set my drink down and placed my hand in his and let him lead me to the dance floor. The last place Jase would ever expect me to be is a bar in Llano. I had to admit when Lauren mentioned this place, my heart began to race at the idea of maybe seeing Jase. I just hadn't planned on seeing him with another girl.

Lucking out, the next song was another slow one. Spinning me around, the guy pulled me closer and asked, "What's your name?"

"Taylor. Yours?"

"Brad."

Oh yuck. Why did he have to have the same name as my dad? Crap.

"Nice to meet you . . . um . . . Brad."

"Pleasure is all mine, Taylor. I can promise you that."

Ugh. Men.

He pulled me closer and I was praying to God this guy had something in his pocket and it wasn't what I thought it was poking my stomach.

Blah.

For a few seconds I totally forgot why I had agreed to dance with him. I quickly looked around until I spotted Jase. He looked miserable and somehow that comforted me.

"So, you couldn't possibly be from around here."

Turning my attention back to the cowboy, I smiled. "No. Fredericksburg originally, but I live in Austin now."

His brows lifted. "Austin? What do you do?"

"I'm a financial analyst."

"Fancy."

With a slight chuckle, I shook my head. "Not really."

His smile was nice, warm almost. I'd give anything to have it affect me in some way.

"What brings you to Llano?"

I glanced around for Lauren and Colt. "My best friends live in Mason. They wanted to check out the band playing here tonight."

With a nod of his head, he accepted my answer. Out of the corner of my eye, I saw Jase walking by. Turning my head in his direction, I watched him as he walked up to another guy. They talked for a few moments when the girl he had been dancing with walked up and stood by his side. My chest tightened as I watched them.

"It's actually kind of cool you live in Austin."

Without taking my eyes off of Jase, I asked, "Why's that?"

"I live there too. That means if I'm lucky, I'll be able to talk you into dinner one night maybe."

Trying not to be rude, I glanced up at him and grinned. "What brought *you* to Llano?"

"Hometown. Visiting the parents."

I pressed my lips together to keep my smile back. For some reason I thought it was kind of sweet he was home visiting his parents. Why, I had no idea.

"Well, if we both live in Austin, I guess that means never say never," I offered.

Brad's eyes lit up while I quickly moved my attention back to Jase. The girl was talking to him and placed her hand on his arm. I couldn't help but notice his reaction when he stepped back, shook his head and said something to her. The look of disappointment on her face was evident.

The song ended as Brad and I stepped apart. "Thank you for the dance," I said with a grin.

"I hope it won't be our last for tonight."

Glancing over Brad's shoulder, I watched as Jase headed out of the bar . . . alone. It was time for me to do a little bit of research. Putting my attention back to Brad, I nodded. "Same here. If you'll excuse me, I need to get a drink."

Before he had a chance to offer, I quickly walked away and headed straight to the girl who Jase had been dancing with. Not having a clue as to where I was getting my courage from, I made a mental note to let Meagan and Grace know. The two of them wouldn't believe what I was about to do, even if I told them.

As I stepped up to the bar next to her, I couldn't help but overhear the conversation.

"Jesus, Rick. You told me he was in a funk, but you didn't tell me he was in that big of a funk. He barely even looked at me."

I turned to see her talking to a guy my age. He was tall with blond hair and looked to have been raised on a ranch with the way he was built.

"I told you, Jill, he's hung up on some girl. Now if you'll excuse me, I've got some fun to make up for."

Rick walked away as Jill turned and stared straight ahead. I motioned to the bartender and sat down next to her. I had no idea what I was doing. All I knew was I wanted to know who this girl was.

"Is anyone sitting here?" I asked.

Turning to look at me, she shook her head. "No."

After placing my drink order, I glanced around for Colt and Lauren. Smiling, I watched the two of them dance. I wanted a love like theirs so desperately.

"I don't think I'll ever understand men."

My attention was drawn back to Jill. My head was spinning with different reasons why Jase left alone. I only allowed myself one brief second to think it might have had something to do with me. "Join the club," I said with a chuckle.

She shook her head and took a drink. "I practically threw myself at an old boyfriend tonight only to be turned down flat."

The feeling of relief swept across my body when she said Jase had turned her advances down. I let out the breath I hadn't even realized I had been holding when she started talking. "Did he give you a reason why?"

With a sour expression, she replied, "No, but I'm guessing it has something to do with some girl he spent the summer with."

"Are they a couple?" I asked, even though I regretted it the moment the words were out of my mouth. There was no reason for me to play at this game like I was.

Pinching her brows together, she slowly shook her head. "No. Well, honestly I have no idea. It's hard being turned down though, ya know?"

With a curt laugh, I agreed. "Tell me about it." Taking a small sip of beer, I set it down on the counter. "Will you keep after him?"

With an evil smile, she looked directly at me. "Oh, hell yes. I don't think I've ever met someone like him. He's handsome, funny, a great kisser."

Squirming in my seat to ward off the jealousy, I looked away briefly before turning back. "Well, good luck."

Jill lifted her drink and said, "I'll take all the luck I can get."

Spinning around on the stool, I stood. "It was nice chatting with you."

Without really looking at me, she said, "You too."

As I made my way over toward Colt and Lauren, I saw Brad.

Shit.

Taking a quick detour, I finally made my way over to the lovebirds. "So . . . this is . . . fun. The band is great!" I shouted as Colt and Lauren looked at each other.

"You're ready to go?" Lauren asked.

With a shrug, I leaned closer so I didn't have to shout. "It's just hard being the third wheel and all."

Lauren flashed me that smile of hers. "I'm feeling tired anyway. Let's head home!"

The faster we got out of the bar and out of Llano, the better. Seeing Jase had bothered me more than I ever dreamed it would. The only good thing that came out of this was he didn't see me . . . and Brad never got my number.

Eight

Jase

"YOU SURE ARE far away."

My eyes lifted from the pasture as I turned to my mother. "A lot on my mind I guess."

"Courtney called and said Ava was staying in Montana for a bit longer."

With a frown, I replied, "I bet that doesn't make Reed very happy."

She laughed and shook her head. Turning to look at her, I couldn't help but smile. My mother was beautiful. Her dark hair was piled up on her head and her blue eyes were staring into mine.

"Want to talk about her?"

With a slight smile, I asked, "How do you know it's a girl?"

She gave me a smirk. "Please, I know you like I know the back of my hand. You haven't been the same since you got back from France. I can only assume you met someone while you were over there that you're smitten with."

With a hard laugh, I looked back over the pasture. "I'm more than smitten with her, Mom. I love her."

With a gasp, she reached her hand out and touched my arm. "What? Jase, sweetheart, please talk to me. I might be able to help."

My head dropped as I shook it. My entire body felt cold as I thought about what I had done to Taylor. What I continued to do to her. I couldn't walk away as hard as I tried . . . I could never forget her.

"Nah, I don't think so, Mom. She lives in Austin and has her own life. It would have never worked."

Her hand pulled back as she sat back. "Jase Morris, look at me."

Doing as she asked, I looked her in the eyes. "My first and last name. Am I in trouble?"

"Is that your only reason, because she works in Austin?"

"One of them."

With a huff, she snarled her lip. "That's a stupid reason."

My head snapped back as I let out a chuckle. "Damn, Mom. Thanks for that."

She let out a frustrated sigh as she rolled her eyes. "Seriously, Jase. It's not like Austin is Dallas or Houston. It's not that far!"

"Mom, when would I ever have time to go see her? I'm always busy here doing something or helping Walker out so he can spend time with his own family."

"I don't buy that for one second. If a love is true, you'll move heaven and earth for it."

My eyes broke her stare. "Maybe," I whispered.

"Tell me the other reason."

"She's beautiful, smart, innocent beyond belief. She deserves someone so much better than me."

Her eyes narrowed. "Did she say that?"

"No. It's hard to explain, Mom. I took something from her because I was being a typical asshole guy. I wanted her to myself, but I got . . . I got . . ."

"Scared?"

Standing, I laced my fingers through my hair. "I need to head up and help Walker get ready for tomorrow."

"Hey, Jase?"

Turning back to look at her, I said, "Yeah?"

"Can I give you a piece of advice?"

With a shrug, I replied, "Sure."

"Once in a lifetime, someone will walk into your life and turn it upside down. Your whole world will feel like it's spinning out of control and you're going to feel so many different things all at once. Being scared is the first thing you'll feel, but if you let love in and trust it, I promise you it's all worth it."

Looking at the ground, I kicked at nothing. My heart physically felt as if it was aching anytime I thought about what we might have together. It wasn't just that I was scared by how much I loved Taylor, I was also worried about the distance we lived apart from each other. "How do you make it work when I'm here and she's there?"

"Do you love her, Jase?"

My head snapped up as I looked my mother in the eyes. "I've never loved anyone like I love her, Mom."

"Then you'll fight to make it work."

ॐ

STEPPING OFF THE elevator, I took in my surroundings. I had no idea what Taylor's grandfather really did, but from the looks of this building, whatever he did he made money at it.

"May I help you, sir?"

I spun around and grinned at the receptionist. Her eyes lit up when she saw me and I flashed my crooked grin. "Hey there."

Running her tongue quickly along her bottom lip, she smiled. "May I be of service to you?"

"Yes. I'm actually looking for Taylor Atwood."

Her smile faded some while she sat up a bit straighter. "Taylor?"

"Yes," I replied with a nod. "Taylor. Is she in?"

"I'd have to check, may I tell her who is here to see her?"

I wasn't sure if I gave her my real name Taylor would tell her she didn't want to see me. *Maybe I should give her a fake name.* After going back and forth in my head I decided to go with my real name.

"Jase Morris."

As she picked up the phone, she flashed me a flirty smile. "Jase . . . that's a nice name."

"Thank you."

Looking away, she spoke. "Ms. Atwood, there is a Mr. Jase Morris at the front to see you. Yes, I'll let him know."

The back of my throat ached. She didn't want to see me.

The receptionist hung up the phone and gave me a polite smile. "Ms. Atwood asked if you would please take a seat. She'll be with you in a few minutes."

A rush of relief raced through my body as I let out the breath I hadn't known I was holding in. With a quick spin on my heels, I made my way over to the chairs and sat down.

Five minutes passed before I heard her voice coming from down the hall. "I'll get those numbers on the investments over to you this afternoon."

Taylor and a guy a few years older than me rounded the corner. When she put her hand for him to shake it, I couldn't help but notice the way he looked her over like he wanted to devour her.

Fucker.

"Thanks so much, Ms. Atwood. You wouldn't happen to be free for lunch would you?"

Taylor stole a glance in my direction. "I'm sorry, Mr. Burns, I wish. I've got another appointment right now."

Ouch. That one hurt. Standing, I cleared my throat while the asshole looked me over. Turning his attention back to Taylor, he said, "Well then, we'll have to make it for another day."

"Sounds like a plan. Have a good day, Mr. Burns."

When he placed his hand on Taylor's arm, I squeezed my hand into a fist. "Have a good afternoon, Taylor."

Taylor walked up to me with a blank expression. "Jase, what are you doing here?"

My smile quickly faded. "I was wondering if I could speak with you."

"You couldn't call?"

Glancing over to the receptionist, I lowered my voice. "You haven't answered any of my calls, Taylor. Otherwise I would have."

"Follow me," she said making her way back down the hall.

Once we got into her office, she shut the door and motioned for me to sit down.

"Man, I feel like this is a serious meeting or something," I said with a chuckle. Trying to lighten up the tension in the air.

Her eyebrow arched as she stared while waiting for me to start the conversation.

"I um . . . well, I wanted to first off apologize for what happened in Paris. I regret what happened."

Her face turned white as a ghost. "What?" she whispered.

"No! I don't mean I regret making love to you; I would never regret that, Taylor. It was the most amazing time of my life."

Taylor looked away as her cheeks flushed. "I see. What exactly are you regretting then?"

"What I said afterwards . . . what happened. For pushing you away because I was scared."

"Scared? Why were you scared?"

Everything! Hurting you, letting you into my heart to hurt me. The insane way I feel about you that has my heart stopping every time you smile at me. My heart was pounding in my chest as I drew in a deep breath and slowly let it out. Hell if I wasn't scared shitless now.

"Taylor, I've never felt like this before. You know I love you and I would never do anything to hurt you."

"Really? Because making love to me and then telling me it wouldn't work between us and leaving with another woman hurt me. A lot."

Pulling my head back in confusion, I asked, "What are you talking about? I didn't leave with anyone."

Taylor let out a gruff laugh. "Really? Cammie left with you, or have you forgotten that?"

"She followed me out the door; I didn't go anywhere with her. I walked around Paris for hours by myself."

Taylor sat back in her chair. "You . . . you didn't spend the day with her?"

"Fuck no. Jesus, Taylor, do you really think I'm that much of an asshole?"

With a smirk, she replied, "If the shoe fits."

Well damn.

"I freaked out and got spooked, but I honestly was and still am worried about dating and living so far apart from each other. But I think we can make it work."

Folding her arms across her chest, Taylor slowly shook her head. "So just like that, huh? You think you can walk in here and give me some sorry excuse for an apology and I'm going to fall at your feet and thank you for coming back to me?"

"Sorry excuse?"

Drumming her fingers on her arm, she nodded.

Swallowing hard, I stuttered. "I . . . I don't really know what to say."

With a frustrated sigh, Taylor stood. "I'm really busy, Jase, so if that was all you stopped by for?"

I narrowed my eyes and stood. "Really? This is how you're going to do this?"

"I can't give you anything right now, Jase."

"What in the hell is that supposed to mean? I love you, Taylor."

Her breath hitched while she quickly looked away for a few moments before turning back and piercing me with her beautiful eyes. "If you loved me you would never have pushed me away in the first place. You took something from me that night, Jase, and it was more than my virginity. Besides, you're right. It would never work with me living in Austin and you living in Llano."

My stomach felt sick as I tried to stop my hands from shaking. "Are . . . are you seeing someone?"

Something moved across her face. She looked conflicted, but stood her ground. "It doesn't matter."

Slamming my hand down on her desk, Taylor jumped. "It does to me! Please don't do this because of some stupid mistake on my part. Give me another chance, I beg of you."

Her eyes filled with tears.

Walking around her desk, I placed my hands on her arms. "If you tell me you don't love me and there is no chance of us, I'll leave. But you have to look me in the eyes and say it."

A small sob slipped from her mouth. "I . . . I'm sorry, Jase. I need you to leave now."

My hands dropped to my sides as I took a few steps back. She didn't have to say the words. I could see it in her eyes.

Dropping my gaze, I fought to keep my voice controlled. "I won't bother you again, Taylor."

Her mouth parted up, but she stopped herself from talking.

Turning, I headed to the door and opened it. Before walking out, I glanced over my shoulder.

"I really thought you felt it too."

"Felt what?" she asked in a quiet voice.

"It doesn't matter anymore."

I walked through the door and quietly shut it behind me. I filled my lungs with a deep breath of air and headed for the elevators. My heart felt as if it had just been ripped from my chest.

The worst part was I deserved it.

Nine

Taylor

COLLAPSING INTO MY chair, I covered my face with my hands and cried.

What did I just do?

The light knock at my door had me spinning my chair around to face the window. My grandfather made sure I had one of the best views in the building. His favoritism caused me more problems than he could ever imagine.

"Ms. Atwood, Mr. Atwood would like to see you in his office."

Luckily the chair hid me enough that Denise wouldn't see me wiping my tears away.

"Th-thank you. I'll be there in a few minutes."

"Um . . . he said now and he seemed a bit upset."

Rolling my eyes, I now knew why my father warned me about coming to work for Granddad.

"I'll be there in a second, Denise," I said firmly.

"Yes, ma'am. I'll let him know."

Why in the hell didn't she just call me? She had to come in here and tell me.

Once the door shut, I spun around and grabbed my purse. Searching for my cell phone, I pulled up my favorites. If I called my sister, she would try to reason with me.

I didn't want to call Lauren. She was too happy with her pregnancy news.

That left Libby, Grace, or Alex.

Looking up, I stared off into space.

He was scared.

Sitting up straighter, I pulled up my address book and found the number I was looking for.

After three rings he answered.

"Taylor, I mean Ms. Atwood, it's a pleasure hearing from you so soon."

Smiling, I tried to ignore the tightness in my chest.

"Mr. Burns, I was wondering if your invite to lunch was still open?"

I could practically hear the excitement in his voice. "Yes, it is."

"I'll meet you in the lobby in ten minutes."

"See you then."

Hitting End, I dropped the phone back into my purse and grabbed my compact. Checking to make sure my make-up was okay, I snapped it shut and stood. I smoothed out my pencil skirt and took a deep breath.

The phone on my desk buzzed. "Ms. Atwood, he is waiting."

Heat surged through me as I moved around the desk and made my way to Grandfather's office.

"I'm done letting men walk over me. It's time I was the one in control."

Pulling the door to my office open, I walked out and headed toward his office.

"As of this moment, I'm starting a new life."

MY FATHER AND mother stood in front of me with stunned expressions as I chewed on the corner of my lip.

"What do you mean . . . you quit?" my father asked in a stunned voice.

Rubbing my elbow in a nervous manner, I repeated what I had just said in a wavering voice. "I quit. Granddad wasn't very pleased, but . . ."

"I could imagine he wouldn't be very happy about that, Taylor. Why in the world would you leave a perfectly good paying job? Do you know how many college graduates would give their right arm for a job like that?"

My posture stooped and I stood there feeling like a fool. What was I thinking trying to do something like this? One look at my mother and I knew what I had to do. She gave me a weak smile and nodded her head in a show of support.

Standing straight again, I dropped my hands to my hips. "I know what you think, Dad."

With a huff, he asked, "Do you really?"

"I wasn't happy there and we both know I was put in a position I was not qualified to do. You want to talk about being in over your head." I let out a gruff laugh. "Dad . . . I was so over my head I was drowning. Needless to say, it was stressful having to listen to Granddad every single day point out every little thing I did wrong and then expected me to fix it, not having a damn clue what I was doing."

My mother frowned. "Taylor, don't use that language; it isn't you."

Rolling my eyes, I looked away. "Don't you roll your eyes at your mother."

Cutting my gaze over to my father, I shook my head. "I can't do this anymore."

A concerned expression moved across my parents' faces. "What do you mean?"

"This!" I said waving my hands about. "I've been so sheltered my entire life I feel like I have no life. Ever since I was little, I was told I could do no wrong. Well . . . I've done wrong. A few times and there are certain things I regret doing."

Tears built in my eyes as I thought about the other night.

"Oh dear," my mother mumbled, pushing away from the counter. "Taylor, if working for your grandfather felt too stressful, then that's okay. He is supposed to be retired, so why he is up there every day is beyond any of us."

"Your mother is right, sweetheart. I don't want you being upset about it. You will easily find another job."

My hands came up to my mouth as I attempted to hold myself together. "It's not about the job."

I quickly turned and ran up the stairs to my room before I lost it completely in front of my parents. Slamming the door behind me, I fell to the bed and buried my face in the pillow. I'd give anything to take back what I did.

Anything.

The light knock at the door caused me to sit up. "Come in."

I breathed a sigh of relief when I saw it was my mother.

"May I come in?"

With a slight nod, I motioned for her to come in.

She softly shut the door then walked over and sat on the bed next to me.

"Do you want to tell me what's really bothering you?"

No longer able to hold it in, tears streamed down my face as my mother pulled me into her arms. The smell of her perfume brought me back to when I was a little girl. Any time I fell and got hurt, she would hold me close to her and I would breathe in her perfume.

"Shh . . . it can't be that bad. So you quit your job. You'll find another one."

I sobbed harder as I tried to fight past my throat closing. "It's worse than that, Mom. I did something terrible. Something I regret and wish I could take back."

Pushing me back, she looked me in the eyes. Her eyes filled with worry. "What did you do, sweetheart? You can trust me."

My lips were pressed tightly together as I shook my head. "You'll think I'm . . . I can't believe I did it . . . oh God."

Dropping my head, my body trembled. "Taylor, you're starting to scare me. Tell me right now what happened."

With a quick wipe of my face, I attempted to calm myself down, but all I could see was Jase standing in front of me . . . asking for a second chance and me turning him down.

"Jase came to see me at the office a couple days ago."

"He did? What did he want?"

After I came back from Paris, I'd told my mother everything about Jase. Even him taking my virginity. The one thing I could always count on was my mother's support. She was there for me in a time I really needed someone to lean on. Never once judging me. "He wanted to apologize for how things went in Paris and he asked for a second chance."

With a slight smile, she grabbed my hands and softly said, "Oh, Taylor. Isn't that what you've been wanting? Did you ask him about the girl he left with?"

A swoosh of air escaped from my mouth as I looked away. "He didn't spend the day with her. He was alone walking around Paris and he said he didn't mean the things he said; he was just scared."

She squeezed my hands and leaned in closer with a wide grin. "That's a good thing, right?"

Sniffling, I nodded my head. "Yes. But something came over me when he was there and I got so mad. All my confused feelings came rushing back seeing him standing there and I told him to leave. He said if I really wanted him gone I had to tell him . . . and I did. I told him to leave and he said if he left he would never bother me again. I let him go." Again, tears rolled down my face. "I let him walk out the door and I didn't say a word to him. Mom, I think I made the biggest mistake of my life."

"So you got angry and let your emotions lead your thoughts. We've all done it and I'm guessing that is what led to all of this in the first place. Taylor, just call him and tell him you were upset."

I frantically shook my head. "You don't understand. I've done something terrible and I feel so . . . so guilty. So . . . dirty."

Her eyes widened in horror. "Wh-what did you do?"

"After I talked to Granddad and quit, I met Mr. Burns for lunch."

Narrowing her eyes, she asked, "Who is Mr. Burns?"

"Clark. His name is Clark and he is a VP in accounting. He's about three or four years older than me and he has been flirting with me since I started. We had lunch and I came back to the office and packed up my desk. When I was leaving, I ran into him again and we made plans for dinner."

Burying my face in my hands, I started crying again while my stomach cramped. Placing her arm around me, my mother held me close to her. "Go on, Taylor."

I could hear how tense her voice was. "We went to dinner and I asked him back to my apartment and we slept together. I thought if I just had sex with someone else, I'd prove to myself I was over Jase and that I could move on. When he got up and went into the restroom, I cried."

"Did he force you to do anything you didn't want to do?"

Gasping, I lifted my head and looked at her. "No! I was the one who asked him to my apartment and flirted endlessly with him. I came on to him and . . . and now . . ." My voice trembled as I wiped my tears away. "And now I'd give anything to have Jase standing in front of me again so I could have a do-over. Oh, Mom. Wh-what did I do? I didn't want to be with anyone but Jase! Why did I do that? I'm nothing but a whore."

Her mouth dropped open as she pushed me back at arm's length. "Do not ever say that again. Please, Taylor. You're not the first woman to seduce a man and have sex with him. Did you use protection?"

My heart dropped at the idea.

"Yes! Of course I did."

She closed her eyes and spoke under her breath. "Thank God."

"What about Jase? I told him to leave when he asked for another chance. He told me he loved me and I never said it back. I've lost him forever. And to make matters worse, I went off and slept with another man."

I'd never felt my heart ache like it was. I was beginning to believe a broken heart was not just a metaphor. The thought of Jase being out of my life forever made me physically sick.

"What you need to do is take a break. You've been working too hard and you need some time off to figure out what you want to do. Spend some time with the girls. I know Meagan would love to see you, especially with the twins. Why don't you go and spend a few days there? I'm sure she could use the help."

Wiping under my nose, I nodded. "That's a good idea. I've got most of my apartment in Austin packed up and ready to move. A few days with Meagan and the twins is just what I need."

My mother smiled and nodded. "Everything will be much clearer when you have some time to yourself. You'll see."

A part of me instantly felt relieved to have gotten what happened with Jase and Clark off my chest. Being able to share it with my mother and have her offer advice was something I was grateful for. I hoped to have such a relationship like ours someday if I ever had a daughter.

Returning her smile, I agreed. If only I believed everything would be clearer. Nothing would ever be able to erase the memory of Clark's touch and how I had tried hard not to let it make my skin crawl.

Nothing.

Ten

Taylor

I WRAPPED THE blanket closer around me as I watched the sun slowly dip below the horizon. Taking in a deep breath, I let the clean crisp air filter through my nose.

"Arabella and Charlotte are finally both asleep."

Glancing up, I smiled. "Meg, you're such an amazing mom."

"I'm a tired one that's for sure," Meagan said as she sank down in the chair next to me. "It's getting colder out here. The front must be moving in earlier than they thought."

I nodded and looked back out to the orange and pink sky. "I can't believe Christmas is in a few days."

"Yeah, I know. I think we might have gone overboard with presents for the twins. Gray especially."

I giggled and shook my head. "They'll never know."

"So, are we going to make small talk or are you going to tell me what is bothering you. You've been in such a funk the last few weeks and I don't know why."

"I'm sorry I'm not much company."

"Tay, if you really think I'm worried about you entertaining me then you are very wrong. I'm worried. The last two days you've been walking around like you've lost everything."

My eyes closed as I swallowed the lump in my throat. "I have, Meg."

"Bullshit. Lauren told me she offered you a job. Why haven't you taken her up on it, or at the very least gone and talked to her and Scott?"

Inhaling a slow breath through my nose, I opened my eyes. "I told her tonight I'd stop by tomorrow and talk to them."

"Good. You need to stop pouting. So you quit your job and slept with a guy. It's not like you cheated on anyone. You think you're the first person to ever have sex and regret it? My God, I could fill your head with tales."

Her words slowly started to fade as I got lost in the memory of Jase's eyes as he said goodbye to me. Every time I'd tried to think of Paris an image of Clark would pop into my mind.

"Are you even listening to me?"

"Yep."

With a sigh, Meagan asked, "What did I say then?"

"I'm not the only person to have meaningless sex and I need to get over it."

With a wide smile, she stared at me. "I said a lot more than that. Have you called him? Tried to text him?"

Shrugging, I asked, "What good would it do me? I told him to leave and then I slept with another guy. I'm no better than what I accused him of."

"Oh, for the love of Pete." Meagan stood up and glared at me. "Taylor, I never in my life thought I would see the day when you would be sitting around feeling sorry for yourself. You had a brief moment of standing up for yourself and having the balls to live life and now you regret it. Well tough shit. You told him to leave, you sought out another man, fucked him, and woke up the next morning regretting it. Welcome to the real world. Daddy is no longer sheltering you, so get the fuck over it. Now, it's time to pull those big girl panties up again and stop sulking. You're either going to call him or you're going to move on with your life. Either way, you better snap the hell out of it by the time Christmas comes."

And just like that, she stormed off into the house . . . leaving me sitting there with her words screaming in my head. Turning my attention to the red sky, I slowly shook my head. "Damn her," I whispered. Knowing she was right.

❧

AFTER TAKING A horseback ride around the ranch with Lauren, Colt, and Scott, we headed back to the house. Lauren and Colt hadn't shared their news with anyone yet and I knew they were bursting at the seams to do so.

Walking into the house, Jessie greeted us with a buffet spread of food. "Y'all are back just in time."

Inhaling the heavenly scent, I moaned. "My goodness that smells good."

"Take the job and you'll eat like this every day," Lauren whispered in my ear.

With a smirk, I looked over to Colt who was totally lost in the sea of food.

"Colt, why don't you open a bottle of wine and pour each of us a glass," Jessie said.

I froze, alongside Colt and Lauren. Jessie glanced up and looked at each of us. "Is something wrong?"

Lauren stumbled over her words. "Um . . . well . . . I um . . ."

Clearing my throat, I looked at Lauren and then Jessie. "I've stopped drinking . . . wine and beer and all that stuff; you know it's bad for you and . . . all that stuff."

Ugh.

I moaned internally. I never was a good liar.

Jessie arched a brow. "Really? Why?"

"Well . . . ah . . . I um . . . I got really drunk and did something stupid. So I gave it up."

Crossing her arms over her chest, Jessie peered at me as if she could see through the lies. All the lies that were about to pile up one on top of each other. "I know, hard to believe, but there it is. It was . . . um . . . illegal."

"Illegal?"

Colt groaned behind me as he sunk down into a chair. "Uh-huh," I mumbled.

"Wow. This is a whole new side of you, Taylor. I'm not sure about hiring you if you've done something illegal."

Oh damn. I stuck my foot in my mouth.

"Well, I mean it wasn't really illegal-illegal. It was just . . . you know."

Scott stood next to Jessie and smiled. "No, I don't think we know. Why don't you tell us?"

"Tell you? You mean tell you what I did that wasn't illegal but was?"

For goodness sakes. Even I thought I sounded crazy.

I could tell Scott was trying to hold back his smile as he and Jessie both attempted to stare me down.

"Well . . . if you're sure you want to know," I mumbled as I glanced at Lauren.

"Oh . . . we want to know. Don't we, Jessie?"

Jessie chuckled. "More than you could imagine."

Swallowing hard, I tried to think of something. Panic was building and I was about to blurt out I slept with a practical stranger.

"I . . . I slept with—"

"I'm pregnant!" Lauren called out.

Jessie and Scott both turned and looked at her with disbelieving faces. "What did you say?" Jessie asked.

Lauren looked at Colt who stood and made his way over to her where he lovingly placed his hand over her stomach. "We weren't going to say anything until after Christmas, but Lauren is two months pregnant."

Jessie quickly made her way over to Lauren and wrapped her in her arms. My heart was bubbling over with happiness while I watched them both start crying. I was so happy for my best friend, yet a small part of me was jealous. I excused myself and headed outside.

Taking in a deep breath, I let the smells of the ranch take over. There was something about the smell of horse manure that I had always loved. I hadn't realized how much I missed being in the country.

I strolled down to the barn and walked up to a paint horse who was begging for some attention.

"Hey there, beautiful girl." Running my hand down her strong neck, I closed my eyes and tried to clear my mind. The horse made it clear she wanted something more from me as she nickered. Looking at her, I laughed.

"Do you want to go for a ride, girl?"

"Tay? Is everything okay?"

Glancing over my shoulder, I smiled at Lauren. "Yes. I wanted to give y'all some privacy. Are they happy?"

Lauren chuckled as she nodded. "Very happy."

"I'm so happy for you both; I hope you know that."

"I do, but I'd really wish you would tell me what's wrong. You seem so unhappy."

With a weak smile, I turned back to the horse and gently stroked her neck. "I'm feeling a bit . . . lost right now."

She sat down on the hay bale next to me. "Want to talk about it?"

With a quiet voice, I replied, "I sometimes think what happened in Paris with Jase was a dream. Like it never happened."

"Why?"

My shoulders dropped as I wiped at my nose. "Because for a few hours I felt the happiest I'd ever felt."

"Maybe you should call Jase."

Shaking my head, I tried to ignore the ache in my chest. "It's too late. I told him to leave and then I slept with Clark. That's such a stupid name. Why in the hell would I have sex with a guy with the name Clark?"

"So what if you slept with him, Taylor? It's not like you cheated on Jase. Besides, how many girls do you think he's been with since Paris?"

My eyes snapped down to her. "Thanks, Lauren. That makes me feel so much better."

Her face fell as she whispered, "I'm sorry."

"I feel like I'm so lost right now, and that alone throws me off even more. I've always had it so together. The one who knew what she wanted in life. I was never going to settle for any guy, and I certainly wasn't going to have meaningless sex."

Breaking down, I buried my face in my hands. Lauren jumped up and engulfed me in her arms.

"Taylor, you made a mistake. You thought by sleeping with Clark you'd be able to prove something to yourself and maybe you did."

I shook my head and pulled back. "What though? I have no clue what I was trying to prove. That I could do it? That I could stand up for myself and leave my job. That I could attract a guy into my bed and hopefully if Jase ever found out he'd be sorry he ever left me that day in Paris."

"Yes. I believe that last part is exactly what you wanted."

My shoulders slumped as I let out an exasperated breath. "I'm such an idiot. I gave up everything I wanted in one day." Lifting my hand, I snapped my fingers. "Just like that. Gone."

"No, that's not true. We're serious about you coming to work here. I really think with your help we can truly get a better handle on the finances. You'd be invaluable with analyzing everything from the supplies we use to the rate we pay for the studs. Think about it, Tay. Daddy was impressed with the suggestions you made earlier just after looking through the inventory of the cleaning supplies!"

With a small chuckle, I nodded. "I think if you looked at all the suppliers, you'd be able to cut the costs by half."

"See! You could stay in the hunter's cabin and have a place all to yourself. It's been remodeled and sits empty."

With a deep breath in, I slowly blew it out. I knew she was right. This was exactly what I needed. "To starting over?"

Lauren flashed me the biggest grin I'd ever seen. "Oh my glitter! We're going to work together!"

With a smile of my own, I squeezed her hands and said, "We're going to work together."

"And you never know when fate will step in again, Taylor. She seems to do that a lot with you and Jase."

Trying to stay positive, I nodded and smiled a bit bigger. "Yeah, she does. Here's hoping she doesn't let me down."

Eleven

Jase

"JASE, I NEED to take a trip into Mason. You want to go?"

Glancing over my shoulder, I looked at my brother-in-law, Walker. "What for?"

"There's a breeder there Dad has worked with in the past. I want to look into using him."

Dropping the brush into the bucket, I stepped out of the stall and wiped my hands on my jeans. "You gonna breed Lady?"

With a bright-eyed smile, he nodded his head. "I think so. There's something about that horse. I feel like with the right match, we could have a good racehorse on our hands. This Scott guy dabbles in racing as well. He told me he has the perfect stud.

Sighing, I shook my head. "I don't know. Isn't your prodigal sister coming in this afternoon?"

"So? My parents are picking Ava up."

With a short chuckle, I grabbed my cowboy hat and motioned for him to lead the way.

"Did Ava mention if she was coming back for good or just for

Christmas?"

Walker laughed. "If I know my sister . . . she's fixin' to drop some kind of bombshell that will rock my father's world."

"Damn if that ain't the truth."

The drive to Mason wasn't a long one and we sat in silence most of the trip. "You gonna tell me what happened when you went to see that girl?"

"Her name is Taylor, and no . . . I don't want to talk about it."

"Fair enough."

We drove another few miles in silence.

"I don't understand women at all," I blurted out.

"Join the club."

My hand rubbed the back of my neck as I let out a frustrated breath. "I mean . . . I made a mistake and I tried to tell her that. I acted like an asshole and I fully admitted to it. She knows I love her and I know she loves me."

"But?"

"She's angry and punishing me."

Walker let out a roar of laughter. "You think she is punishing you? Why?"

"I asked her for a second chance and she told me to leave. Made it seem like she didn't love me. Then she tried to prove it to herself."

Walker turned his attention to me and asked, "How?"

"She slept with some asshole she worked with."

"Damn. Did she tell you that?"

My body tensed as the memory came back. Fisting my hands, I looked out the window. "No. I waited outside her apartment and saw her coming home with him. He went up and never came back down until late in the middle of the night."

"How do you know?"

I wasn't sure if I wanted to admit to Walker I had sat in my truck all night watching Taylor's place. Swallowing hard, I stared out the passenger window.

"Holy shit. You stalked her."

My head turned to look at him. "I didn't stalk her, you dickhead. I sat in my truck all night and just watched her apartment."

Walker pinched his brows together. "You stalked her."

"Whatever. Call it what you want. The point is she slept with him and I know she regrets it."

Walker pulled over to the side of the road and put the truck in park. "And how in the world do you know she regrets it?"

"After the guy left I stayed there for a while. Taylor opened her balcony door and sat out there for a bit and she . . . well . . . she cried the entire time. I wanted so badly to go to her."

"Dude, why didn't you?"

With a shrug of my shoulders, I replied, "I don't know. She told me to leave and the last thing I wanted her to find out was that I had spent the night outside her apartment."

"Stalking her."

Clenching my teeth, I rolled my eyes. "I wasn't stalking her!"

Maybe I was a little.

"Have you called her since?"

"Nah . . . I figured if she really wanted to talk to me she'd call. I'm always the one calling her and it's clear she wants to move on."

Walker reached for the gearshift and put it in Drive. "Jase, if there is one thing I learned from your sister it is that what you think women want is usually the exact opposite of what they want."

"So you don't think she really wanted me to leave?"

With a nod, he said, "I don't. And when you did it probably made her angry and then that made her turn to this work guy. Clearly she didn't want to be with him . . . or he hurt her in some way."

The thought had me livid. "I'll fucking kill him if he hurt her."

"Down boy," Walker said with a chuckle and pulled back onto the highway. "I think if things are meant to be with this girl they'll work themselves out, but you might have to push it along. Especially if she lives in Austin."

With a gruff laugh, I nodded. "Yeah. It's not like fate is going to have me run into her in Llano."

"Never ever doubt fate, especially when she teams up with destiny."

My heart felt so heavy as I smiled weakly.

"This is it."

Dipping my head down, I glanced up at the sign.

Reynolds Breeding.

"Do they know we're coming?"

Walker grunted. "Of course they do. Jesus, Jase. I'm not that un-professional to just show up."

With a shrug, I grinned and mumbled, "Just checking."

As we pulled up, I couldn't believe the massive house in front of me. "Wow. This place is nice."

Throwing it in Park, Walker opened the truck door and jumped out. Walking around the front, he shook his head. "Damn. Reminds me of your parents' house."

"It's fucking huge," I said under my breath as the front door opened and an older man came walking out along with a younger guy.

"Walker Moore?" the older gentleman asked as he extended his hand.

"Yes, sir." They shook hands as he replied, "Scott Reynolds. This is my son-in-law, Colt Mathews."

That caught my attention. "Colt Mathews, as in the Mathews Cattle Ranch?"

Colt smiled and nodded. "Yes. Gunner Mathews is my father."

"It's a pleasure meeting you," I said as I shook his hand. "Jase Morris."

Scott and Colt both lifted their eyes as Scott replied, "Don't tell me your dad is Layton Morris?"

It must have then hit Scott who Walker was, because he turned to Walker. "Reed Moore. It's all coming together. Jesus, the last time I saw you two boys you were running around playing cowboys and Indians."

Everyone laughed.

"I'm sorry I didn't put the name together when you mentioned Llano."

Walker lifted his hand. "Nah, don't even think twice about it."

"Your fathers have some pretty good racehorses. We worked to-gether a number of years ago."

"Yes, sir, they do. I've always been interested in that side of the busi-ness as well, hence the reason I'm here today."

Scott nodded his head. "Then let's get right to business. From what you've told me about Lady's lineage, I'd say you've got a great start in her."

"I have a feeling. I know that might be crazy to hear, but something tells me with the right stud, she could foal a real racehorse."

Scott grinned from ear to ear. "Then, son, do I have the stud for you. Let's go meet Whiskey. He's in the main barn right behind the house."

"Whiskey and Lady . . . what a combo," I mumbled under my breath as Colt laughed.

We walked behind Walker and Scott and made our way to the barn. "So, you work here, Colt?"

"Yeah, horses have always been my kind of thing since I was young. Don't get me wrong, I love the cattle business, but this is where my heart is."

"I admire you for following your dreams."

Colt smiled weakly and asked, "You haven't?"

"Oh, there were a brief few months where I declared I wanted to do something other than ranch. It's in my blood though, and it didn't take me long to come to my senses."

Colt placed his hand on my shoulder and gave me a slight push. "Once that shit is in your blood you can't get it out."

With a nod, I agreed. "Amen to that."

Lifting his gaze to in front of him, Colt lit up and smiled like a man in love. Turning, I saw a beautiful girl with blonde hair round the corner coming out of the barn. The way she looked at Colt, I knew that must have been his wife.

"Lauren, this is Walker Moore," Scott said as Lauren shook Walker's hand.

Why did she look so familiar to me?

Turning to me, her smile dropped as she gasped. "This is Jase Morris. Jase, my daughter, Lauren. She is the one really in charge."

Her eyes looked me over as her mouth snapped shut for a brief moment before she flashed a brilliant smile and said, "What a crazy thing fate is. It's a pleasure to finally meet you formally, Jase."

Frowning, I looked over at everyone else with a confused expression before focusing back on Lauren. "I'm sorry?"

The air around me instantly changed as I saw her walking out of the barn. When our eyes met, she came to a stop.

"Taylor," I whispered as her eyes widened in shock.

Her mouth opened and shut quickly as she looked around. Lauren walked up to her and said, "I told you that, girl; fate has a way of taking care of things."

My eyes snapped over to Walker who wore a huge grin on his face.

Clearing her throat, Taylor asked, "Wh-what are you doing here?"

I couldn't help but look her over quickly. She looked tired. Focusing back on her beautiful green eyes, I smiled. "Walker wants to breed a horse and asked me to drive along with him. What are you doing here?"

"Taylor works for us now."

My head snapped over to look at Lauren. "Here?"

She nodded her head and wiggled her eyebrows. "She's even going to be staying in the hunter's cabin . . . isn't she, Daddy?" Lauren asked as she turned to her very confused father.

All eyes went to Scott. "Um . . . yes she is, but do the two of you know each other?"

"Yes," Taylor said sharply.

Colt clapped his hands together causing both Taylor and I to jump. "So, let's look at that horse and let Taylor and Jase catch up, shall we."

With a tip of my hat, I silently thanked Colt and stole a look at Walker. His eyes widened and he silently pleaded for me to talk to Taylor.

"I think I'll head in with them in case Walker has any questions," Lauren said.

Taylor reached out to grab Lauren. "Wait!" Lauren stopped and leaned in to whisper something to Taylor. I couldn't help but notice how hard Taylor was breathing, and I wanted more than anything to pull her into my arms and beg her to start over.

With a sincere smile directed toward me, Lauren turned and headed into the barn.

Taylor pushed her long brown hair behind her ear and peeked up at me. "I . . . I've been wanting to . . . I mean." Sighing, she turned her head away from me.

My heart couldn't have been beating any harder than it was at that point. I knew deep in my heart Taylor deserved so much better than me, but I was tired of caring. I loved her and wanted her so damn much. "You look beautiful, Taylor."

She slowly shook her head while pressing her lips together. I knew she was about to get upset. Walking up to her, I wrapped her in my arms and held her as her shoulders shook with sobs.

"I'm so sorry for hurting you, Taylor. I'd give anything to go back to that day in Paris and change it. I pray to God you believe me."

Burying her face into my chest, she nodded. I moved my body and held her to my side as we walked over toward a gazebo. Stopping, I motioned for her to sit down.

The moment she looked into my eyes, I felt my stomach drop. She looked emotionally drained and her eyes were filled with such sadness. "I was so angry and I wanted you to hurt like you hurt me. I didn't really want you to leave and I didn't mean to . . ." Her eyes snapped shut as she slumped over and cried harder.

I knew she was thinking about the night she spent with that asshole. I'd love to punch his face. If I ever saw him again I probably would.

"We both did enough hurting of each other to last a lifetime . . . me especially to you, sweetness. Can't we just forget all of that and start over? I mean really start over and do all of this right. I feel like fate is giving us a second chance."

She sniffled and wiped her tears away. "What do you mean?"

With a grin, I looked around before turning back to her. "Are you really working here?"

Her expression softened as she nodded her head. "I am. And I guess I'll be living here too. It makes sense since my parents live in Fredericksburg."

Is this really happening? Was Taylor going to be living less than thirty minutes from me? My heart beat rapidly in my chest at the thought. I'd never felt so happy in my life.

"Please tell me I'm not dreaming because there is no way fate would be so cruel."

With a giggle, she shook her head. "Fate. Lauren was just talking about how fate always seems to step in where we're concerned."

A single tear rolled slowly down her cheek.

Lifting my hand, I wiped the wetness away and brushed my thumb across her skin. "I love you, Taylor. I've always loved you and hope you know that is why I acted so fucking crazy."

Her smile faded. "I know you have. I've done something though and I think you should know. It . . . it might change how you feel about me."

It killed me knowing she was beating herself up over what happened. "Nothing else matters except for you telling me right now you forgive me for being a total ass in Paris and all those other times I played tug of war with your heart. I'll make you this promise right now . . . I will never be the reason you cry again unless they are tears of happiness."

Her hand came up to cover her mouth. Closing her eyes, she said something I couldn't understand.

"Sweetness, please don't cry."

Tears streamed down her face and it destroyed me. "Jase, that day you left."

Shaking my head, I held up my hand. "None of that matters."

She grabbed my hand and pushed it down. "Please let me tell you this because I don't want anything between us. We've always had something between us and I don't want that. Like you said, I want to start over clean, and the only way I can do that is if I tell you everything."

With a slight nod, I held my breath and waited for her to tell me she slept with that asshole.

"I . . . I was angry and trying to prove something to myself. I slept with another man the night you left my office. The guy you saw me talking to, Clark . . . er . . . Mr. Burns. Oh no wait, that sounds creepy."

Shaking her head trying to rid herself of the memory, she rolled her eyes. "Well, I mean I guess it doesn't matter what his name was. It was only that one time and I regretted it so much. I've been so torn up about it because I didn't really want you to leave my office!"

Walker was right. What you thought women wanted was the total opposite of what they really wanted.

Cupping her face with my hands, I pressed my lips against hers and kissed her. "Shh . . . none of that matters. I'm not going to let anything take you from me again. It wasn't fate that brought us back together today."

She wiped her nose and sniffled as I let out a chuckle. "It wasn't?" she asked.

My thumbs moved across her beautiful face as I looked deep into her eyes that were filled with hope. "No. It was destiny."

Twelve

Taylor

MY SKIN WAS on fire everywhere Jase touched me. I still couldn't believe he was here. When I walked out of that barn and saw him standing there I lost all control of my emotions and it took everything out of me not to rush into his arms and beg him to kiss me.

Jase was looking at me liked he adored me. My heart felt light in my chest while the same feeling I felt after he made love to me came rushing back.

"Destiny," I repeated.

Jase smiled lovingly at me and I knew he was right. I couldn't contain the smile that spread across my face. "What do we do now?"

Jase's eyes began to glow. "I think I should ask you out for dinner."

"I am hungry." She looked back toward the barn. "But I didn't bring a change of clothes and I still need to figure out how to get my stuff from my apartment in Austin to my new place here."

"Then consider that our first official date."

"Moving me?"

His wide smile had me grinning so hard my cheeks were beginning to ache. "Why not? We've done everything else ass-backwards, why should our first official date as boyfriend and girlfriend be any different."

Lifting my brow, I softly said, "Boyfriend and girlfriend?"

"Yes. Boyfriend and girlfriend.

Every single one of my nerve endings tingled at his words.

"I could call you my ball and chain if you'd rather."

With a chuckle, I hit him on the chest.

"I'm perfectly fine with boyfriend and girlfriend."

The wind blew my hair about as Jase pushed another piece behind my ear.

His eyes filled with love while they searched my face. "Kiss me and make it official then."

I launched myself into him as our lips found one another. The kiss wasn't frantic, but it wasn't slow either. I wanted him more than ever. When we finally broke apart, our eyes searched each other's face.

"Would Walker mind if you left with me?"

"Even if he did, I wouldn't care."

With a light-hearted laugh, I turned to the barn. "I should probably officially accept the job then."

Jase stood up and pulled me up with him. "Yes! You really should."

When his fingers laced with mine, I couldn't ignore the way my heart was beating so rapidly. It felt like a million butterflies fluttered in my stomach.

We headed back to the barn and joined the others. Scott and I talked for a bit about the job, what I would be paid and what I would pay to live in the hunter's cabin. It was dirt cheap and I could see it in his eyes he didn't even want me to pay rent, but I had insisted.

Colt, Jase, and Walker hit it off instantly and talked non-stop. I got Lauren caught up on everything. When I told her the things Jase said to me, she got all teary eyed and said it sounded like something Colt would have said.

Never in a million years would I have dreamed Jase Morris was so romantic.

"You ready to go?" I asked walking up to the guys.

Walker slapped Jase on the back and winked. "Don't forget tomorrow afternoon I'll need your help with that fence."

"I won't forget," Jase said walking up to me and wrapping his arm around me. Every time he touched me, my heart either skipped a beat or my stomach dropped.

"Let's go get you packed up and ready to move."

I was sure my face was beaming as I rapidly nodded my head. Jase followed me to my car. Trying like hell to walk normal, I fought not to break out into a run as I calmly made it to my car. After picking up his truck in Llano, Jase followed me to Austin. I couldn't help but look in my mirror every two minutes at the handsome cowboy in the black Ford truck.

The moment we got to my apartment I knew what I wanted to happen. Peeking over to Jase, I couldn't help but smile when I saw his face.

He was hoping for the same thing.

◦───◦

THE SECOND THE door to my apartment shut, Jase pushed me against it and kissed me like I'd never been kissed. Things quickly heated up as we each undressed one another as fast as we could.

"Jase," I panted into his mouth, "I want you so much."

His hands were everywhere on my body. It was as if he was trying to memorize everywhere he touched.

"Sweetness, we need to slow down."

Lifting his shirt over his head, I took in his amazing body. Years of working on his father's cattle ranch gave him a broad chest and abs I'd forgotten were so amazing. My hands gently rested on his skin. Warmth radiated through my body as our eyes met.

"I'm so glad everything is packed up," I said quickly.

Jase looked around and smiled. "You're all packed?"

"Yep. That means you can take your time making love to me."

He turned back and pierced my eyes with his. I'd never seen them so blue before. He lifted me up while I wrapped my legs around his waist.

"Bedroom?" he asked against my lips.

My breathing was labored as I felt his hard-on pressed into my body. Stammering, I said, "Down the hall, last door on the right."

Before I knew it, Jase was gently laying me on the bed where he slowly peeled the rest of my clothes off until I was in nothing but my panties.

He feasted his eyes on me while licking his lips. "Jesus . . . you're so beautiful."

My cheeks heated as I watched him unbutton his jeans and take them off.

"Do you always go commando, Mr. Morris?"

With a wink, he crawled onto the bed as I held my breath. His lips began to kiss my neck while he whispered into my ear, "Most of the time."

"Oh God . . . what a thought," my breathy voice spoke.

The smell of his cologne felt like a warm blanket wrapping around my body. I wasn't sure when he did it, but he had turned on music as I attempted to look around for the source.

His hand cupped my breast, causing me to arch my back and moan.

"I want to touch every inch of your body, sweetness."

My hands twisted the bedspread while I gasped for air when he took my nipple in his mouth.

The way he worshipped my body and took his time was driving me insane, yet made it even more amazing.

Moving to my other nipple, I closed my eyes and dreamed of what was coming next.

Goose bumps spread over my body when his hand slipped inside my panties. My legs spread open wider, inviting him to take me with his fingers.

"Fuck . . . you're so wet."

Lifting my head, I watched him kiss down my stomach and run his tongue around my belly button. My head dropped back to the bed as I let out a long moan.

When I felt him removing my panties, I barely had the energy to lift my hips for him to slip them off. His hands were everywhere but where I wanted them.

Kisses peppered along my hips as he moved his fingers lightly over the inside of my leg. If I had more courage, I'd tell him what I really wanted him to do with his mouth and fingers.

"I want to taste you."

My head lifted while my chest rose up and down rapidly. "Okay! Yes! Please . . . now!"

The desperation in my voice shocked me, but I didn't care. It had been too long since he had touched me. I wanted him to do everything to me all at once.

And everything is what he gave me. His fingers pushed in at the same time as his mouth worked magic on my clit.

My orgasm hit me so fast and hard I saw stars while I rocked my hips against his face.

"Jase!" I screamed out. He had stopped and then started again, throwing me into a second, more powerful orgasm.

The room felt as if it was spinning and I was floating in the air. When I felt him moving up my body, I wrapped my legs around him, pulling him to me.

"So greedy today," he said with a crooked smile and those damn dimples.

Lost.

I was completely lost in this man.

His smile. His blue eyes that were staring back at me with nothing but love in them. Utterly lost.

"You're mine," I whispered.

His eyes pooled with tears as he replied, "Thank God."

"I feel so lost in you, Jase."

Resting on his elbows, he laced his fingers in my hair and slowly pushed into me as we both sucked in a breath of air. "Better to be lost together than apart."

His lips brushed against mine. Each movement in and out of me was heavenly. Jase took his time at first. Kissing me so deeply I was sure we were one.

My eyes pierced his while I demanded, "More."

With that crooked smile of his, he lifted me and grabbed onto my hips and gave me exactly what I asked for.

It was fast . . . hard . . . and the most wonderful experience of my life. Even better than the first time we were together.

He called out my name as my entire body trembled.

Leaning over me, Jase breathed heavily while I wrapped my arms around him.

"My God, Taylor. That was . . ."

My fingertips grazed lightly across his back. "Magical."

Lifting his body off of mine, he pierced my eyes with his. "Yes. That's the only word to use."

When he pulled out of me, I felt the loss immediately. He quickly got off the bed and headed into the bathroom. When he returned, he gently cleaned me off with a warm washcloth. "We never ate," he said with a quick kiss on the lips.

"I'll order a pizza and we can pack up the last of my stuff."

Jase emerged from my bathroom again and said, "What about all the furniture?"

"It came furnished. I only have to worry about my stuff."

I could see something on his face. He looked . . . worried. I quickly got up and made my way over to him. "What's wrong?"

Swallowing hard, he closed his eyes and shook his head. "I know why it felt so fucking amazing."

With a smile, I felt my face grow hot. "It did feel even better than before."

His eyes opened and he placed his hand on the side of my face. "Taylor, we didn't use a condom."

My face dropped and my chest tightened. "Oh no."

"You're not on the pill, are you?"

My hand covered my mouth as my heart dropped. *Oh no. What did I do? How could I be so stupid!* Quickly dropping it, I shook my head. Stumbling on my words, I replied, "I'm not on the pill right now. I swear I didn't forget a condom with him. I swear to you!"

Jase frowned and I knew I shouldn't have brought up Clark, but I didn't want him to think I was having unprotected sex. "I'm sorry . . . I just don't want you to think I . . ." Shaking my head, I looked away. My stomach felt sick as a million and one things raced through my mind.

I jumped when he placed his hands on my shoulders and turned me to him.

"I got as caught up in the moment as you did, Taylor. We both forgot, and I swear to you I've never had unprotected sex. But I won't lie and say it didn't feel good, because it was the most amazing thing ever."

Pressing my lips together, I fought to hold my smile back. He pulled me to him and buried my face in his chest. "Let's not worry about it now. There's nothing we can do about it."

The thought of being pregnant at twenty-four scared the hell out of me. I knew all of my friends had kids young . . . well almost all of them. But hell, even Lauren was pregnant.

But Jase and I were not ready for a baby. We had to work on us first.

"We have to be more careful from now on, Jase. As much as I would love to have a baby with you . . ."

His face lit up as he smiled. "I really want it to be us for a while. I think it's important for the two of us to spend time together."

The moment his hand laced through my hair, my body came to life. "I agree with you. I'm so sorry I put you in this situation."

"We both did. The bigger question is, do you have any condoms?"

With a chuckle, he nodded. "Yes, sweetness, I do."

Reaching for a shirt I had on the chair, I slipped it over my head. "Good. Let's get the rest of this stuff packed up."

Jase pulled his jeans on and said, "I'm glad I talked you into taking me to Llano and picking up my truck. I think we can get everything into your car and my truck."

Pulling on a pair of boy shorts and some sweats, I noticed Jase staring at me. "What?"

He slowly shook his head. "Nothing . . . it's just you look so sexy right now."

Glancing down, I took in the old sweats and faded T-shirt. "I do?"

"Fuck yes. If I thought my dick would come back up this soon, I'd take you again."

My lower stomach pulled with desire. "I'm glad to see you're easy to please."

Jase laughed and walked over to me. Pulling me into his arms, he kissed me deeply. "Let's get you moved. The faster you're in Mason, the better."

Thirteen

Jase

AFTER THE LAST box was placed in the back of my truck bed, I leaned against it and smiled. *I can't believe Taylor will be living and working so close to me.* Who would have thought this would all work out like this?

Pushing off the truck, I headed back to her apartment. Walking in, I watched as she stood in the middle of the living room vacuuming. The entire place was emptied of her stuff. What she wasn't taking she dropped off at a neighbor's who was going to donate it for Taylor.

She turned and saw me watching her. Turning off the vacuum, she gave me the cutest smile ever. "I had a cleaner come in and clean the whole place up for me, but I thought I would at least vacuum."

I headed into the kitchen and checked all the cabinets. "How did you get packed up so fast?"

"I never really unpacked; I only had out the stuff I really needed. I didn't like this apartment that much. I had a feeling I wouldn't be staying long. Most of the stuff was packed still from when I moved in and was from my place when I was in college."

I let out a chuckle. "Made it easy for me!"

"And you got pizza out of it," she said with a sexy look.

"That's true. But you did get free labor out of me."

With a lift of her eyebrows, she tilted her head. "I believe I get more out of you."

"You are very right. Where should we say goodbye to your apartment?"

Taylor glanced around and walked up to me, pressing her body to mine. "How about right here in the kitchen?"

My dick jumped at the thought. My hands moved to her hips where I pushed her sweats down. Kicking them off to the side, she quickly unbuttoned my jeans and ever so slowly pulled them down while taking me in her hand.

Sucking in a breath of air, I knew I wouldn't last long if she played with me. When she licked her lips and went to put me in her mouth, I stopped her. "Don't. I'll come the second your mouth wraps around me."

Biting on her lip, she asked, "Even if I don't know what I'm doing?"

My eyes closed and moaned. "Jesus, Taylor. Knowing I'm the first guy you've done it to almost has me about to now."

"I want you to teach me how to make you feel good, Jase. There are so many things I want to try."

My heart slammed against my chest as I pulled her to me and lifted her and set her on the counter. "What's the first lesson you want, sweetness?"

Her cheeks flushed and she struggled with what she wanted to say. "I . . . I really want . . . um . . ."

Spreading her legs, I took myself in my hand as her eyes widened. "Tell me."

"I want to know what it feels like to just be fucked."

My eyes closed and my knees wobbled. Reaching down, I grabbed my wallet out of my pocket. Taking the condom out, I ripped it open and quickly put it on.

"You want to be fucked?"

With a quick nod of her head, I pulled her to the edge of the counter. "Promise me you'll tell me if I hurt you."

Her chest heaved as my heartbeat raced. "I promise."

Slipping my fingers into her, we both moaned. She was so wet and ready.

Positioning myself at her entrance, I grabbed a hold of her and pushed myself in, causing her to gasp.

"Taylor—"

"I'm fine!" she called out as she placed her hands on my shoulders. "It feels so different."

"Good different?" I asked with a wicked smile.

Nodding her head, she panted out, "Move, Jase. God, please move."

Moving slowly at first, I relished in the feel of being inside of her. I picked up the speed, fucking her like she asked. My eyes about rolling to the back of my head. I loved making love to Taylor, but this was so raw and felt so damn good.

"Yes!" she cried out as I pulled out and pushed back in deeper. "Jase . . . oh God!"

Her legs shook as I pushed in deeper, this time feeling my own release as I moaned and called out her name.

When we both finally came down from our highs, I rested my forehead to hers.

"Holy crap. That was . . . even better . . . than . . . before," Taylor spoke between breaths.

Laughing, I pulled back and looked at her. God, she was so beautiful. I wanted to pinch myself. Was this really happening? This morning it I couldn't have cared less if the world had gone on without me. Now, all I wanted to do was get her moved into her place so I could start showing her how much I loved her and wanted to make her happy.

"I have to say . . . this day is certainly going to end a hell of a lot better than it started."

The smile that spread over her face made my knees weak. "I love you, Jase. And in a strange way, I feel like everything that happened led us to this moment."

Before I had a chance to answer her, someone knocked on her door. Looking down, my jeans were around my ankles. Laughing, Taylor pushed me out of the way as she hopped down, and quickly put her panties and sweats back on.

Pulling the condom off, I tossed it in the trash and pulled up my jeans.

"One second!" Taylor called out as she glanced over her shoulder. Giving her the thumbs up, she opened the door.

"Clark. What . . . why are you here?"

Anger instantly swept over my body as I stood in the kitchen. I wasn't sure if I should move or not.

"Are you moving? I found out today you quit your job and I wanted to make sure it had nothing to do with me or what happened between us."

"Um . . . no it had nothing to do with you. I quit before . . . well . . . I left before we met for dinner."

"I see . . . well would you maybe like some help moving or can I take you to dinner?"

Walking out of the kitchen, I made my way to the front door. Slipping my arm around her waist, I could feel Taylor tense up.

"Everything okay?" I asked.

Clark looked me over and forced a smile. "And who are you?"

"Taylor's boyfriend."

His head snapped back over to Taylor. "You had a boyfriend?" Looking back at me, he held up his hands. "Dude, I had no idea. If I had I wouldn't have . . . um . . . shit."

In a strange way, I felt sorry for this guy. Taylor quickly said, "We weren't together so it's fine, Clark. But if you'll excuse me, we really need to finish up and head out."

His eyes bounced between the two of us. "Right, well I guess I'll see you around. Or not. Okay. Bye."

Clark quickly turned and walked away as Taylor shut the door and looked up at me. "I'm so sorry."

Cupping her face with my hands, I kissed her gently. "Let's get out of here and get you settled in. I've got plans for us tonight."

Taylor's eyes lit up. "I really like the sound of that. Will you stay with me tonight? I'm not sure how I feel staying there by myself in the middle of that giant ranch!"

My stomach did the damn flutter thing, just like it did every time Taylor smiled at me, or told me she loved me. "Nothing would make me happier."

Pressing her palms to her cheeks, Taylor giggled. "Oh my goodness! Is this really happening? I'm moving to Mason! I'm starting a new job and I have a boyfriend!" Knowing I had something to do with how happy she was did crazy things to my own emotions. There wasn't anything I wouldn't do to make every single one of Taylor's dreams come true.

"Um . . . what about your parents? Your father wasn't too pleased when you called him earlier and told him."

With a wave of her hand, Taylor grabbed the vacuum, wrapped the cord around it and handed it to me. "He'll get over it. He knew I was moving back home; I just had a little change of plans."

"And me?"

She chewed on the corner of her lip. "I think we should let my father get used to the idea that I started a new job and moved into another place before we drop you into the mix."

With a huff, I asked, "Won't Scott tell him?"

Shrugging, Taylor looked around one last time before reaching for her purse.

"If he does, I'll deal with it then. Right now I really want to get back to Mason. We have a lot of time to make up for and another new place to break in."

I pulled her into my arms. The smell of her perfume filled my senses. "Then we have my place when I move into it."

"Yes," she whispered. "And your truck. My car. So many new places and things to learn."

Closing my eyes, a low growl came from the back of my throat as I said, "I can't wait."

Fourteen

Jase

TAYLOR AND I left Austin and headed straight back to the Reynolds'
place. I called my mother to let her know what was happening. I could
hear it in her voice she was happy, but she tried not to get to excited or
ask too many questions. I was positive the moment I got home I was
going to be hit with questions from my parents, my sister, and Walker.

When we pulled up to the main house, there was another truck
parked out front. I parked behind Taylor and got out of my truck.
Lauren said Taylor needed to stop at the main house to pick up the key.

She sat in her car staring ahead. I knocked on the window, causing
her to scream. Laughing, I opened her car door.

"Sweetness, what in the world is wrong?"

Turning back to look at the house, Taylor said, "I don't even know
where to begin."

"What do you mean?"

Quickly getting out of the car, she shut the door and faced me.

"No matter what my father says, please ignore him."

My stomach felt sick as I stole a look at the truck that was parked in front of Taylor's car. "Your father is here?"

She squeezed my hands. "Looks like you get to meet my parents. Yay!"

My mouth fell open as I looked back at her. "Yay? Did you really just say yay? Your father is going to kill me."

Taylor hit me on the chest lightly. "Don't be silly. He'll be . . . happy."

"Uh-huh. Oh, I'm sure he will be. The man who took your virginity, broke your heart, then came back in and had hot passionate sex with you twice today and now has wicked plans to make you come every possible way imaginable tonight."

"Oh God. Jase, I want you so much right now."

Pushing her hands away from me, I took a step away. "No! If he sees the way you're looking at me, he'll cut my dick off, and I'm rather fond of my dick."

Her tongue slowly traveled across her upper teeth as she softly said, "I'm rather fond of it as well."

And there went the betraying bastard. Jumping around in my pants like he hadn't seen enough action today. Greedy cock.

"Taylor?"

Spinning on her heels, Taylor grabbed my hand and pulled me along after her. I couldn't hear anything from my heart pounding in my ears.

"Daddy! Mom! What are y'all doing here?"

Shit! What is his name? Bill. No, that's not right.

Taylor's father glared at me as he replied, "We thought we'd come and check out where our daughter had decided to move in the flash of a second."

Brody? Bryan! No . . . fuck. Brock. Benji? What the fuck, Jase!

"Daddy, this is Jase. Jase Morris."

Brantly. Brendon.

"Jase, this is my father."

Taylor's father stuck his hand out as I saw my whole life flash before my eyes.

"Mr. Atwood, it's a pleasure to meet you."

He gripped the hell out of my hand as I tried not to show the pain. "So, you're the boy my daughter has been pining over for the last few months. Crazy you'll now be living less than an hour away from her. How lucky for us."

The lump in my throat kept me from saying a word. Taylor dropped my hand and balled her fists as she stood directly in front of her father.

"Dad! I can't even believe how rude you're being right now."

"Why? This kid is the reason you've lost your damn mind, isn't he?"

The woman standing next to him I assumed was Taylor's mom. She hit him lightly on the chest. "Brad, stop acting like this."

"Brad!" I shouted as I snapped my fingers and smiled. All eyes were now on me. "Oh. I was trying to remember what your first name was, sir."

Rolling his eyes, Brad turned to Taylor's mom.

"Jase, this is my mother, Amanda. Mom, this is Jase."

Amanda walked up and held her hand out for me. "It's a pleasure to meet you ma'am."

She grinned sweetly and said, "Please, call me Amanda and ignore Taylor's father. He seems to forget she is twenty-four and a grown woman."

"I have not. I just hate seeing her making bad decisions."

Taylor's mouth dropped practically to the ground. "What? Is that what you think I'm doing?"

"Um, Brad why don't you come on in and we'll have a beer. Taylor, here is the key to the cabin. Everything is clean and ready to go," Scott said.

"I'll help you get settled in," Amanda said as she glared at Brad.

Walking up to Scott, Taylor took the key. "Thank you so much, Scott. Thank you for taking a chance and giving me this amazing opportunity. Even if my father thinks I'm making a *bad* decision."

With a frustrated sigh, Brad threw his hands up. "Not with the job. With him!"

All eyes were back on me again, and I was beginning to wish I had just talked Taylor into doing this tomorrow. We would be back in her apartment right now wrapped up in each other instead of being here with Brad ready to beat the shit out of me.

"Ugh! I'm not listening to this. Mom, you're more than welcome to come and help Jase and I, but Dad is *not* welcome."

Taylor stormed off to her car, got in and started it. I stood there bouncing my eyes from the car back to Brad. *What would my father tell me to do?*

"Mr. Atwood, I know you don't think very highly of me, but I love your daughter and I plan on spending the rest of my life making her happy and making up for the heartbreak I caused her. There isn't a day that goes by that I don't wish I had done things differently. But I can't change the past, so I'm going to focus on the future and she is the only thing I see in my future."

Scott cleared his throat and smiled as Brad took a deep breath in and slowly pushed it out. "You say you love her? How do you know you love her?"

With a smile, I simply said what I felt. "I can't imagine my life without her in it."

Brad narrowed his eyes and turned his head slightly away from me. He looked at Scott and then Amanda. "That girl is my life. My baby. I swear if you ever hurt her again, I'll break both your legs and arms and trust me, when I'm done with you, you will never be able to spawn children."

The instant pain I felt in my dick would insure I wouldn't have a hard-on anytime soon. With a nod of my head, I stumbled on my words. "Y-yes, sir. I promise you."

Taylor laid down on her horn as Brad rolled his eyes. "For fuck's sake. She is so much like you, Amanda."

With a chuckle, Amanda walked up and got into the passenger seat of Taylor's car. Scott winked and mouthed, *good job* before turning and following Brad back into the house.

My legs trembled as I forced them to move and take me back to my truck. At least I got the whole *meet Taylor's parents* out of the way.

⌒

I SET THE box down on the small kitchen table and smiled. "This is the last box."

"Oh, Taylor, most of this stuff is from when you were in college. Honey, didn't you go and buy anything new when you moved into your apartment?"

Amanda was trying to break down a box while Taylor wiped her forehead. "Let me do that," I said reaching for the box.

"My pleasure. I hate moving. I hate anything to do with moving."

Taylor giggled. "That must be where I get it from. That's probably why I didn't have that much stuff and I never really unpacked."

"Well, I think as soon as you get settled in we need to go shopping and make this place a little more . . ."

Both women looked around while scrunching up their noses. "Feminine," they both said at once.

"I think it looks nice in here."

Taylor gave me a *really* look while her mother chuckled.

"Where do you live Jase?"

"I've been staying with my parents. Their house is about the size of Scott's, so I practically have the whole upstairs to myself. We have a cabin on our ranch as well that I was going to start staying in. I think my mother would rather not hear me coming and going."

Amanda smiled. "I don't blame her. Is your place just as . . . drab?"

"Mom! This is a cute little cabin. I love it and think it's perfect!"

"Mine is a bit smaller, but I'm actually getting ready to have a house designed to be built."

Amanda and Taylor stopped what they were doing and looked at me. "What? Where?" Taylor asked surprised.

Taking another box they emptied, I started to break it down. "Um . . . my parents went in with their best friends and business partners and bought the ranch next to us. They split up the land between the four kids."

Amanda smiled. "Oh, how nice of them!"

I nodded. "Yes, it was."

"That's kind of cool. How much land did y'all get?"

I didn't really want to keep talking and sound like I was bragging. "A good piece. And I've been working for my father since I swear I was old enough to walk. I've been putting away money since I was about thirteen, so I have a nice nest egg built up."

The look on Amanda's face was hard to read. "I have to tell you, Jase. That is such a breath of fresh air to hear you say you've had the common sense to save up like that. I take it you're doing this all on your own?"

"Yes, ma'am. My sister, Liza, and her husband, Walker, are using their place now to raise their own cattle."

"Impressive."

Taylor walked up and kissed me quickly on the lips before turning back to her mother. "Now you can go back and tell Daddy that Jase is a responsible young man with a clear head on his shoulders."

I let out a gruff laugh and sat down on the couch. "I don't know about that. I just didn't want to live with my parents forever. It's kind of awkward bringing home a date with Mom and Dad watching a movie in the living room."

Amanda laughed when Taylor hit me on the chest.

"At any rate, I'm glad you have a plan. It's important to have a plan."

I couldn't help but notice Amanda looking at Taylor. "I have one, Mom. I'm going to learn this new business I'm starting in, I'm going to learn to garden, and someday I'll get married and push out a few kids. The last one will come much later."

My stomach dropped when Taylor mentioned kids.

With a slight chuckle, Amanda nodded. "I hope so. I'm perfectly happy with the two grandbabies I have now."

Taylor stole a glance my way and smiled nervously as I gave her a reassuring nod. I was still pissed at myself for being so careless today with both of our futures.

"Jase, will you be heading back to Llano soon?"

"Mom! Please don't go there."

Amanda rolled her eyes. "You may be an adult, Taylor, but I still would rather live in my own little bubble."

Taylor hugged her mother and kissed her on the cheek. "Thank you for helping. Tell Dad I love him."

"He's going to want to talk to you."

"Well, not tonight. Jase is taking me out to dinner."

With a look my way, Amanda smiled. "Well, it's getting late so be careful driving."

"Yes ma'am, always. Let me take you back up to the main house."

Giving me a hug and a kiss on the cheek, Amanda gave me a grin and said, "That would be great."

Giving Taylor a wave, she headed to the door. "Why don't you and Jase come by for dinner this weekend? It will give your father a chance to get to know Jase a bit more."

Holding the door open for her mother, Taylor nodded. "Maybe, we'll see. Today has been a whirlwind day and I honestly can't think about next weekend."

Amanda smiled lovingly. "I'm sure. Okay, we'll talk later. Bye, sweetheart. Love you."

"Bye, Mom, I love you too."

I opened the door for Amanda and helped her up into the truck. "Thank you, Jase," she said with a wink. "If you're buttering me up . . . save it for Brad. I'm afraid he's the one you have to win over."

With a light-hearted chuckle, I replied, "I'll remember that."

Of course when I pulled up to the house, Brad, Scott, and Jessie were all sitting on the back porch.

"Do I dare get out or should I just floor it and flee?"

Amanda laughed as she looked over at me. "Jase, I know the two of you have been through a lot. I have to be honest, I haven't seen Taylor with this much life in her eyes in a long time. Not to mention the smile she's wearing."

"I want you to know if I could go back and do it again, I wouldn't be so stupid. The last thing I ever want to do is hurt her. I love her, Mrs. At . . . I mean . . . Amanda."

"Life is all about mistakes. It's how we learn from them that matters. Now come on, let's risk it, shall we?"

My heart stopped as I pushed the door open and got out of the safety of my truck. Swallowing hard, I followed Amanda up to everyone.

"Mr. Reynolds, I have to tell you your ranch is beautiful."

Scott grinned as Brad looked away and mumbled, "Kiss ass."

"Stop it, Brad," Amanda whispered while hitting him lightly on the stomach.

Clearing his throat, Brad glared at me. "So. You helped my daughter move her stuff; are you heading to your own house now?"

Glancing over my shoulder to my truck quickly, I stumbled on my words as I faced Brad again. "Well . . . um . . . she's kind of expecting me to come back."

"I see."

Stepping between Brad and me, Scott winked at me. "Jessie made a casserole for Taylor. Why don't you take it to her and y'all can have it for a late dinner?"

"I figured she won't make it to the store for a few days, so will you please let her know she can join us for breakfast tomorrow?"

With a smile, I replied, "Yes ma'am, I'll let her know."

Jessie moaned, "Please call me Jessie, Jase. You don't have to be so formal. Now, follow me in and I'll get that casserole."

"Yes ma'am. I mean, Jessie." Walking up to Brad, I extended my hand. "It was a pleasure meeting you, sir."

With the look he was giving me, I should have been down on the ground laid out dead. Gripping my hand tightly again, he pulled me closer to him. "I know people who will bust your knee caps and make it so you don't walk for months."

"Ah . . . that's good to know, sir."

Lifting his eyebrows, he slowly nodded. "Yes, it is good to know. That means if you hurt her ever again . . . you'll be hurting a lot worse than her."

"May I be honest with you, sir?"

"Yes. I expect it always."

My eyes drifted over to Scott who was attempting to hold back his smile. Placing my attention back on Brad, I fought for my mouth to form words to speak. "You scare the hell out of me."

I don't think I'd ever seen anyone smile like how Brad was. "Good. That means I've done my job."

Amanda walked up and pulled Brad back. "All right, that's enough, Rocky. Don't pay any attention to him, Jase. He's trying to scare you."

"He certainly succeeded," I mumbled under my breath.

Fifteen

Taylor

STANDING IN THE middle of my new little place I smiled. "What a day," I whispered.

Pulling my phone out, I sent a text to Meagan.

Me: So I took the job. I'm now in the breeding business.

Meg: OMG! And the cabin?

Me: Standing in it as I type!

Meg: I'm so glad you will be closer to me and the twins.

Me: Same here. Oh. Jase and I got together today.

I stared at my phone waiting for her to respond. When my phone rang in my hand, I screamed.

"Hey. That was fast."

"What? Jase? Back together? How? Why? When? Where?"

Laughing, I dropped onto the couch. "Well, if you would stop asking one-word questions, I'll tell you."

"Taylor, this is huge. What do you mean by together? Do you mean bumping uglies together or dating together?"

Rolling my eyes, I shook my head. "God. Why are you and Grace so . . . ugh?"

"It's called keeping it real and start talking! Wait! Do Mom and Dad know?"

I couldn't hold in how happy I was. All those years dreaming of being in Jase's arms. Wondering what life would be like if we were together. My heart felt as if it was about to burst. "Yep. And they've already met him and that was not planned. Really, nothing today was planned and that's okay because it was the best day of my life!" I said with a giggle.

Meagan tittered. "Okay, spill it and start from the beginning."

After I told her everything there was silence on the phone. "Meg?"

"Wow. That's all I can say right now. I mean . . . I won't argue and say fate certainly had a hand in all of that, but Taylor are you sure you should have run back into his arms? I mean, I know how sad you've been and I want to make sure you weren't reacting with your heart only."

I closed my eyes and pulled in a deep breath before speaking again. "Do I think Jase and I rushed into things? Yes, and I'm sure he does too, but it felt so right, Meg. The moment he held me in his arms and told me how sorry he was and I told him about Clark—"

"You told him about Clark! Why?"

With a shrug, I replied, "Why not? I don't want anything to be between us and the reason I even slept with Clark was because I was angry with Jase."

"I don't understand you two. You're not dating yet you both tell each other when you've slept with other people . . . as if you were cheating. So weird."

"It doesn't matter . . . we spent the most amazing afternoon together. It was magical."

I heard rustling and then Meagan mumbled something to Grayson. "Hold on, Tay, let me go on the back porch."

A few moments later, I heard the screen door open and close.

"Okay . . . I want details. How was it? It had to have been better than the first time."

I could feel my cheeks burning as I pulled my knees up to my chest. "Meagan . . . oh my gosh. It was beyond amazing. He is so . . . good!"

Meagan let out a roar of laughter before finally saying, "That's good! How many times? Does the boy have stamina?"

Peeking out the window, I didn't see Jase coming. "I feel funny talking about it."

"What? Nonsense. Get used to it because tomorrow we are all meeting for lunch and talking about it. You're the last of the group to fully have your cherry popped. Clark doesn't count. From this day forward we never mention him again."

"Done," I mumbled.

"So? How many times."

"Twice. And the second time was . . . very different."

Meagan was silent for a few moments before she said, "Okay, new ground rules. I don't want to hear any kinky shit like you are preparing for anal or anything."

"What?" I gasped. "I just finally got used to sex in my vajayjay and you're talking anal? Can I at least graduate from regular sex before you have me starring in porn flicks?"

"Well, you were the one who said it was different."

"It was! It was in the kitchen and we . . . well, he was different."

I could hear Meagan chuckling. "He fucked you?"

The lights to Jase's truck flashed through the window.

"Jase just pulled up from dropping Mom off. I've got to go."

Meagan screamed. "No! You can't tell me he fucked you and then leave it at that? Did you like it like that? Was he gentle at least? What did Dad do when he met Jase? Ohmygawd! The questions I have!"

"Will have to wait until tomorrow." Jase walked in carrying a casserole dish and my stomach decided to make itself known I was in need of food. "I'll call you tomorrow."

"Wait!" Meagan called out as I hit End and tossed my phone on the sofa.

Inhaling a deep breath, I let the aroma of the food engulf me as I let out a low moan. "That smells so good!"

With a huge grin, Jase brought it over to the stove. "Yeah, it does. Jessie made it and said you're more than welcome to join them for breakfast tomorrow."

The idea of Jase leaving and not staying with me was unsettling. "Do you have to work early tomorrow?" I asked as I lifted the foil and smelled the chicken enchilada casserole, which was one of my favorites from Jessie. "Mmm, Jessie made my favorite."

"Nope. I already called my father and told him I was staying with you tonight since it was your first night alone here."

Turning, I leaned against the counter and took in Jase. He was so handsome. That dark-brown hair made his blue eyes pop. His smile was one of my favorite things about him. It always had been. He had so many different ones. The playful crooked smile that made my stomach drop. And the serious heartfelt smile that made my chest tighten, and then you had Jase's wicked smile with those sexy dimples. Oh how it filled my head with naughty thoughts.

Then there was his body. He was built, but not overly built like some guys are today. There was no doubt he worked out and his arms were to die for. I loved that he wasn't too tall, but he wasn't short either.

He was perfect.

"Taylor?"

"Yeah?" I mumbled as I continued to study him.

"You couldn't eye fuck me any harder if you tried, baby."

Lifting my eyebrows, I slowly let a smile play across my face. "You told your dad about me?"

"Of course I did. I told my parents everything about what happened. At the time my father was not too happy with me when I told him, but he sounded pretty happy on the phone just now."

My cheeks heated at the idea of Jase telling his father he took my virginity. I didn't mind really. I was proud of the fact that I had saved myself for when I thought it was the right time.

"Are you sure you don't mind staying here with me tonight?"

"Of course I'm sure. You're in a new place, in the middle of a huge ranch all alone. Besides, I don't want you being alone out here. I'd rather stay with you until you feel more comfortable . . . and I can talk to Scott about putting in an alarm system."

I let out a chuckle. "Seriously? Do you honestly think people would just be walking around the ranch and stumble upon the cabin?"

"No, but I'd feel better knowing you had an alarm."

My breath stalled at the notion Jase was concerned enough about me to worry.

"Are you hungry?" I asked.

With moves faster than a cougar, Jase was in front of me with both hands on the counter, pinning me in. "I'm hungry . . . but not for casserole."

My body shuddered as my eyes searched his face. "My dad didn't scare you away?"

Jase made a shuddering motion before saying, "Oh, he scared me, but nothing would make me walk away from you ever again."

Lifting my arms, I wrapped them around his neck. I'd never felt so content in my life. "Promise? Because today has been the best day of my life. Even better than Paris. I'd love to have many more days like this."

"I promise and so would I." Leaning over, he kissed the tip of my nose before leaning his forehead to mine. "To be honest, this whole day has felt like a dream."

Meagan's words replayed in my head as I placed my hands on Jase's chest. "You don't feel like we are rushing into this do you? I mean, I guess it's a little too late to ask that."

Jase placed his hand on the side of my face and gently glided his thumb across my cheek. "I know how I feel about you and I know how much of stupid idiot I was when I pushed you away. This feels like a second chance and I don't want to risk playing it safe anymore. Do you?"

My breathing increased as I looked into his eyes. "The only thing I want is for you to make love to me."

"We have one condom left, sweetness."

With a wide grin, I replied, "Better make it a good one then."

Taking me in his arms, Jase carried me over to the couch, the only surface not covered by boxes where he made sweet love to me.

Best. Day. Ever.

MY BODY ACHED as I stretched my arms above my head and let out a soft moan. Turning to my left, I smiled when I saw Jase sleeping. Lightly using my finger tip, I drew circles across his chest. Last night had been amazing. After Jase made love to me on the couch, we searched for my box with towels and sheets in it. When we took a shower together, I couldn't believe how Jase took care of me. He totally took control and washed every inch of my body. It felt more like a massage than a shower.

After the shower, we made the bed and collapsed in it. Before falling asleep in each other's arms, we spent about two hours just talking about everything and anything.

"Waking up to you touching me is probably the best feeling in the world," Jase mumbled in a sleepy voice.

Resting my chin on his chest, I giggled. "I'd say waking up to you in my bed *is* the best feeling in the world."

His arm wrapped around me, pulling me closer to him. "That too. Is today your first day at the new job?"

"Nope. Lauren told me they have a ton of stuff to do today, so she said for me to start after Christmas."

Pulling his head back and looking at me, Jase wore a wide grin. "So we can spend the day together?"

"Yep."

"How would you feel about getting this place unpacked some and heading in to meet my parents."

I was pretty sure my face turned white as I held my breath.

His parents? Oh God.

"Um . . . your parents?"

When he gave me that crooked smile, I knew what was coming. "I had to meet yours, now you have to meet mine. Besides, I want to stay here another night with you and I need clothes."

I quickly pushed off of him and swung my legs over the bed. "Okay. Let me let this sink in for a few minutes."

The bed moved when Jase got out. When I looked at him walking by, my lips parted as I sucked in a small gasp of air. His naked body walking across the room and into the bathroom had to have been the most glorious sight I'd ever seen. My teeth sunk into my lip as I felt my lower stomach pull with desire.

Man oh man, have I been missing out on things.

The water in the bathroom turned on, causing me to finally get ahold of myself. Reaching for Jase's T-shirt, I slipped it over my head and headed into the bathroom.

When I walked in he looked at me and grinned like a crazy fool. "What's wrong?" I asked.

"Nothing. It's just . . . you look so damn good in my T-shirt."

Glancing down, I noticed it came to my mid thighs. I needed to file this little bit of information away in my *things that turn Jase on* file.

His hands were under the T-shirt before I even had a chance to say anything. His fingers dipping inside my body, causing me to hiss while pumping my hips. I'd never imagine I would be so greedy when it came to sex. I craved it. Craved his touch, his kiss, the way he felt inside me. All of it was like a drug.

"Jase," I whispered as he moved his lips along my neck. I was thankful he hadn't tried to kiss me. Morning breath and kissing didn't sound sexy at all.

"Sweetness, you're so wet. Are you sore?"

I was, but there was no way in hell I was going to pass up sex with Jase. We had too much to make up for.

"No," I panted as I pushed my hips into his hand.

"Fuck. I used the last condom last night."

My mind was spinning as he moved his fingers expertly. Gripping onto his arms, I dropped my head back and let a low groan slip from my lips.

"Are you close to coming?"

"Yes. Oh yes . . . so . . . close."

When he pulled his fingers out from me, I groaned in protest. "How about our first lesson, sweetness."

With a confused look, I tried to keep my legs from going out from under me. I had been so close to coming, and having it denied was something I wasn't sure I liked.

"Lesson?"

Jase took my hand and led me back to the bed. He laid on the bed and motioned for me to crawl on top of him. "No, spin around and sit the other way."

Frowning, I shook my head. "Why?"

"We're going to do a sixty-nine, Tay."

My heart dropped. "Six . . . sixty . . . nine? You mean . . . what if I do it wrong?"

When he laughed, I felt the rumble move straight to the area between my legs. "I promise you won't. I'll tap you when I'm going to come, that way you can finish with your hand if you want."

Oh, dear lord. I really wish I had time to call the girls. *What would Grace do? Hell, I already know . . . she'd swallow.*

The blowjob workshop! I just needed to remember what Anna had taught us. She told me my cucumber had to have been the happiest one in the bunch and that I was a natural. At the time I didn't take it as a compliment, but now I was happy I paid attention to her!

Crawling over Jase, I stopped and said, "Should we shower first?"

"We showered last night, but if you want to we can."

With a shake of my head, I continued to move into position. *Make use of your hand. You don't have to take the whole dick in your mouth.*

Jase grabbed my hips and pulled me to him. The feel of his warm breath instantly had me anticipating the feel of his lips and tongue on me.

"You're shaking."

"I'm excited and nervous at the same time."

His hands moved over my body, eliciting even more trembling as my excitement built.

"Does it taste bad?"

"You?"

Jerking my head around, I stared at him. "No, not me! I mean . . . I guess I'd want to know that, but I was talking about your cum!"

With a chuckle, he winked. "First off . . . you taste like fucking heaven . . . and I'm sorry, baby, I have no clue what cum tastes like, nor do I have the desire to ever find out."

My face burned with embarrassment. "You need to eat lots of kiwi."

Pinching his brows together, he asked, "Why?"

"I heard it makes the cum taste better."

"Dully noted. I'll buy some today."

I turned back and looked at his dick. It was hard and at attention. "What if I suck?"

"Oh geesh, Taylor. That is exactly what I want you to do."

Laughing, I hit him on the side. "You know what I mean."

"Practice. Practice makes perfect. Now I have to be honest, your pussy is in my face and I want to taste you. Now."

Gasping at his dirty talk, he pulled me back and licked my clit with his tongue. "Oh my," I whimpered as I focused back in on him. I wrapped my hand along his shaft and spit on it. When my hand moved, Jase moaned, pulling me in closer to him . . . causing my entire body to fill with desire.

"Jase," I mumbled as I lowered my mouth and took him in. Everything Anna had taught us that day was running through my mind. *Start off slow.*

Slow. I can do slow.

Moving my hand and mouth, I moved ever so slowly. It wasn't so bad. The cucumber tasted better, but this was not bad. I remembered Anna saying to lick up and down the shaft to learn what he would like best. I did and Jase's body trembled.

Breathe and relax.

Moving my mouth completely over him, I picked up the pace some as Jase continued to bring me closer to an orgasm. I was concentrating so much on him, I almost forgot how amazing it felt for me. I needed to focus, though. The moment Jase tapped me out, I was pulling my mouth off and letting him cum on himself. Meagan's words of advice to let him cum on himself was stuck in the back of my head.

Jase moaned and the vibration rushed through my body, causing me to moan. "Oh fuuuck," he called out.

Smiling, I couldn't help myself. I was making him feel good with my mouth and that made me feel good in return.

I started to go faster and remembered Anna mentioned something about the balls. Moving my other hand down, I started playing with them. Jase jerked and pushed further into my mouth, causing me to almost gag. "Mmm," was all I could do in response as he focused on my clit. Clearly he liked me touching his balls. I did it again and he responded by pushing his fingers inside of me and sucking harder.

My body quickly began to build. I was close. Oh God I was so close.

My orgasm hit me hard and fast. I could feel my legs shaking as euphoria swept through my body. My moans were evident as I tried to focus both on the mind-blowing orgasm I was having and Jase's blow-job. Pulling me closer to his mouth, I swear he brought out another orgasm . . . or the one I was having intensified.

I squeezed on the bottom of his shaft and sucked harder. The next thing I knew, something warm was hitting the back of my throat.

Oh. Holy. Hell. No.

Quickly pulling my mouth away, I spit out the nasty tasting cum. "Gross! Oh gawd!" I started gagging as I flung myself off of Jase and to the floor. I was desperate for water. Anything to get the taste out.

"Water!" I screamed as I heard Jase start laughing.

"Oh, come on! It's not that bad!"

Glancing over my shoulder, I glared at him. His smile faded as I headed into the bathroom.

After rinsing my mouth out with water, I brushed . . . twice.

Jase held his finger out and put toothpaste on it. My mouth fell open when he stuck his finger in his mouth and started brushing. "What are you doing?" I asked.

Turning to look at me, he smiled and mumbled, "Brushing."

"With your finger?"

With a nonchalant shrug, he replied. "Yep."

I cleared my throat and gave him a stern look. "So, what happened to tapping on me to let me know you were about to come?"

Jase spit and quickly rinsed off his finger and then his mouth. Standing, he turned to me and gave me the cutest damn smile I'd ever seen. "I guess I got so caught up in you coming and how great it felt I kind of . . . forgot."

My brow lifted. "You forgot? Or you just didn't want me to stop?"

"Maybe a little bit of both."

Slapping him on the chest, we both laughed. "Gross, Jase! I was not prepared for that. It was so . . . so . . . salty and warm and thick!"

He pulled me closer to him and pressed his lips to mine. The kiss was slow as we explored each other's mouths. When he stopped, he looked into my eyes. "I'm sorry. I promise to let you know next time."

"You better and I hope you have plans on making it up to me."

Taking my hand in his, we headed back into the bedroom. The cabin was three rooms. The living room, kitchen, and dining area was all in one big open room. The bedroom and the bathroom made up the other two rooms. Everything had been remodeled and was actually nicer than my apartment in Austin. It was just small, which was okay.

"Let's get dressed and we'll head into Llano. I'm sure my mother is on pins and needles waiting to finally meet you. You can also meet Ava, Walker and Liza."

My heartbeat increased as I frantically looked for boxes that held all of my clothes. Most of my stuff I wore a lot I had brought with me to my parents'. I made a mental note to head over there and get it all as quickly as possible.

"I have nothing to wear! All my good stuff is at my parents' house."

Jase pulled his jeans on and looked me up and down. "Anything you put on will look amazing on you."

With a frustrated sigh, I looked around. "I can't just wear anything! It's your parents. Your sister!"

He stood there staring at me with a dumbfounded look on his face. "Just wear the sweats you had on yesterday and a T-shirt. You looked adorable."

With a stony expression, I rolled my eyes and grabbed a pair of jeans and a sweater.

Men.

Luckily it was chilly outside. I could wear my boots and add a scarf to dress it up some. By the time I was finished getting dressed, Jase had found the box with the Keurig and made us each a cup of coffee.

Glancing up, he grinned and took a sip before slowly shaking his head. "Damn, you look beautiful, Tay."

I had pulled my long brown hair up and put it in a ponytail. With just a few light touches of make-up on, and a quick spray of perfume I was able to find, I felt like I was ready to meet the parents. Of course with the way Jase was looking at me, I felt like a princess.

"Thank you for the compliment and the coffee!"

He handed me a cup he found packed away in a box. "Good thing you take it black since you don't have any food in the house."

My stomach fluttered at the notion he knew how I drank my coffee. "I'm impressed you remembered how I take my coffee."

"I've tried to memorize everything about you."

My tongue ran along my upper lip while I tried to give him the sexiest look I could. "Keep talking like that and we'll be here all day."

Jase pushed off the counter and stopped directly in front of me. "I'd normally be okay with that, but we need condoms."

Chewing on the corner of my lip, I nodded. "Right. That is our number one priority today."

After finishing off our coffee, we unpacked the rest of the kitchen stuff and headed out to Jase's truck.

"Should I drive and follow you?"

Jase stopped and looked at me like I had grown two heads. "Hell no. The more time we are together, the better. I'll drive since I know where I'm going. I've texted my mom to let her know we are on our way."

"I feel sick," I whined while placing my hand on my stomach.

Grabbing me, Jase spun me around as I screamed and threw my head back laughing. "Stop it! You put me through hell yesterday, so now it's your turn."

When he set me down, I shook my head and pointed at him. "The difference is, I didn't knowingly lead you into the wolf's den. My parents just showed up. You're lucky they didn't drive into Austin and catch us in the act."

Jase shuddered and opened his truck door for me. "Point taken."

He took my hand and helped me into the truck, causing that ever-growing feeling of happiness in the pit of my stomach. "Such a gentleman," I whispered. He reached in and kissed me gently on the lips while flashing the dimples.

Watching him walk around the front of the truck, I pinched my arm.

"Yep, I'm awake," I mumbled under my breath.

Sixteen

Taylor

THE DRIVE TO Llano was beautiful. *I can't believe I ever thought I would be happy living in Austin.* The Texas hill country was and always would be my home.

"What are you smiling about over there?" Jase asked while taking my hand in his.

"How beautiful it is in the hill country. I wonder how long I would have been happy living in Austin?"

His lips pressed against my wrist. "I'm not going to lie and say I'm not over the moon you're not in Austin. I hate that you left your job, but damn I'm glad you're so close to me."

With a giggle, I took in Jase's features. His jaw was strong and he had the most beautiful eyelashes. I'd kill to have them. Everything about him was perfection. Even his nose was beautiful. We would have beautiful babies.

My head snapped forward as that thought hit me a little too close to home. Closing my eyes, I said a quick prayer I wasn't pregnant.

I jumped when Jase started to speak again. "I love Texas and couldn't imagine living anywhere else."

"You said your sister's best friend Ava was in town? Does she live out of the state?"

"Ava, no she lives in Austin. Both my family and her family went to Montana, remember?"

I nodded as he kept talking. "Well, it turns out she knows one of the guys who is helping us go organic. His family owns a huge ranch up there and they invited us up to see how an organic cattle ranch runs. While we were there, Ava broke her leg and her ankle. She's been playing house with Ryder."

"Ryder? He's the guy she knew?"

"Yep. I will bet you a million dollars she is not home to stay."

"Why?" I asked.

Jase laughed and shook his head. "If I know Ava, she's fallen in love with Ryder and coming home to pack up her shit and head right back up there."

"So Ryder lives there?"

Looking at me he winked, "I know it's so damn confusing. No, he lives in Austin but will be moving back to Montana."

"Wow. It's like a soap opera."

"When it comes to Ava, you have no idea. I'm pretty sure there were bets placed that the two of us would end up together."

My interest was piqued. "And? Did y'all ever date?"

"Nah. We messed around together a few times in high school with a bit of kissing and touching, but it never led anywhere. Afterwards we laughed our asses off. She really is like a sister to me. I like this guy Ryder, so I hope things work out for both of them."

A streak of jealousy zipped quickly through me before I pushed it away. It was high school and I had no reason to be jealous.

I studied him more before he turned and captured my eyes. "What?"

Slowly shaking my head, I softly spoke, "Nothing. I'm just trying to figure out how this all happened. I feel so happy and I'm so afraid something is going to pull the rug out from under us."

With a squeeze of my hand, he replied, "I refuse to believe anything will ever come between the two of us again."

He turned left and took off down another country road.

Deciding I needed to push my negative thoughts away, I looked back out the window. "So, your parents and Walker's bought y'all land? That was really nice of them."

"Yeah it was. An older couple, Mimi and Frank, had a huge working cattle ranch next to ours. Not as big as my dad and Reed's, but big. Frank got too old to take care of it and offered to sell to my father. They bought it up and left some land for Mimi and Frank and divided up some for the four of us."

"What will Ava do with hers if she moves?"

He shrugged and said, "I don't know. I never even thought about that. If she wants to keep it great, if not I may buy it from her since it backs to mine."

We drove for a little bit in silence when Jase pulled over on the side of the road. "What are we doing?"

"Come on, I want to show you something."

Opening the truck door, I went to get out, but Jase quickly was there helping me down. "Do you often stop on the side of the road for no reason?"

With a smirk, he took my hand and led me up to the fence. Looking out over the land, I smiled. "Wow. It's beautiful. Whose land is this?"

"Ours. In this very spot is where my father saw my mother for the very first time."

My heart skipped a beat. "How do you know?"

Pointing to the fence, it was painted red. "My father and mother have told us so many times how they met. They didn't hit it off at first. My mother was a city girl from New York with a broken down car and my father was as much of a cowboy as humanely possible."

My smile grew bigger while I watched Jase's face light up when talking about his parents. "My father comes to this exact spot and sprays it with paint so he never forgets the spot where his life changed."

Dropping my shoulders, I teared up. "That's so romantic."

Jase's grin grew wider. "Yeah they are disgustingly romantic, but I love when they both talk about each other. You see the love in their eyes, their smile. Hell the way their voice changes. I've always looked at that and wished like hell I would be lucky to find it."

My heart rate spiked as Jase looked away. "For the longest time I thought I wasn't good enough for you." His eyes met mine. "You're so beautiful, Taylor. Not only on the outside, but on the inside as well. The thought of you looking at me like my mother looks at my father . . . it's something I have never wanted so badly before in my life like I do with you. After all the shit I put you through, I wanted to stop here . . . in this spot were true love first found each other. To tell you I swear I will do everything in my power to make you the happiest woman on earth if you let me."

Tears pooled in my eyes as my heartbeat filled my ears. No one had ever made me feel like Jase had. Even when he pushed me away, he had a way of letting me know how much he loved me.

I searched for the words to say. His eyes focused on my face for some kind of clue to what I was thinking.

"I . . . I've never been so happy as I am right now. I keep saying it, but I feel like I'm in a dream that I never want to wake up from."

Taking my hands in his, he smiled the most beautiful smile I'd ever seen. In that moment I knew, we would be together forever. "God I feel the same way. I love you, Taylor."

"Oh, Jase," Throwing myself into his body, he wrapped me up in his arms and lifted me off the ground. "I love you too."

A horn honked as Jase put me down and we both turned to see a Ford F-350. "Who's that?"

"My dad."

"Oh," I mumbled.

"Come on, he's probably wondering what in the hell I'm doing and praying I'm not asking you to marry me."

Marry me.

The idea made me happy and scared me at the same time.

The window rolled down and I almost gasped when I saw Jase's father. He was an older version of Jase. His blue eyes stood out against the black cowboy hat he had on. I imagined he had dark hair under the hat and would look even more like Jase when he took it off. Turning to look at Jase, my mouth dropped open. They looked almost alike. "I know. Everyone says I'm a mini version of my father."

"I'd say," I replied so only he could hear.

"Dad, this is Taylor Atwood. Taylor, this is my father, Layton Morris."

I attempted to reach up and in to the truck to shake his hand and failed. Everyone laughed as I made a face and felt my cheeks heat up. "I guess I'm shorter than I thought."

"It's a pleasure to finally meet you, Taylor." Layton looked over to Jase. "What are y'all doing on the side of the road?"

Jase pointed back to the fence and the exact spot we were standing at. "I was showing Taylor where you and Mom met."

Layton's eyes lit up and I could see the love for his wife on his face as he glanced over to the spot. "One of the best days of my life. That's a good spot."

"Yes, sir, I'm sure it is," I said peeking back over to it.

"Well, get her back in the truck and head on to the house. I'm sure your mother is wearing the floors out waiting to finally meet Taylor."

With a light chuckle, I looked away and then to Jase as he replied to his father, "Yes sir, we're right behind you."

Placing his hand on my lower back, I got that silly feeling in my stomach again as he led me to his truck.

After helping me up into the truck, he stepped up and slid his hand behind my neck, pulling my lips to his. With a fast kiss, he whispered, "One down. One to go."

MY HANDS SHOOK as I walked up the stairs to Jase's parents' house. His father must have floored it to get here and in the house before us.

Stopping short of the door, I grabbed onto Jase's arm and pulled him to a stop. "Wait. I know you said before you told your parents everything, but . . . what if they don't like me?"

Jase cupped my face with his hands and gave me a panty-melting smile. "Yes. They know everything and they are happy we're together. It's the past. All we have in front of us is our future. That's all we concentrate on from this point on? Okay?"

Pressing my lips together, I nodded my head. "O-okay."

With a kiss on my lips, he took my hand in his and we walked through the front door. Standing in front of me was Layton, Walker, and a gorgeous woman I was assuming was Jase's mom, and a beautiful brown-haired, blue-eyed woman holding a little boy who was trying with all his might to get down.

All eyes were on me as I focused on the baby for a little too long. "This is Nickolas and all he wants to do is get down and crawl," Jase said with a chuckle.

Smiling, my eyes bounced between everyone.

"Holy hell. Nothing like overwhelming her with a welcome committee," Layton said while giving me a reassuring smile.

"We were just so excited to meet you, Taylor. I hope you don't mind if I asked Walker and Liza to be here when you got here," Whitley said.

"Um . . . no of course not," I said trying to do something with my nervous hands.

Jase placed his hand on my lower back again, guiding me into the living room. "This is my sister; Taylor is her name also. She goes by Liza though."

"It's a pleasure to meet you, Liza."

Her blue eyes sparkled as she looked at Jase and then me. "I've heard so much about you, Taylor. It's so wonderful to have you here. It really is."

Feeling the heat sweep across my face, I replied, "Thank you. It's been an amazing couple of days."

She winked as she leaned in closer. "I bet."

Oh lord.

"You already know Walker."

Reaching my hand out to Walker, he pulled me in for a hug and whispered, "Don't worry. They won't bite."

When I pulled away, he winked and I couldn't help but chuckle.

Next came Jase's mom. Please don't let me say something stupid.

"Taylor, this is my beautiful mother, Whitley. Mom, this is my Taylor."

My Taylor.

Both Whitley and I looked at Jase and smiled. "*Your* Taylor, huh?" Whitley said with a chuckle.

When he wrapped his arm around my waist, I couldn't help but relax into his side. I felt so safe with him.

"Let her go this instant, Jase Adam Morris."

Letting his arm drop, Whitley engulfed me in a hug and whispered, "It's so wonderful to finally meet you. You have no idea how happy I am right now."

She pushed me back at arm's length and looked me over. "You're more beautiful than Jase said."

Tingling swept the back of my neck and I was pretty sure even my ears were red. "All right, Mom. You're embarrassing her. You've already met my father."

"Mr. Morris," I softly spoke with a slight nod.

"It's Layton. Please no Mr. or Mrs. Morris in this house." Layton turned to Jase and grinned. "I only need you to do me one favor and that is to mend the fence in the southwest pasture next to the gate. It looks like someone was trying to get in. After that you're free to spend the next few days off."

"I've got the fence, Layton. Jase has been working non-stop and deserves a few days off."

Jase shook Walker's hand and said, "I owe you one."

Clearing her throat, Whitley asked, "Will you be home for dinner? Reed, Courtney, and Ava will be here. I'm sure they would love to meet Taylor."

With a quick peek at me, I nodded. "What time?"

"Seven."

With his arm back around my waist, Jase replied, "We'll be here."

Whitley's expression was one of pure elation. "Perfect!" Taking my hands in hers, Whitley forced the wetness in her eyes down. "Taylor, it really was so wonderful to meet you. I'll see you tonight."

"Sounds great," I replied with a polite smile. I wasn't sure why, but I had the strangest feeling after tonight my life would never be the same.

Seventeen

Taylor

JASE LED ME away from everyone and to the stairs. I quickly peeked around the house. It was huge.

"Want a tour?"

"How about tonight," I replied as we headed up the steps. Walking down the hall, Jase opened the door to his room and I instantly grinned from ear to ear. It looked like we were walking back in time. Trophies adorned the dresser, a collection of baseball caps hung on the wall along with a football jersey. The thing I noticed the most was how clean it was. Even the bed was made.

"Wow. Are you a neat freak or something?"

Looking around, Jase asked, "No, why?"

"It's so clean in here. There isn't anything out of place."

With a quick laugh, Jase pulled me over to the bed and pushed me down. "Maybe we should mess up the sheets."

I held up my hands and pointed to him. "No! Stay away, Jase. Your parents are right downstairs!"

He crawled over me and sucked my lower lip into his mouth. A low growl came from the back of his throat as I fought to keep my libido in check.

"No," I whispered against his lips. "It's not right."

His hand laced through my hair where he pulled, exposing my neck to him. Running his tongue along my skin, I trembled. "You're right, but remember this is where we left off because I intend on picking back up when we get back to your place and unpack."

My thoughts were scattered. A part of me wanted to beg him to take me right there and the other part was excited for what waited for me later.

"What about you? You said you were going to use your days off to move and now you're wasting them on me."

Jase's face fell. "Wasting. I'm not wasting anything. I only want to be with you, Taylor."

Pushing off the bed, he walked to his closet and grabbed a duffle bag. Without much thought, he began throwing clothes into the bag. He wasn't even folding them.

"Are you even paying attention to what you're packing?"

"Yeah. Why?"

Shrugging, I took this as the chance to really look around his room. Standing, I made my way over to the dresser and looked at the few pictures stuck between the mirror and frame. My eyes immediately zeroed in on the blonde in a lot of the pictures. She was gorgeous.

"Who's this beautiful blonde?"

Jase walked over and pulled one of the photos down. It was of him and a blonde who was on his shoulders. "That's, Ava."

Swallowing hard, I wasn't sure why the tinge of jealousy rippled through my body. "She's very pretty."

Jase glanced at me and looked again. "Yeah, I guess she's cute."

Cute? She was a knock out.

Chewing on my lip, I looked at the next picture. It was of Jase and Ava again, but this time there were two other people in the photo. Ava was looking at Jase laughing when the picture was taken.

"You two must have been really close if you've got pictures of her in your room."

The words came out of my mouth before I could take them back.

Jase reached over and pulled the other photos down, opened the desk drawer and tossed them in there. He pointed to another photo of him and Liza. Then another with Walker on what looked like a racehorse. "They were just good memories, Tay, that's all." He took the rest of them down and put them in the drawer as well.

I felt like a fool for feeling jealous. "I didn't mean anything by it and I certainly don't want you to think I'm being jealous, even though I was being jealous, but I know I have no reason to be so—"

His lips captured mine, bringing my rambling to a halt. "Stop," he softly spoke against my lips. "I'd be upset if you had pictures of some guy in your room no matter how close you were to him. I really haven't touched this room since high school. I sleep in here and that's about all."

I glanced down to the floor, feeling like a twelve-year-old. "Still, I shouldn't have acted like that. I'm sorry."

His finger lifted my chin as he captured my eyes. "There is nothing to say sorry for. Now let me grab my toothbrush so I don't have to use my finger again."

Giggling, I nodded and walked back over to his bed. The view from the window caught my eye as I leaned forward.

"Wow . . . the view from your room is amazing."

All I could hear was banging in the bathroom before Jase rounded the corner. "You should see it at sunset. When I was little I would run up here to watch the sun go down. My mother would get so mad at me. I would have my phone set and even if we were at dinner, I would jump up and come here. I was obsessed with it. Even now I love to watch the sun set."

I found myself breathless as I listened to Jase talk. "That's not something you would normally hear a guy saying."

"Well, I was eight so . . . I guess I had an excuse."

Jase turned and started rummaging through his closet. Cocking my head to the side, I asked, "What in the world are you looking for?"

"Found it!" he called out as he held a blanket in his hands. What in the world did he need a blanket for? "Are you ready?"

Smiling slightly, I asked, "Ready for what?"

"The plans I have for you today . . . and tonight."

I was positive my face was beaming with happiness. "I'm more than ready."

"Good, let's get going."

He grabbed the duffle bag and threw it over his shoulder and took my hand in his. There went my silly stomach. I swear every time he touched me, my body reacted in some way.

As we made our way back downstairs, I prayed this day would never end. The thought of going back to a somewhat normal life and not spending every moment with Jase made me feel sad.

"Are you heading out?" Whitley asked.

"Yep. We're gonna stop at the store and pick up some food for Taylor and then head back to her new place."

With an upturned face, Whitley's eyes danced. "Taylor, are you excited about living in your own place? I know it's a bit different from an apartment in the city."

"I am. I'm excited about so many things, truth be told. The new job, learning something new. I've been around horses my whole life, but nothing this deep. It's a bit strange to think I'll be in a cabin in the middle of nowhere all alone, but in a way I think it will be good for me also." Peeking up at Jase, I couldn't help but grin bigger. "And I know I'm not that far from Jase, which is the most exciting."

"That is a *very* good thing," Whitley said as she walked up and hugged me. Pushing me back at arm's length, she took me in with loving eyes. It was as if she was also trying to make sure this wasn't a dream. "See you both tonight."

"It was a pleasure meeting you, Whitley."

Jase leaned over and kissed his mother on the cheek. "See ya later, Mom."

As we made our way out to his truck, I glanced over my shoulder back at the house. It was so beautiful. I didn't want to do it because I would never want to jinx what Jase and I had, but I let myself dare dream of how beautiful a wedding would be here.

"What are you thinking about?" Jase asked while helping me up into the truck.

With a bubbly voice, I replied, "Our day today."

His face lit up like Christmas morning. "Then let's get it started, shall we?"

JASE CARRIED IN the last few bags of groceries I had bought at the HEB in Llano and set them on the kitchen counter. I couldn't help but feel so domesticated right now. I was living in a bubble of happiness which was a far cry from a few days ago when I was more depressed than I had ever been.

After putting the food away, I turned and looked at the boxes. "Yuck. This does not look like fun." Looking up at Jase through my eye lashes, I offered up another plan. "Do you want to put this off and, I don't know . . . do something else?"

With a smirk, he shook his head. "Oh no. We are getting you unpacked and settled young lady. Afterwards we can play. Right now it is work time."

Rolling my eyes, I sighed. "Ugh. All work and no play makes for a dull boy."

"Dull?" Jase asked with his brow arched. "Once we get this finished and I take you to bed we'll see how you feel about that statement."

Swallowing hard, I quietly replied, "Oh my."

Ideas filled my head with what Jase would do. I wanted to try everything with him and I wasn't the least bit embarrassed by my lack of sexual knowledge. Something about Jase being the one to teach and guide me made it all the more special.

"If you keep looking at me like that, Taylor, I'm going to do something about it."

My lips parted open and I could feel myself getting wet between my legs. "Wh-what would you do?"

His smile grew wicked and his eyes dark. "Do you really want to know?"

Frantically, I nodded my head. "Y-yes."

"I'd turn you around and make you bend over the table."

My breathing increased tenfold as my chest rose up and down. "Then what would you do?"

Taking a step closer to me, Jase unbuttoned his jeans as my heart dropped to my stomach. "Slowly pull your pants and panties down so nothing but your sweet little ass was facing me."

"Oh God," I gasped. Jase talking dirty was something I was pretty sure I would love to hear more of.

"Then?"

His crooked smile and dimples had me pushing my pants down and kicking them off to the side. This was a side of me I never knew. A side I only wanted to share with him.

My body trembled as his eyes roamed over me. "What about your panties, Taylor? Take them off too."

Doing as he said, I quickly pulled them off and tossed them to the side. I turned around and placed my hands on the table. My breathing was labored and I was positive the moment he touched me I would explode. "What then, Jase? Please tell me."

My voice sounded desperate. I should be embarrassed exposing myself to him like this, but I wasn't. I was more turned on than I ever had been before.

Jase's breath caught as he placed his hands on my ass. Leaning over, he placed soft kisses across my back. Dropping my head back, I let out a long soft moan.

"I'd spread your legs apart and bury myself deep inside you."

His foot moved my leg out. I gasped when I felt him bury his fingers inside of me.

"So fucking ready for me. Do you want me, Taylor?"

Fighting to hold myself up on my shaking legs, I nodded. "God yes. I want you so much."

The movement of his fingers was heavenly. Lifting my head, I saw the condoms on the table. Jase must have looked as well. Pulling his fingers out of me, I groaned in protest while he reached for the box and tore it open.

Glancing over my shoulder, I watched him rip the condom open and sheath himself. Licking my lips, I spoke what was on my mind. "What . . . what will you do once you are inside of me, Jase?"

His eyes held mine. They were burning with passion. "Jesus, Taylor. You're driving me fucking insane and I don't want to hurt you."

Each breath felt forced. "Why would you hurt me?"

"Because I want to fuck you from behind. Hard."

"I want that too. *Please*. Please don't make me wait."

His eyes closed as he positioned himself at my entrance. Holding my breath, I got ready for this to feel very different. I'd heard the girls talking about how much they liked being taken from behind. It felt deeper . . . more full. I was still sore, but I didn't care. I wanted this more than I could stand.

Pushing myself back against him, he cursed under his breath and pushed in fast and hard, causing me to gasp.

"Are you okay?"

The feeling was beyond amazing. He felt so big . . . so deep.

"Y-yes! Don't. Stop!"

Jase gripped my hips, digging his fingers into me, and moved fast and hard. It wasn't going to take long before I was going to be completely undone.

Just as I felt it building, a knock on the door had Jase coming to an immediate halt.

Pulling out of me, we both quickly got dressed without saying a word. It felt like I had been running a marathon as I attempted to calm my breathing down. Pushing Jase away, he quickly grabbed a box and went into the bathroom.

I pulled in one last deep breath and opened the door. To my surprise, my parents were standing there.

You've got to be kidding me.

"Mom! Dad! What are y'all doing here?"

"Well, Jessie said you and Jase had come back from Llano and were here unpacking, so we thought we'd stop by and see your new place."

Turning to look over my shoulder, I called out, "Hey, Jase. My mom and dad are here."

When I looked back, my father was scanning the cabin and my mother was looking at me like she knew what they had just interrupted. Smirking, she asked, "Did we come at a bad time?"

My chest felt like a weight was sitting on it. Avoiding total eye contact with her, I looked at my father. "No. Not at all. We were unpacking."

It was then I remembered the box of condoms on the table and the one Jase had ripped open. Quickly turning around, I noticed they were gone. My eyes scanned the floor but all looked good.

Jase walked out of the bathroom with a huge smile on his face. I wanted to giggle thinking about how he was just talking so dirty to me while taking me from behind.

"Amanda, Brad, it's great seeing you again."

My father lifted his hand and mumbled something. My mother on the other hand walked up and gave Jase a small hug. "So what have you two been up to?"

"Well, we went to Llano and I met Jase's family. Well, almost everyone. I met his parents, his sister, and his nephew. They invited us back to dinner tonight to meet Walker's parents and his sister, Ava."

My mother grinned. "Oh, that's so nice. You know, Taylor, you should invite Jase over for Grams' birthday celebration."

Doing a little jump, I clapped my hands together. "Yes! You can meet everyone."

Jase smiled. "Is it here in Mason or Austin?"

"Oh, not my grandmother. Grams is Colt's great-grandmother. She'll be ninety-five. We're all like family, though. I swear there were hardly any weekends that went by where we weren't all hanging out at one of our houses."

"Wow, ninety-five!" Jase said.

With a chuckle, I nodded. "I know. Her husband, Gramps, is ninety-eight and they are both still going strong."

Jase pulled his head back in surprise. "That's wonderful. Do they still live at home or in a nursing home?"

Clearing his throat, he walked up to us. "They're both still at home. Jack has in-home health care for them both."

Turning to Jase, I said, "Jack is Colt's grandfather."

Jase nodded his head. "That's so awesome. To live such a long life together is amazing and such a blessing to still be at home."

Oh my.

Jase's words caused my heart to skip a beat. My mother gushed at them and my father looked at him skeptically. "Yes, it's pretty amazing," my father said looking between Jase and me.

There was a weird silence filling the room. Since my parents were there, I decided I might as well embrace it. "Well, since y'all are here, want to help unpack? You were a huge help yesterday, Mom."

Perking up, my mom took off her jacket. "I thought you would never ask! I never got to help you move into your place in Austin. This will be fun."

Jase laughed and headed back into the bathroom. I wasn't even sure he had the right box.

Everyone quickly got to work and before I knew it, Jase and my father were talking up a storm. With a quick peek in their direction, I couldn't help but get teary eyed. As much as my father was trying to fight it . . . he liked Jase. They were getting along beautifully.

Nothing could ever ruin this high I was on.

Nothing.

Eighteen

Jase

THE DAY FLEW by and we quickly had Taylor's whole place unpacked and almost everything put away. Brad and I ended up spending much of the early afternoon talking about sports. Of course, he had his subtle ways of asking me what my future plans were, how long I would be living with my parents, and how involved I was with the running of the ranch.

"You're having a house built then?"

"Not right now. I meet with the architect after the holidays. We had to bump our appointment back a few weeks."

Brad nodded. "That's good that you have a plan, Jase. I'm impressed with how much you've thought this through."

I nodded and gave him a grin.

Brad looked around and let out a satisfied sigh. "Well, I think we probably should call it a day."

Reaching his hand out to me, we shook. "It was a pleasure getting to know you better, Jase. I see why my daughter is so taken by you. You've got a good head on your shoulders and I like where your thinking is."

Holy shit. Could it really be that easy?

He gripped my hand harder and pulled me closer to him. "But if you ever hurt my daughter again, I'll be at your doorstep. With a gun."

My eyes widened in shock as I gulped and said, "No, sir. I'll never . . . no um never."

"Daddy, stop it," Taylor said as she gently pushed her father back.

Amanda walked up and kissed me on the cheek and gave me a hug. Turning to Taylor, she kissed her and said, "I'll let you know about Gram's birthday so Jase can plan on coming."

"Sounds good, Mom. Love you both."

When Amanda and Brad were out the door, Taylor shut it and turned to face me. She fell back against the door and gave me a horrified look. "Oh. My. Goodness."

Covering her mouth with her hands, she broke down laughing. "That was so close! What if they had walked in? We would have been caught in the act."

Letting out a laugh of my own, I shook my head as my hand pushed through my hair. "That was very close. I'm pretty sure your dad knew."

Horror washed across Taylor's face. "No!"

"Yes. He was pissed when he first got here and he kept making little comments here and there."

"That makes me feel a little sick. I mean, I'm sure my parents know we are sleeping together, but to have them show up when we are . . . well . . . doing what we were doing."

My heart stopped for a brief moment at the thought of Brad walking in on us. My body trembled as I pushed the image away quickly.

The concerned look on Taylor's face had me holding back my chuckle. *God how I love her.* With a wicked smile I said, "Playing?"

Her face curved into a grin so enticing I wanted to take her right this very second. "Is that what you would call it?"

We moved closer to each other while our breathing increased. Her beautiful green eyes turned dark with desire as I replied, "I wish we could finish playing, but we probably should head to Llano for dinner."

Taylor jetted out her lip in a pout. "My parents kind of put a damper on today, I'm sorry."

Kissing her on the forehead, I grinned. "Nah, it was kind of nice getting to know them. Plus, they helped us get you unpacked and settled so the next couple of days we can spend together doing whatever you want."

Her voice was breathy as she said, "I like the sound of that." Her lips pressed against mine while my body heated the longer the kiss lingered on.

"I should go get dressed for dinner."

Taylor started to her bedroom when I reached for her arm. "Don't dress up. Wear jeans and layers. I have plans for after dinner."

With a delighted expression, her cheeks blushed as she grinned. "Okay, jeans and layers. Got it."

While Taylor got dressed, I got her DVD player and TV hooked up. I couldn't help but smile like a fool thinking about all the nights we would curl up and watch movies together.

Closing my eyes, I took in a long deep breath and held it for a few moments before letting it out. *This has been like a dream.* One I never wanted to wake up from.

"Do I look okay?"

I quickly stood and spun around. My heart dropped and I swear my knees wobbled. Taylor stood before me dressed in jeans and a beige dress shirt. The lace on the shirt somehow made her look so damn innocent. But the way it scooped down showed just enough to make me curious and had my dick jumping in my pants. Her hair was pulled up and piled in a sloppy bun on the top of her head. I swore I could see her hazel eyes sparkling from where I was standing.

Sauntering over, she stopped right in front of me. In a quiet voice, she asked, "Do you want me to change? You're not saying anything."

"Your beauty has left me speechless."

Her lips parted slightly open as she let out a soft chuckle. "You do crazy things to me, Jase. You always have."

My hand cradled the side of her face as she leaned into it. "Sweetness, you drive me mad. From the first moment I saw you, I had to fight the attraction."

"No more fighting though, right?"

Leaning my forehead against hers, I whispered, "Never again."

❦

PULLING IN, I parked behind Reed's truck. "Looks like everyone is here if Ava rode over with her parents.

Taylor wrung her hands in her lap as she looked at the house.

"Hey, look at me, Tay."

She snapped her head and tried like hell to smile. "There isn't anything to be nervous about. You met my parents already; they are who really count."

With a slight nod, her voice wobbled as she talked. "I don't know why. . . . I'm just so nervous."

Pulling her hand to my mouth, I kissed the back of it. "I promise I won't leave your side for a minute. Everyone is going to love you."

"How do you know that?"

I fought against the lump in my throat. She really had no idea how much she meant to me. How since the moment she walked out of that barn I've been in a world of utopia. "You have no idea how happy you make me, do you?"

Sniffling, she blinked her eyes quickly to keep from crying. "You make me happy, Jase. So very happy and I'm so scared I'm going to wake up and this is all going to be a dream and I hate that I keep thinking like that."

My hand slid behind her neck, pulling her closer to me. "It's not a dream," I spoke against her lips. "I love you, Taylor."

She didn't have a chance to answer me when I pulled her closer and kissed her. I wanted her to feel how much I loved her in that one single kiss. Her soft whimper traveled through my body and warmed it instantly.

The loud knock on the window caused us both to jump. Glancing over Taylor's shoulder, I saw Walker standing there with a shit-eating grin on his face.

"Asshole!" I shouted as Taylor blushed. Turning my attention back to her, I kissed her quickly on the lips. "Hold on and I'll help you out."

Racing out of the truck and over to her, I pushed Walker out of the way. "Don't you have anything better to do . . . like go be with your wife and son?"

"Nah, harassing you is so much more fun." Walker turned to Taylor and smiled. "Hey, Taylor! You ready for the nightmare to begin?"

"I . . . I um . . . I think so?"

Walker laughed and confessed, "I'm kidding. It's going to be fine and everyone is going to love you. All they have to do is look at Jase and see how happy he is."

I slipped my arm around her waist and led her toward the front door. "Is everyone here?"

"Yep. Ava is chomping at the bit to finally meet Taylor."

"Me?" Taylor asked in surprise.

"Hell yeah. Jase has been talking about you for a while now."

Taylor looked at me with a blank expression. "Relax, sweetness. Take a deep breath and let it out."

Walker headed in first. Everyone must have been in the kitchen, or at least that was where all the talking was coming from. The second we walked in everyone stopped talking and turned to us.

Oh great. If Taylor was nervous before, I'm sure now she was freaking out. Everyone was staring at us.

Ava popped around my mother and took one look at Taylor and screamed.

"I'd run to you, but I have a broken leg! Jase pushed me."

Scowling at Ava, I pointed to her. "I did not push you!"

"Jase, she is just screwing around with you," Liza said with a chuckle.

Ava made her way over to Taylor and engulfed her in a hug. She whispered something into Taylor's ear, causing her to frown.

When she pulled back from her, Ava wore a huge smile. My mind raced in a million and one different directions as to what Ava might have said to Taylor. Probably that I picked my nose or some shit like that. "I'm so happy y'all found your way to each other."

With a shy smile, Taylor agreed. "So am I. Very happy."

"I bet." Ava turned and looked at everyone. "So, this is amazing isn't it? Our Jase in love!"

Courtney smiled and made her way over to Taylor. "Hi Taylor, I'm Ava and Walker's mom, Courtney. This is my husband, Reed."

Shaking everyone's hands, Taylor stole a peek over to me. I quickly made my way back to her side and pulled her to my side. Leaning over, I put my lips to her. "What did Ava say to you?"

Taylor pressed her lips together and glanced around the room before turning to me and speaking so only I could hear her. "She told me she was so happy for us and the distraction we provided."

"What's that supposed to mean?"

With a shrug, she replied, "I was going to ask you the very same thing."

"Taylor, Whitley said you're going to be working for a friends breeding business."

Clearing her throat, Taylor nodded. "Um, yes. I'm a financial analyst. My job is to see where they can best cut back in their expenses."

Whitley and Liza both raised a brow. "Really? Do you know much about the breeding world?"

"Nope. Not a darn thing. But I do know horses along with the cost of up keep for them. I'm a quick learner so I don't think it will take me long to get a game plan down."

My father wore a thoughtful look as he turned to Taylor. "What about cattle? Do you know anything about them?"

"I've practically grown up on the Mathews cattle ranch in Mason."

I couldn't believe the smile that appeared on my father's face. "No kidding. I've met with Gunner and Jeff a lot over the years. I admire them both, not only for the cattle knowledge but also with racehorses. Jeff and I actually co-own a racehorse."

Taylor's eyes widened in shock. "I thought you looked familiar! I must have seen you before if you've been to the Mathews' place before."

"I have, a lot. So has Reed."

Taylor turned to me and I couldn't help but return the happy look she was giving me. "What a crazy small world."

With a chuckle, I nodded my head. "It is." I turned to my father and said, "I wonder if Gunner is related to the architect I have a meeting with in a few weeks. His last name is Mathews."

Taylor gasped. "Drew! Drew Mathews?"

"Yeah, how did you know?"

"Jase! That's Gunner! Drew is his real name." Shaking her head in disbelief, she covered her mouth and laughed.

"Now this *is* crazy. It appears our worlds were meant to collide one way or another doesn't it?" my mother said as she took an apple pie out of the oven.

Reed slapped me on the back and said, "I'm shocked the two of you didn't meet before college."

Everyone laughed as my mom and Courtney started bringing the food into the dining room. "Let me help, please," Taylor said.

Whitley drew her attention over to Jase. "No! You're a guest, Walker and Jase can help, you visit with Liza and Ava and get to know them."

Liza walked up to Taylor and hugged her. "I know we keep saying it, but it is really wonderful that things worked out the way they have. I haven't seen Jase this happy in a very long time."

"I don't think I've ever seen Jase this happy," Ava said with a giggle. Taylor's face blushed even more.

Once we got all the food in the dining room, I led Taylor in and pulled a chair out for her. Ava quickly sat down next to Taylor. Peeking up at me she said, "I'm going to need a neutral supporter."

"Oh no," Taylor said under her breath.

Narrowing my eye at Ava, I asked, "What are you planning on doing?"

She leaned in closer as I sat down and answered, "Ryder asked me to marry him."

"Is that a bad thing?" Taylor asked.

Ava screwed her face up. "It will be for my parents. But it most certainly isn't for me."

"Your dad is going to freak, Ava!" I whispered.

She sighed. "You don't think I know that?"

"When are you going to tell them?" Taylor asked.

Ava glanced around at everyone. "Probably when my dad has had a few drinks. I thought about drugging him, but I figured he might not like that."

Taylor's face dropped as I took her hand in mine. "She's kidding. I think."

"Half-heartedly," Ava mumbled.

"So, Ava, how was Montana? Are you glad to be home?" my mother asked.

Walker and Liza must have known as well because they froze just like Taylor and I did.

Ava giggled nervously. "Well, I'm not actually home to stay."

Reed and Courtney both said together, "What?"

"This just got interesting," my father said as Taylor tried to hide her smile.

Ava turned to Taylor. "So, Taylor, when was the first time you and Jase met?"

"Oh God," I said as I picked up my beer and took a gulp.

Taylor kicked me under the table as she stumbled over her words. "Um . . . well we ah . . . freshman year I guess? Right, Jase?"

"I'd rather hear about Ava not staying in Texas," I said with a smirk.

"Oh dear," Taylor spoke under her breath.

Ava glared at me as I winked. "It's like you're pushing me all over again," she hissed through her teeth.

Leaning forward, I said in a flat voice, "I. Didn't. Push. You."

Taylor looked between the two of us with a confused expression. "Wait. Why did you push, Ava?"

Snapping my eyes, to Taylor I shook my head. "I didn't push her! She slipped and fell. That's how she broke her ankle and leg."

Taylor turned to Ava. "How much longer do you have to wear the cast?"

Ava's face dropped as she pouted. "The doctors say—"

"Stop! Everyone stop talking for two minutes!"

All eyes fell on Reed. Ava's little plan of trying to pull me into a fight with her was never going to work.

"Ava Grace Reed. What do you mean you're not staying here?"

Ava sat up straighter and looked at Taylor. "So . . . tell us about Paris!"

Nineteen

Taylor

I SAT THERE stunned as Ava looked at me with pleading eyes.

"Ah . . . Paris is amazing?"

"The city of love! Did you and Jase first have se—"

"Ava!" Reed and Courtney both shouted.

Turning back to me, she smiled. "If they try to come after me, I'm counting on you to block them so I get a head start."

My mouth fell open, but nothing came out.

Dropping her shoulders, she put her fork down. "Fine. Let's just get this over with. Ryder asked me to marry him and I really think I want to make Montana my permanent home."

Jase took my hand under the table and squeezed it. "I'm so sorry I brought you here. Now you're going to be a witness to murder and this puts a real damper on my plans for tonight."

I couldn't help but laugh. Covering my mouth, I dropped my eyes to my plate and bit on the side of my cheek. It was so refreshing to see Jase's family was normal like mine. Crazy normal.

Courtney held up her hands to hush Jase. "Wait. Did I just hear you say Ryder asked you to marry him? Ava! Didn't you learn anything from the last time with Johnny?"

"Who's Johnny?"

Jase replied, "I'll tell you later."

"Mom, don't bring him up. What I feel for Ryder is so much more."

Whitley cleared her throat and announced, "I think maybe we should save this conversation for another time, don't y'all agree?"

Ava and Courtney both nodded. Reed stared at Ava. "I agree. Nice try though, Ava."

"Can't blame a girl for trying," Ava said with an innocent grin.

The rest of dinner was spent with conversations around the table. Ava and I talked mostly about Paris. I could see the passion in her eyes as she talked about her love of designing wedding gowns.

Leaning in closer to her so no one would hear, I asked, "Will you design your own?"

Her eyes lit up and I knew that no matter what her parents had to say, none of it would matter. She was in love and you clearly saw it in her eyes.

"Yes! I already have most of it planned out in my head, but, I've stumbled upon a design that Ryder's sister, Kate, was working on before she passed away."

My stomach dropped. "Oh no!"

Ava frowned, "I know. She was so young and she was pre . . . um . . . well it was really sad."

I nodded and quickly changed the subject. It was obvious she was about to say Kate was pregnant.

Dinner finished and the kids cleaned off the table as the parents happily let us take care of the clean up.

When the last dish was dried and put away, Jase winked and motioned for me to walk over to him.

"Have you had enough of my crazy family?"

With a titter, I hit him lightly on the chest. "Nonsense. I've had a wonderful time. It's nice to see they're normal just like mine. I have to admit; I give Ava props for trying to use me being there as a way to soften the blow of her news."

Jase rolled his eyes. "Typical Ava. Come on, let's head out back and let my parents know we are heading out."

"So soon?"

Without so much as looking back at me, Jase took my hand and pulled me along behind him. "I don't want to miss the sunset."

Grinning from ear to ear, I said, "Because we know how much you love the sunset."

Glancing over his shoulder, he gave me a wicked smile. "Yes, I do. And I will love it even more sharing it with you."

Thud. There went my heart against my chest. I never imagined I'd find someone as romantic as Colt, Will, and Luke. I dare say Jase could give them a run for their money.

Meagan, Lauren, Grace, and Alex had all been texting me throughout the day. I texted them each back and told them to give me twenty-four hours and then I'd fill them in on everything. Lauren pretty much told them everything so far. I knew they would hit me up with questions like how is the sex or is he hung well.

"What are you smiling about over there?" Jase asked as we walked up to his parents.

"Nothing, I'm just happy."

He stopped walking and cupped my face in his hands. "And you have no idea how happy that makes me hearing you say that."

Kissing me lightly on the lips, he took my hand again. Stopping in front of Whitley and Layton, I smiled at them as Jase told them our plans.

"I'm gonna show Taylor the ranch before the sun goes down. We probably won't be stopping back by before we leave. We've got a date under the stars tonight."

Courtney sighed as Whitley beamed. "How romantic." Turning to look at me, she asked, "Taylor sweetheart, did you bring a jacket?"

"Yes ma'am, I did."

Turning to Courtney and Reed, I smiled brightly. "It was such a pleasure meeting you both."

They both stood and hugged me. "I'm so sorry Ava dropped her bomb on us at dinner," Courtney said in a frustrated voice.

"It's really okay. She kind of gave me a heads up. For what it's worth, she really seems to be happy."

Tears built in Courtney's eyes as she looked at Reed who barely smiled. "That's what scares me," he barely said.

Jase clapped his hands together and said, "Okay, let's go. The sun is dipping further down and we need time to get to my spot I have picked out."

Whitley kissed Jase and then me. "Have fun and be careful, Jase," Layton said as he kissed me on the cheek. "We'll see you soon, Taylor."

"Thank you again for dinner."

"Any time, sweetheart. You're always welcome here," Whitley said as her voice cracked.

Jase took my hand and pulled gently. "That's our cue to leave before she gets all emotional."

Laughing, I waved goodbye to everyone. I was on a high the whole way to Jase's truck. There was a feeling in my bones telling me tonight was going to be a night I would never forget.

JASE DROVE THROUGH pasture after pasture and through a couple gates. We had passed the cattle a few miles back not to mention the endless amount of deer that were out.

"So, is this really your spot?" I asked watching the beautiful countryside pass by in the window.

"Yep. I come here a lot when I need to think."

Peeking over to him, I asked, "So, you're sharing your thinking place with me?"

With a chuckle he nodded. "I am. After that dinner we needed a place where the only thing we hear is the crickets singing."

Staring at him, I couldn't believe how he made me feel. The things he said to me made me feel like I was on a constant thrill ride with as much as my stomach dropped with not only his touch, but his words as well.

"The suns starting to set. It's perfect timing."

My attention was drawn to the view in front of me. The sun was sinking lower on the horizon and the colors were breathtaking. "Wow," I quietly said.

Jase turned the truck around so the bed was facing the west. "Wait. This is nothing."

Excitement built up as Jase parked and jumped out of the truck.

When he opened my door, he held his hand in to help me down. He made me feel like a princess with everything he did.

"What do you think about my spot?"

Turning in a circle, I took it all in. We were up on a hill and the view to the west was stunning. "It's beautiful. I don't think I've ever seen a view this beautiful and I've seen some beautiful views."

I let my eyes scan the horizon as Jase got a bag out of the backseat. Placing my hands over my stomach, I let my imagination run wild. Closing my eyes, I pictured Jase running after a little girl with brown curls bouncing while she ran. As much as I wanted to have a baby with Jase it was too soon. We needed to get to know each other. Be a couple before we took any other steps. But I didn't see the harm in dreaming.

"All ready."

Getting my senses about myself, I spun around and gasped. "Jase!"

The back of his truck had a blanket laid out with a picnic basket sitting in the middle. A few pillows were piled up making it look inviting enough to sleep.

My hands covered my mouth as I giggled and made my way over to the bed of the truck. Jase stood behind me and moved my hair, exposing my neck to his soft lips. "I want to learn every curve of your body. Every touch that makes you tremble. Words that make your pulse beat harder. Ways to make love to you that have you whispering for more. Tonight is all about you, Tay. Lead me where you want me to go."

Each breath was heavy as my body was covered in goose bumps. Moving to face him, I searched his face. With trembling hands, I placed them on his chest. I'd never felt so moved by words in my entire life. It felt as if we were one. "I come alive when I'm with you, Jase. It feels like our hearts beat in a syncopated harmony."

His hand came up and traced his finger along my jawline. "I never want to take what we have for granted. We've been given another shot at this and I swear to you I'm going to do everything in my power to show you every single chance I get how much I love you."

"I'd say you're off to a great start. This spot of yours is pretty incredible."

His eyes searched my face as he wet his lips. My lack of concentration was evident while I focused on his beautiful baby blues. The feeling of love was almost overwhelming.

"It's our spot now, Taylor. Our future."

My stomach fluttered. "Our future?"

Lifting my hands to his lips, he nodded. "Yes. This is the spot where I'd like to build a house. Where someday I'd love to sit and watch a couple kids running around playing while we sit on the back porch and watch the sun go down." Jase looked away toward the sun that was now touching the ground. "The last few months I'd come here and would sit for hours. I'd wonder if this would be the type of life you would want. Then I'd verbally beat myself up for letting you go and hurting you."

I shook my head. "None of that matters anymore." His eyes came back to mine. "All that matters now is that we have each other and I want all of this. I just need to know if you do as well."

His eyes grew wide and glowed with happiness.

"I want all of this with you, Jase. I can't imagine my life without you in it."

Cupping my face with his hands, he tried to speak but his voice cracked, causing tears to build in my eyes.

"I . . . I love you so much, Taylor." His thumb gently wiped my tears away.

My heart felt as if it would burst I was so happy. The sounds of crickets filled the air as they played what I would now always think of as our song. Jase reached down, picked me up, and placed me into the bed of the truck.

When he crawled up into the truck bed, I moved back against the pillows while he made his way over to me. My heart was pounding so loudly I was sure Jase could hear it.

"My heart's pounding," he whispered.

I giggled and asked, "Why does it feel like our first time again?"

My smile faded as we got lost in one another's eyes. The breeze lightly blew giving just the right amount of chill to the air. When I finally found my voice again, I breathed out, "Please make love to me."

"I thought you'd never ask."

Twenty

Taylor

Christmas Day

THE MOMENT I walked out onto the back porch of Gunner and Ellie's house I was attacked by the mob.

Meagan, Grace, Lauren, Libby, and Alex were all in front of me, eyeing me up and down. Meagan's hands went to her hips as she shook her head and made a tsking sound. "I think we've waited long enough. It's time to spill the beans, little sister."

My face instantly heated as I peeked over to where my parents were standing. "There isn't anything to tell really."

"Bullshit," Grace said as she held Hope in her arms. "Let me find Noah so he can take Hope. Since everyone else is free of their kids, we can talk!"

Rolling my eyes, I let out a groan.

Lauren wrapped her arm with mine as we headed down to the barn with each of our best friends following behind us.

"Have you told anyone else?" I asked in a hushed voice.

Lauren beamed with happiness. "Not yet. I think we'll wait a bit longer. Maybe make the announcement at Gram's birthday party."

I was so happy for Lauren. She looked happier than I had ever seen her. "I'm so happy for you and Colt."

Resting her head on my shoulder, she sighed. "I'm happy too. If only the morning sickness would go away."

We both giggled as Libby came up next to us. "What are you two going on about?"

"How happy we both are," I said with a huge smile.

"It's about time we're all happy and there is no damn drama!" Grace called out.

Walking into the garage, I glanced up and laughed. "Libby, do you remember when you caused Luke to fall back in the chair when he saw you standing there after he talked a bunch of crap?"

She chuckled and nodded her head. "I do remember that. He was talking shit indeed. Oh! Then Alex and Will snuck off."

Alex grinned as she shook her head. "It seems like yesterday, but at the same time it feels like forever ago."

Grace sat on a hay bale and pulled her knees up to her chest. "Can you imagine all the memories this barn as seen? The secrets it must hold."

Lauren sat next to Grace. "I remember playing hide and seek in here so many times."

Meagan laughed and said, "What about the football games we used to play? Luke and Will would get so mad when the girls played better than them."

We all laughed as the memories came flooding back.

Leaning against a stall, I looked at each of my best friends. They were more than friends; they were my sisters. "Now look at us. Grown women managing kids, jobs, and owning businesses. Who would have thought?" Alex said with a huge smile.

"Do you know what makes me so happy?" Grace said as we all focused on her.

"What?" Alex asked sitting down on the other side of Grace.

Her eyes filled with tears as she attempted not to cry. "That we're all together. When Meagan and Noah moved to Texas I couldn't believe how happy I was. Now, Tay is back and it seems like everything is how it's supposed to be. Our kids will now all grow up together and I pray like hell they are as close to each other as we all are."

"They will be," Libby said coming and sitting on the floor in front of Grace. "Look at them all now. They love each other so much. They're going to have beautiful memories here just like we do."

Alex chuckled and looked around in amazement. "Do y'all realize our kids are the fifth generation to grow up here? How crazy is that?"

The idea that so many of us walked and ran around these pastures made my heart feel light. "What about Grams and Gramps? I can only dream of living a long happy life like they have. And when Gramps put's on that song and dances with Grams."

Libby sighed. "It's Nate King Cole's 'Send for Me'."

"Yes!" we all said with a laugh.

Meagan pointed to me and wiggled her eyebrows. "Speaking of . . . spill it. I want to know everything."

My face instantly warmed. I placed my hands over my cheeks to hide my blush.

"Are you blushing?" Libby asked with a snicker.

"Holy shit, Tay. Look at you turning red. I take it the sex is good then," Grace said as she turned to Meagan and winked.

Wrapping my arms around my waist, I couldn't hold it in anymore. I had been bursting to talk to them. "Oh my gosh. The sex is amazing!"

They all laughed except for Meagan who pretended to gag. "Stop it, Meg! You have to be happy for Taylor," Lauren said.

My sister turned to me and gave me the sweetest smile. "I truly am. I'm glad it all worked out. I know how much you love him."

Alex walked up and grabbed my hands, pulling me over to the other girls. We were soon all gathered around talking and giggling. I told them almost everything. I left out a few times when Jase and I got a little into things.

"He made love to you in the back of his truck?" Libby gushed.

I nodded. "It was so wonderful. He's so romantic and treats me like a princess."

"Good. The last time we talked about him he was making you cry more than making you smile."

Looking at Meagan, I nodded. "I know. Sometimes though . . . I worry."

Alex took my hand in hers. "Worry about what?"

"That I'm too happy and something bad is going to happen."

"Oh, Tay. I'm sure I can speak for all of us when I say we have all felt like that before. It's not something you only feel in the beginning either. When I wake up each morning and see Luke sleeping there I want to pinch myself," Libby said.

With a surprised look, I asked, "Really? Still?"

"Yes!" Libby said with a giggle. "Love is funny that way. It brings you so many emotions. Happiness, desire, fear, anger . . ."

"Lust, passion, heat, hunger . . ."

Libby turned to Grace. "Thank you for those added emotions, Grace."

With a shrug, Grace winked. "I'm keeping it real. There is nothing wrong with having a healthy sexual appetite."

"Agreed," Alex said as Libby moaned.

Before I could stop myself, I blurted out, "There is nothing missing in my sexual appetite." I'd sat in the shadows for so long listening to everyone else talk about their sex lives, I was practically bursting at the seams to brag about mine.

All five of them leaned closer to me. "Is that so?" Meagan asked. "Explain."

"Well, all I mean is Jase and I are both very attracted to each other and he is an amazing teacher."

Grace clapped and pointed to me. "There it is! I knew it. What has Jase been teaching you, oh so innocent one?"

"Ugh, I'm not sure I like where this is going," Meagan said with a groan.

I shrugged. "I will say one thing, Grace. Anna's tips have come in handy!"

All six of us started laughing as Meagan buried her face in her hands. "Oh my God! My baby sister is dishing out blow jobs!"

Grace held up her hands to get everyone to stop laughing. "Wait! There is something I have to know." She looked directly into my eyes and asked, "Tay, do you spit or swallow?"

I shuddered at the memory of the first time I gave Jase a blowjob.

"That shit is nasty. I'm a finish yourself off kind of girl."

We all roared with laughter as we spent the next hour talking about sex, the latest in baby toys *and* big girl toys, as well as how utterly happy we each were. It was the perfect way to spend time. All of us going on about our past, our present, and what we all hoped for with our futures.

When we started back up to the house, my heart tugged as I watched Mireya and Bayli come running up to Libby and Alex. Something strange came over me as I watched them. I couldn't help but peek over to Lauren. I was positive she was thinking the same thing I was.

For one crazy moment I let myself dare to dream of what it would be like if I was carrying Jase's baby.

"WHAT ARE YOU doing on the front porch all alone, young lady?"

I jumped up when Grams came walking up to me. With a slight chuckle, I replied, "Just wanted some time alone. It gets a bit overwhelming when the gangs all together, especially on Christmas Day."

Grams nodded and took a seat in the rocking chair next to me.

"I hear you've got yourself a beau."

Grinning from ear to ear, I nodded. "I do. His name is Jase."

"Does he make you laugh?"

I looked at her. "That's an odd question."

She pulled her forehead down. "Is it? I don't think so. But I guess most people would ask you if he makes you happy or treats you well."

"I suppose so."

Grams chuckled. "But if he makes you laugh, then you've already answered all of those other questions. If you're happy and he treats you well, then you'll laugh more. A man who can make a woman laugh knows how to treat her right."

My teeth sunk down into my lip as I nodded. "It must be so wonderful to share so many memories with Gramps."

"Oh my dear, it's been a blessing. Not many people are as lucky as we are. Plus, we both have our wits about us still. That's important. I'm not sure what I would do if I woke up one day and Garrett didn't know who I was."

My heart dropped. I never really imagined life without Grams and Gramps. "That would be sad."

We sat for a few moments in silence before I turned to her. Her blue eyes still sparkled and I wondered how many wonderful memories she held in them. "May I ask you something, Grams?"

"Of course you can, my darling."

"Did you ever feel like you didn't deserve to be so happy? Like the life you were living was a dream and at any moment the rug would be pulled out from underneath you."

She tossed her head back and laughed. "Life is a series of rugs being pulled out from underneath us. I think it's God's way of telling us not to take things for granted. Keep us on our toes if you will." She smiled and looked thoughtfully at me. "Life can change in a moment. Worlds turned upside down, or right side up. It's okay to feel happy, Taylor. Don't get caught up wondering when something will happen. Enjoy each day as if it was your last."

I couldn't contain my smile. "Jase said something like that to me before."

"Then he's a smart young man."

I nodded. "He is. And romantic!"

Grams wiggled her eyebrows. "Really? My Garrett was terribly romantic. Still is. Do you know he puts a fresh flower next to my bedside every morning before I get up?"

"That's so sweet!"

She chuckled. "It is. Crazy old man gets up early every day and walks out with Louise to the garden. She insists on going with him and I know that just makes Garrett so mad." Grams covered her mouth as she smiled.

Rocking in her chair, we talked a bit more about me coming over more often to visit her. She wanted to finish teaching me how to can veggies. Especially now that I had come to my senses and moved back home to the country.

Grace, Gunner's mother, walked out onto the porch with the warmest smile on her face. "Here you two are. We were wondering where you both snuck off to."

"Taylor and I were enjoying the peace," Grams said as she stood up. Taking Grace's arm, she looked back down to me. "Always kiss him goodbye and kiss him when he comes home. A man needs to feel loved and it's usually the simple things that make him feel it."

Standing, I kissed Grams on both cheeks. "I'll remember everything you told me. I love you, Grams. Thank you for all your advice."

Ever since I could remember, Grams had been there to give us all advice. From when was the best time of year to plant certain vegetables to how to get over a broken heart. It seemed like she had a story for everything. And I swear she had some magical gift to tell when someone was pregnant even before they knew. It was weird.

With a nod, she replied, "I love you too, sweet girl."

Glancing over to Grace, I said, "I'll be right in, Grace."

"Take your time, honey."

Once they were inside the house, I sent Jase a text message.

Me: I miss you.

It was less than a minute before my phone beeped.

Jase: I miss you too. Are you going back to your parents' tonight?

Me: Nope. Santa left me a little something in my stocking just for you.

When my phone rang, I couldn't help but laugh.

"That was fast."

"What did he leave you?"

I tried to hold my giggles back. Lauren and I had run into Fredericksburg yesterday for a few last minute gifts. When we stumbled upon a new store tucked away on one of the side streets, I thought Lauren was going to go nuts. It was a lingerie store. We both bought a little something for ourselves and few little things for Alex, Grace, Meagan, and Libby. It was nice to know we didn't have to drive into Austin for something sexy.

"I'll give you one hint."

I could hear him moving away from everyone. "Okay, I'm on the front porch. I only get one hint?"

"Yep!" I said, popping my p. "It's lace."

"Color?"

"That would be two hints," I softly replied.

"I'm coming over tonight."

Desire blazed through my body. "I was hoping you'd say that."

"Shit, I've got to go. They're about to open gifts. Next year we'll be spending all of Christmas day together."

I was on early kitchen duty this year and ended up staying last night at Ellie's house along with Alex. That meant no waking up to Jase this morning, but Alex and I had our own little private slumber party last night, which had been fun.

The thought of waking up Christmas morning in Jase's arms was a wonderful one. "I'll text you when I'm leaving and heading home."

"Sounds good. Taylor?"

My breath caught like it always did when I knew what was coming next. "Yes?"

"I love you."

My eyes closed as the most amazing feeling wrapped my body like a blanket. "I love you too."

Twenty-One

Jase

"YOU'RE OFF IN another world," Ava said as she hit me lightly on the stomach.

Drying off the last dish, I placed it in the cabinet and turned to Ava. "Wondering what Taylor is doing."

A smile grew across her face. Nodding, she said, "Yeah, I can't stop thinking about Ryder. I can't wait to get back to Montana."

Narrowing my eyes, I leaned against the counter and crossed my arms over my chest. "Are you really going to move to Montana?"

Her eyes lit up and her face beamed. "I love him, Jase. I can honestly say I've never felt this way before in my life. It's like he brought a part of me I didn't know existed to life. That's the only way I can describe it."

"You're preaching to the choir."

With a chuckle, she leaned her head back and took me in. "Taylor seems very sweet and . . . innocent."

"She's both."

"Very beautiful too, I might add. The way she looks at you there is no doubt she is madly in love with you."

With a grin, I looked out the window. "I wish I hadn't been so stupid and wasted so much time."

"Everything worked out like it should have and that's all that matters."

I brought my attention back to Ava. "Yeah. So how are Reed and Courtney taking your decision to marry Ryder and set up roots up north?"

She frowned and let out a low moan. "My father must have lectured me for I swear three hours about jumping into something so quickly with Ryder."

"It is kind of fast, Ava."

She glared at me. "Not you too, Jase. Of all people I thought you would understand. Look at you and Taylor."

My hands came up in defense. "Whoa. Hold on a second. I do understand and I get it. I'm just saying it would be different if he was in Austin and all of this was happening. Your parents are trying to deal with not only the fact that you're going to be getting married, but you're moving to Montana also. That's huge."

With regard, she nodded. "I know. The whole time I was flying down here I think I pinched myself at least ten times to make sure this wasn't all a dream. I realize what I'm walking away from. I have a great life in Austin. My job, my badass apartment, friends who are a blast. My family is here in Texas . . . I know what this means."

"But?"

Her eyes filled with tears. "I love him so much. Being away from him the last few days has only shown me how much I love him. I honestly don't think I could even attempt to have a relationship with him where I'm thousands of miles apart. Plus, I feel some sort of connection there."

With a speculative eye, I asked, "What kind of connection?"

She shook her head and frowned. "I can't explain, and if I tried you would think I was insane." Waving off where her thoughts were going, she continued. "But that doesn't matter. What matters is I know being with Ryder is what I want. And he's in Montana so that means I'm in Montana."

"I envy you, Ava."

She lifted her eyes and gave me a funny look. "Why?"

"You knew what you wanted and no matter what the costs, you went after it. You explored it and you found happiness. I'm really happy for you, I really am."

Her face lit up as she pushed off the counter and walked up to me. Kissing me on the cheek, she winked and said, "I'm happy for you too. Are you going to be able to see her tonight?"

Wiggling my eyebrows, I answered, "Hell yeah, I am."

Chuckling, Ava hit me on the chest and walked out of the kitchen.

"Hey, make sure you say goodbye before you head back to Montana!" I called out as Ava turned and blew me a kiss. It was then my phone went off.

> *Taylor: Heading home.*

> *Me: I'll see you in a bit.*

> *Taylor: I can't wait to see you! Be careful driving.*

> *Me: Will do! You too!*

Walking into the game room, I made my way over to my father. "Dad, I'm going to go see Taylor."

He smiled and nodded his head. "You staying with her tonight?"

"Probably. I'll be back home early. We've got a delivery of hay that I need to be here for."

"I can take care of that if you don't want to rush home."

Placing my hand on his shoulder, I gave it a squeeze. "Thanks, Dad. I appreciate it, but this is my job and I have no intentions of slacking off."

He pinched his brows slightly together. "I've got to tell you, Jase, that is a very responsible thing to do. I'm not sure if at your age in a new relationship I would have picked my job over my girlfriend."

Letting out a gruff laugh, I shook my head. "Well, I learned from you so maybe you would have."

Laughing, he nodded. "Maybe. Make sure you say good-bye to everyone before you leave."

"Will do."

I made my way around to everyone and wished them a Merry Christmas before stopping in front of my mother last.

"Thank you for dinner, Mom."

With a soft smile, she placed her hand on the side of my face. "Enjoy your evening, sweetheart. Tell Taylor I said Merry Christmas. Oh! And don't forget her gift, it's under the tree."

"I won't. Night, Mom. I'll see you in the morning."

"Good night, Jase."

✧

PULLING IN BEHIND Taylor's car, I glanced at the cabin. I could see a faint hint of a light coming through the front window. Jumping out of the truck, I shut the door and quickly made my way into the cabin. Taylor had sent a text and told me to come in and head straight to her bedroom. I'd been uncomfortable the whole drive here with a hard-on the entire trip.

"Tay?" I called out as I opened the door and locked it behind me. The last thing I'd want is for her dad to make a surprise visit.

"In the bedroom!"

I dragged in a few deep breaths before making my way to her. The bedroom door was shut some so I pushed it open. The sight before me almost had my legs buckling out.

"Holy. Shit."

Her face was lit up by the candles that flanked either side of her bed. She was dressed in the sexiest piece of lingerie I could ever imagine. It was red and white satin and lace. My eyes swept across her body as I tried to take everything in. I swallowed hard when I saw the thigh-high stockings and garter. To top it all off, she had on red heels.

"I've died and gone to heaven," I mumbled.

Her face blushed as she motioned with her finger for me to come closer.

"I wasn't sure if I could pull off sexy, but Lauren assured me I could."

I ripped my shirt off my body and threw it to the floor. "You sure the hell can. I've never seen anyone so fucking sexy in my life."

With a grin from ear to ear, she softly replied, "Good."

My jeans where the next thing to go as I tried desperately to get my boots off.

"Having a hard time?"

When I finally got my damn boots off, I kicked my jeans off and crawled onto the bed.

Taylor's chest rose and fell fast. Kissing her neck, I softly spoke. "I want to slowly peel everything off of you piece by piece."

"O-okay," she panted. Not being able to stop myself, I smiled. Ava was spot on when she said Taylor was innocent. I loved that about her though. Knowing I was going to be the one to teach her everything made me look forward to so many things.

After giving her a proper greeting, I pulled my lips away and took her hands, standing us both up.

Dropping down, I lifted one foot and slipped her heel off, followed by the other foot. My fingertips gently moved up her legs. Glancing up at her, I smiled as she stared at me with wide eyes. No matter how many times I made love to her, it always felt like it was the first time.

Unclasping the garter, I slowly rolled her stocking down as she mumbled something under her breath. Not taking my eyes off of her face. I moved my hands up her other leg. Taylor's lips parted slightly while her tongue moved across her lips. My dick was aching, I was so hard.

"Jase," she whispered as I did the same thing with the other stocking. My eyes zeroed in on her lace panties. I placed my hands on her hips and pulled her closer to me.

"Dear Lord," she panted. Her fingers laced through my hair as she tugged me closer to her. Placing my mouth over her, I blew hot air as her entire body trembled.

"I want you so much, baby."

Her hands tugged harder as she said, "Please. Take me now. I want to feel you on top of me."

I slipped her lace panties off and moved my hands back up her legs. Removing her garter, I dropped it to the floor and stood.

Searching my face, I could see she was nervous and I wanted her to know how she made me feel. "Do you have any idea how much you mean to me? How you make my body crave yours?"

She chewed nervously on her lip. Reaching up, I pulled it out. "You're so beautiful."

She closed her eyes as I reached behind her and finished undressing her. The lingerie dropped to the floor as I cupped her breasts in my hands. Giving each nipple equal attention, I moved my hand down and pushed my fingers inside her.

My eyes rolled to the back of my head as I moved in and out of her. "You're so wet, sweetness."

"I. Want. You."

Her breathing was heavy as she pierced my eyes with hers.

"Lay down, Taylor."

Doing as I asked, she moved quickly to the bed. Reaching into the side drawer, I pulled out a condom and quickly put it on before moving onto the bed. Positioning myself over her, I teased her entrance.

"Jase, please don't tease! I need you."

With a slow push, I sank into her as we both moaned.

"Fucking hell . . . I can't get deep enough inside you."

Her legs wrapped around my body as we both moved slowly. Nothing on earth would ever compare to making love to Taylor.

Nothing.

Twenty-Two

Taylor

"I CAN'T BELIEVE Grams is ninety-five today!" Lauren said as we walked up to the table Jessie pointed us to. Each of us carrying I swear a hundred cupcakes a piece.

"Why in the world did your mom make so many cupcakes?"

Lauren laughed. "I think she's nervous. I mean after all, this is Grams' birthday celebration *and* Jase's family will be here too! The first time the parents are meeting!"

Rolling my eyes, I set the cupcakes down. "You laugh because you didn't have this stress. Our parents all knew each other."

"That's true," Lauren said as her eyes drifted up in thought. "But Gunner and my dad have both told your father they thought Jase was a fine young man."

I peeked over to Gunner and smiled. "Jase reminds me so much of Gunner. Colt too. He says the most wonderful things to me. I remember being little one time and hearing Gunner and Ellie in the kitchen together. I'll never forget what he told her."

Lauren's smile grew bigger. "What did he tell her?"

"He cupped her face with his hands and kissed her forehead." Glancing back over to Gunner, I continued, "Then he told her, I can't wait to wake up tomorrow to your beautiful face."

Lauren sighed. "So simple, but so utterly romantic."

"I know."

Lauren stole a peek at Colt. "The apple didn't fall from the tree. The things Colt says to me makes me weak in the knees."

"Wow. I think that's amazing. He must have learned it from his father."

Lauren chuckled. "Some guys think they have to swoon their girl-friends to win their hearts, but that's not true. I think they should always be trying to win our hearts no matter how long we've been with them."

"I agree."

My eyes drifted over to Matthew. He was sitting peacefully off to the side painting.

Arms wrapped around my waist while my stomach dropped. "What do you agree with?"

"Jase!" I said, spinning around and throwing myself into his arms. "What are you doing here? I didn't think you were coming until six."

"My father called Gunner and asked if he and Jeff could spare a few minutes to talk about business."

I shook my head. "Don't they ever know how to not work?"

He looked deep into my eyes. "Let's hope I'm not the same way once Walker and I take over full time."

My eyes snapped over to Lauren's as we both smiled. "Come on! I want to introduce you to everyone! My parents are not here yet, but that's all the better."

Jase chuckled as he turned to Lauren and tipped his cowboy hat. "Lauren, how are you?"

"I'm doing good, Jase. Thanks for asking."

Taking his hand in mine, I led him over to Matthew first.

Clearing my throat, I asked, "Matthew? Would you like to meet my boyfriend?"

"Not now."

Jase looked surprised, but then smiled. I had already told him all about Matthew and Fragile X.

"Are you sure? He's right here, maybe you could say hi?"

Matthew turned to Jase and sized him up.

"You look like an assmole."

"Matthew!" I gasped and then giggled.

Jase widened his eyes in surprise. "A what?"

"Asshole. He is saying you look like an asshole, which you are not." Turning to Matthew, I said, "He is very much not an assmole."

Matthew nodded. "I'll paint him a picture then."

"Thank you!" Jase said with a smile. "I love paintings."

Matthew smiled. "Okay. I have to paint now, so bye."

I giggled and took Jase's arm.

"Wow, he is an amazing painter!" Jase said glancing over his shoulder to Matthew.

"I know. He is a sweetheart. He'll be easier to talk to when he isn't painting. It's kind of his escape. His happy place if you will."

I pulled Jase through the back door and into the kitchen where pretty much everyone was standing. Gunner and Ellie's kitchen opened up to a family room that held pretty much all of us at one given time.

"Um . . . everyone. This is Jase!"

Jase nodded his head as Gunner walked up. "Jase, long time no see."

Both Gunner and Jase had met last week to go over ideas for the house Jase was wanting to build.

"Nice to see you again, sir."

"Please, call me Gunner." Turning to take Ellie's hand, Gunner went on. "Jase, this is my wife, Ellie."

"It's a pleasure meeting you, Jase. Gunner has spoken very highly of you. Thank you so much for coming."

With a huge smile, Jase replied, "Thank you for inviting me."

Introductions went around the room. I was worried Jase would be overwhelmed meeting everyone, but he took it like a trooper.

"This is Jeff and Ari," I said as Jase shook Jeff's hand.

"I believe we've met before. I was with my father once when he came to look at a horse he was having trained by Ari."

Ari's eyes lit up. "That's right! Reed brought you along and you couldn't have been but maybe seventeen or so."

With a light-hearted laugh, Jase agreed. "Sounds about right."

"What a small world," Heather said.

Grinning, I pointed and said, "This is Heather and Josh."

Jase shook Josh's hand. "Josh Hayes?"

With a surprised look, Josh nodded his head. "Yes."

"I've heard a lot about your wood working. I actually saw a desk and custom cabinets you made for one of my friend's father. He's a lawyer in Llano."

With a stunned expression, Josh said, "Yes! Rob Price . . . I believe that was his name. Man, that was a long time ago."

"I can't believe how connected we have been all these years yet not connected," I said.

Jase chuckled. "I know."

Spinning around, I smiled. "You already know Scott and Jessie. Now it's time for the real test. The best friends."

Everyone laughed as Jase made a frightened face.

With our arms laced together, we made our way around as I introduced Jase to everyone he hadn't met yet. We'd had dinner at Meagan and Grayson's place twice already. My heart melted with how Jase took to Arabella and Charlotte the way he did. The entire time we were there I went back and forth in my mind about if I would be pleased or disappointed if I turned out being pregnant. In the end, I knew it would be best if I weren't. Jase and I needed to spend time together. I still hadn't had my period and made an appointment for Monday. Jase hadn't asked and I wasn't ready to talk about it so we both simply ignored it.

"Libby, Luke, I'd like you to meet Jase. Libby is Will's sister and Heather and Josh are their parents. Luke's sister is Grace, who is married to Noah. Jeff and Ari are their parents. And this is little Trey and the sweet little girl running around us is Mireya."

Luke shook Jase's hand as he held Trey while Mireya sang a song she clearly had just learned.

"Wow! I sure hope there isn't a quiz after this," Jase said with a chuckle.

Luke slapped him on the back and said, "If you remember half this shit and you decide to stay with Taylor after today, I'll be very impressed."

"Stop that!" Libby said as she playfully hit Luke. "Welcome to the family, Jase. It makes me so happy to see Taylor in love."

I felt my face heat up as I guided Jase on to the next group. "This is Alex and Will."

Jase pointed to Will. "Libby's brother. Parents are Josh and Heather."

Will raised his eyebrows. "Impressive."

Alex reached her hand out for Jase's. "It's so nice to finally formally meet you, Jase. I've heard so much about you. Oh . . . I belong to Gunner and Ellie."

Jase tilted his head. "You have a daughter if I remember right from Taylor. Bayli?"

All three of us turned to look at Jase while Will replied, "Dude, you've impressed me. I sure as hell hope you like football and beer."

"Very much so," Jase answered.

Turning to me, Will kissed me on the cheek. "I like him."

With a chortle, I pushed Will away. "One more and you've met them all."

Jase wiped his forehead. "This is Grace and Noah."

Noah and Jase shook hands as Jase smiled and said hello to Hope. "And who is this beautiful princess?"

"Oh, yes. I do indeed like you. Good looking, goes right for the kid and starts giving her attention." Grace turned to me. "I hope he's good in bed because this one is a keeper."

"Grace!" I gasped.

Noah laughed and slapped Jase on the back. "So, do you like football?"

They walked off toward the kitchen as Grace pushed me with her shoulder. "Damn that boy is good looking, Taylor. And the whole cowboy hat thing. Meow."

Pressing my lips together to contain my smile, I nodded and said, "I know."

"Those blue eyes. Dreamy."

Glancing over to her, I scowled. "I can't believe you said that!"

Grace smiled and winked. "Yes you can."

Rolling my eyes, I let out a quick chuckle. "You're right. I can believe it. Don't scare him off, Grace."

Her mouth fell open. "Like I could scare that boy off? If meeting all of us and spending the day with this crazy-ass family isn't enough to scare him off, I seriously doubt anything I say would."

I stared at her in disbelief. "Don't underestimate your power with words, Grace. You have a gift."

With an evil laugh, she handed me Hope. "Go see your Aunt Taylor and slobber all over her."

Hope smiled as I took her in my arms. "She's getting so big."

With an adoring smile, Grace traced her fingertip along Hope's jaw. "I know. I can't wait for another one."

My head snapped up to meet her eyes. "What? Are y'all trying?"

Grace never blushed, but when her cheeks turned red I couldn't help but feel such excitement for her. "I know it's soon, but we decided one more and we wanted them to be close together. We haven't told anyone yet I'm pregnant."

"Oh Grace, I'm so happy for you both."

Her eyes danced with happiness as she gazed back down at Hope. "Thanks. So things will be crazy at the shop with both me and Alex pregnant."

Sucking in a breath, I whispered, "Alex is pregnant too?"

Graze froze. "Oh shit."

My eyes quickly dashed around until I found Alex. How did I not notice? Look at her face glowing. "Holy crap. You, Alex, and La . . . um . . . you and Alex! Wow!"

"Oh no. No way, Taylor Atwood. You were about to say . . ." Grace did a once over and turned back to me. "Lauren. You were about to say Lauren!" She started jumping up and down as she covered her mouth.

"Don't you dare say a word, Grace. They don't want to tell anyone yet. They were going to tell everyone today I think."

"Our little Lauren is pregnant!"

With a giant grin, I nodded. "Yep."

"Now we just need you to pop one out and we'll all have kids."

My smile quickly faded as I looked back at Hope.

"Oh hell. Taylor please tell me you're not."

Swallowing hard, I looked at Grace as tears filled my eyes. "I really hope not. I'm not ready."

"Oh, sweets." Pulling me into her arms, Grace held me while I held onto her daughter and fought to keep my tears in.

Twenty-Three

Jase

THE REST OF the afternoon was filled with meeting more family. I was positive I'd be quizzed after this. There was Jack, Gunner's father. I'd already met his mother Grace. Ellie's mother and stepfather were there, Sharon and Philip.

My eyes scanned everyone as I saw Greg and Elizabeth. *Shit. Whose parents are they again?* When I saw Bayli running into Greg's arms it hit me. Josh's parents!

And to think there are even more I haven't met yet. I'm going to have to ask Taylor for a family tree.

Blowing out a breath, I caught sight of Taylor. She was talking to Grams and Gramps. They had to have been the nicest people I'd ever met. Both still so sharp, especially Gramps for being in his late nineties.

Taylor leaned over and kissed Grams on the cheek and made her way over to me. Smiling, she stopped in front of me and said, "So, has anyone scared you off yet?"

Pulling her into my arms, I gently kissed her lips then whispered, "Never."

"You've never said, do you have a big family?"

"No not really. My father's parents died years before Liza and I were born. His brother, Mike, died in the military when my father was young and Mike's daughter Kate got married a few years back and lives in Phoenix with her husband. We don't get to see her very often which sucks. But her mom, Jen, still lives in Llano. My mother's mom and dad live in New York. They used to come to Texas a lot to visit, but have slowed it down some the older they have gotten. They'll be here this summer though."

Taylor softly smiled. "I'd love to meet them," she said before glancing over her shoulder. "They've already done the whole happy birthday thing. We're just waiting on one more announcement and then we can leave if you want."

Pushing a piece of hair behind her ear, I nodded. "I'm in no rush, sweetness. It's whenever you want to leave."

Colt called out to get everyone's attention as Taylor took my hand and pulled me closer to everyone. "This is it!" she said with excitement in her voice.

"First. I'd like to wish my grams a very happy birthday again. You're rocking it at ninety-five, Grams!"

Everyone clapped as cheers rang out. Colt motioned for Alex to stand next to him as well as Lauren and Will.

"Alex and Will, as well as Lauren and I, have an announcement to make."

Colt turned to Alex who smiled and wiped a tear from her cheek. "You first," she said.

With his arm wrapped around Lauren's waist, Colt beamed with pride and happiness. "Lauren and I will be welcoming our first child July 7."

Cheers erupted as everyone rushed up and started hugging both Lauren and Colt. Ellie was crying as she pulled Lauren to her and held her for the longest time.

When things finally died down, all attention was on Alex and Will. Alex cleared her throat and said, "We didn't want to ruin this day for Colt and Lauren, but once Colt found out he insisted we make our announcement as well."

Ellie's hands went to her mouth as she started crying . . . again. "Will and I are expecting our second child . . ." Alex turned to face Colt and started laughing. "On July 6!"

Taylor jumped as she rushed over to Alex and hugged her. I couldn't ignore the pit in the middle of my stomach. Taylor hadn't mentioned anything and I knew she had to have missed her period. We'd been together for just over a month now.

As much as I dreamed of marrying her and having kids, I really wanted to get my life settled. That meant building a house, setting up roots and settling in with Walker on running the ranch. Not to mention the change to taking everything organic. Walker invested a lot of time in the horseracing side of the ranch while I focused more on the cattle. It was a good arrangement and I liked it. It meant long hours though and if I threw a baby into the mix, it meant I would hardly see him or her.

Letting out a frustrated sigh, I pushed my hand through my hair and did what I have been doing for the last few weeks. Ignored it.

Once everything settled down, Alex got everyone's attention. "So . . . I'm not really sure if she is ready to say anything or not . . . but I really wish she would so we can really turn this into an even bigger party. Grace?"

All eyes turned to Grace. She looked around with a shocked look on her face before turning back to Alex. She blew out a quick breath and walked up next to her. "Well. I guess we might as well tell y'all. We're going to be needing to hire some help at the flower shop."

"That's wonderful, sweetheart!" Ellie called out. "Means your business is thriving."

Grace pinched her face up and said, "Well . . . yes it is but obviously there is something in the water here in Mason. Noah and I are expecting our second child in . . . you guessed it. July. July 24 to be exact."

"Three new babies! July is going to be busy!" Jeff called out as he wrapped his daughter up in his arms while Ari started crying.

Taylor turned to me and laughed. "Jesus, what in the hell is in the water here?" I asked as she laughed. "I'm not sure, but I've got a ton of baby shower planning to do!"

It wasn't lost on me how much Taylor was ignoring our potential problem just like I was.

$\swarrow$

TAYLOR SAT NERVOUSLY on the end of the table, swinging her legs and wringing her hands. "You know you didn't have to come."

"I wanted to."

When Taylor told me she was coming in to talk about getting on birth control and to take a pregnancy test, there was no way I was going to let her come alone.

"So you know this doctor?"

Taylor nodded. "Well, her father mainly. I've been to see her once. Her dad delivered almost all of us, I swear. He retired and his daughter took over."

The door opened and a young female doctor and nurse walked in. "Hi, Taylor. How are you doing?"

"Good," she answered in a shaky voice.

The nurse sat down and pulled up the screen on the computer. Standing, I introduced myself. "Jase Moore."

Dr. Johnson looked between Taylor and myself. "Jase is my boyfriend."

With a satisfied nod, she leaned against the bed. "So, we're here to talk about birth control and I believe you took a pregnancy test as well."

"Y-yes. The one I took at home was negative, but I haven't started so I wanted to be sure."

Dr. Johnson gave Taylor an understanding smile. The nurse turned to the doctor and nodded yes.

Pressing her lips together, Dr. Johnson turned and looked at Taylor, then me, then back to Taylor. "Honey, I'm guessing since you are here to start the pill, pregnancy is not something you are wanting anytime soon."

My heart was pounding so hard in my chest I could hardly hear.

I stood next to Taylor as she reached for my hand. "No . . . I mean at least not right now."

"I want to go ahead and draw some blood to confirm this, but your urine sample came back positive for being pregnant."

Taylor gasped and squeezed my hand. My stomach instantly felt sick as my entire future flashed before my eyes. Brad was going to castrate me.

Closing my eyes, I pushed all the negative thoughts away. I needed to show Taylor we were in this together. Rubbing my thumb across the top of her hand, I kissed her on the forehead and whispered, "It's okay, sweetness. It's okay."

The nurse quickly stood up and blurted out, "Dr. Johnson, I'm so very sorry. I had the wrong chart pulled up!"

Dr. Johnson pushed off the counter and glanced down at the screen. Speaking softly, she replied, "Oh, Nelly."

She quickly closed the chart and typed something in and began reading another chart. Turning to look at the nurse, she politely said, "Would you mind stepping outside of the room for a moment, Nelly?"

Nelly looked panicked. "No, Dr. Johnson, not at all." She rushed out of the room, shutting the door behind her.

Dr. Johnson turned back to us. "Both of you take a deep breath and blow it out."

Doing as she said, Taylor let off on her death grip some. "We have two girls in here today by the name of Taylor and your appointments were at the same time. Nelly had the other Taylor's chart pulled up. I'm so very sorry for that, but I am happy to say you tested negative for being pregnant."

Taylor collapsed into my side as a sob escaped from her lips. I silently thanked God as I held Taylor up against me.

Dr. Johnson grinned slightly. "Again, I'm so sorry for the mini heart attack I'm sure you both had."

"It's okay, no harm no foul," I said with a weak smile. Taylor stayed quiet at my side as Dr. Johnson continued on talking. I wasn't sure how much Taylor heard before she finally snapped out of it and asked a few questions.

When it was all said and done, Dr. Johnson prescribed birth control pills and had Nelly come back in and apologize.

We weren't even out the front door when Taylor spun around and flung herself into my body. Her body shook as she buried her head in my chest and cried.

Moving my hand over her back, I attempted to get her to calm down. "Shh . . . it's all right, Tay."

She pulled back slightly, and my chest hurt when I saw her tear-soaked face. I lifted my hands up to her face and wiped them away.

"I was so scared, Jase. The only thing I could think about was how mad my father was going to be."

Lifting my brows, I pulled my head back and said, "Your dad? Mine would have cut my dick off."

When she laughed, I felt the tension letting go of my body. "It's over, we made that one mistake and it will never happen again."

Placing her hands on my chest, she took in a deep breath before slowly expelling it. "I want kids, Jase. I really do. And this may sound selfish, but I want you all to myself for a while before we have them. I mean . . . we just started dating and I'm not expecting anything from you."

"Taylor you don't have to explain anything. I feel the same way. I want to date, get engaged, plan the wedding of your dreams, and then we can talk about kids."

"You just made my heart flutter."

With a smirk, I leaned in closer and barely spoke against her ear. "My mother would say I swooned you."

With a good laugh, Taylor wrapped her arms around me. "Thank you for coming today. I'm not sure how I would have reacted had you not been there."

Kissing her quickly on the lips, we headed to my truck. "So did you decide if you were moving out of your parents' house?"

"I don't think so. I'm always at your place and never home really, so why move?"

"I was thinking and please don't feel like you have to say yes . . . but why don't you move in with me? I know it's still a good drive to the ranch, but we'd be together every night."

My chest tightened and I couldn't decide if the idea thrilled me or scared the piss out of me. The idea of holding Taylor in my arms every night was amazing. To wake up to those beautiful green eyes had my stomach flipping. And it meant we were moving in together.

Stealing a look in her direction, I asked, "Are you sure? I mean there might be some nights I'd have to stay with my parents or the cabin when I had an early start, but the thought of waking up to your beautiful face each day makes my heart race."

Her teeth sunk into her lip. "I'm positive. Life is short and I don't want to take a day for granted."

"You have to let me split the bills with you."

Trying to contain her smile she agreed. "Deal!"

I reached my hand out for hers. Pulling it to my lips, I gently kissed it. "Then it looks like you've got a roommate."

Twenty-Four

Taylor

Late March

"TAYLOR, ARE YOU sure you want to go?"

"Of course I am! Jase, these are your friends. You hang with my friends all the time. I want to meet some of your friends."

"You've met Rick."

Rolling my eyes, I mumbled under my breath, "He doesn't count."

Jase laughed and pulled me into his arms. "Why do you not like him?"

With a shrug, I replied. "He makes comments to me all the time that make me feel uncomfortable."

With a glower, he asked, "What kind of comments?"

Waving it off, I replied, "Nothing really. I'm just being silly."

"Taylor, if Rick is saying something to you I want to know about it."

Swallowing hard, I chewed on the corner of my lip. The last thing I wanted to do was cause problems between Jase and his best friend. It was true though that I didn't care for Rick at all.

"He's made comments about how nice my ass is and how he sees why you were hung up on me."

Anger built in Jase's eyes. "Please let it go . . . I shouldn't have said anything."

"The fuck you shouldn't have. You should have told me before. What else has he said to you?"

I shook my head. "Nothing really. He just puts his hands on me all the time and I don't like it."

"Explain please."

Ugh. This is exactly why I didn't say anything before to Jase. "Jase, honestly it's just me being me."

His face grew red the angrier he got. When he balled up his fists, I was silently wishing I hadn't said a word.

"Taylor," he bit.

Sighing, I answered him. "He puts his arm around my shoulders and will pull me close to him. Or he puts his hand on my lower back and he always does it when you're not looking or not in the room because I know he knows it makes me uncomfortable and you wouldn't like it."

"I'm gonna pummel his fucking face in when I see him."

Grabbing his arm, I pleaded with him, "Jase no! This is exactly why I didn't say anything to you. I've already decided when he does it again I'm going to say something. Please let me handle this. Maybe he doesn't realize he is doing it . . . doubtful, but possible."

Shaking his head, Jase turned away from me and paced. Both hands pushed through his hair and I couldn't help the ache between my legs. I loved when he did that. It left his hair with that just-fucked look as Meagan called it.

"I swear if I see him touch you or hear him make any comments I'm going to take care of it myself."

This was the first time I'd seen the jealous side of Jase. Pressing my lips together, I nodded.

"Should I bring my swimsuit?"

"I don't think anyone will be swimming. The water is still pretty cold and it's only getting up to the mid-seventies."

I was glad my change of subject worked. I packed a bag and put my swimsuit in anyway just in case.

An hour later and we were walking up to a large group of people. One of Jase's friends rented out a few cabins at a park that was right on the Llano River. It was beautiful. There was a huge fire going and someone had brought a giant grill they were grilling hamburgers on.

Rick turned and smiled as he waved. Jase lifted his hand and waved. "Fucker," he whispered as I bumped my shoulder against him.

The same girl I had talked to that night at the bar came walking over. I didn't think she would recognize me and she didn't. Of course, she acted as if I wasn't even standing there when she threw her arms around Jase. To his credit he didn't hug her and she quickly stepped back.

"Jase! I'm so glad you decided to come. I've hardly seen you in the last few months."

Jase put his arm around my waist and looked at me with a loving smile. "I've been pretty busy."

"Oh, I bet the ranch keeps you busy."

Jase and I both looked at her. "Jill, I'd like to introduce you to my girlfriend, Taylor."

Jill gave me a once over. With a fake smile she said, "Any friend of Jase's is a friend of mine."

"Thanks," I politely answered.

Putting her attention back on Jase, she let out a yell as a song started. I couldn't see where the speakers were or where the music was coming from, but clearly she liked this song with the way she was reacting.

"Jase it's 'Young and Crazy' . . . our song! We have to dance."

Reaching for his arm, she tried to pull him away.

"That's okay, Jill. I'm going to pass."

Her smile dropped and was replaced by a look of shock. "Oh." Her eyes flashed over to me. "I see, well maybe later."

With a polite smile, Jase replied, "I doubt it, but it was nice seeing you again."

When Jase led me away, I took a chance at looking back at Jill.

That was a mistake. She was shooting daggers straight at me.

"Sorry about that, Tay. Jill and I used to date in high school."

I was somewhat surprised Jase told me he used to date Jill. But then again, why not tell me.

My stomach was in knots as Jase began introducing me to everyone. *What if his friends didn't like me? What if I didn't fit in with them?* I felt so bad that Jase had been spending all his spare time with me. When Rick mentioned this party I knew Jase wanted to go.

"So, Taylor, Jase mentioned you live in Mason?"

With a grin, I replied, "I do. I work for Reynolds Breeding."

"Oh really?" the girl who I was pretty sure was named Shay said. "What do you do there?"

"I work in the office as a financial analyst."

"Interesting. Did you grow up in the country?"

I would have loved to ask her where she was going with this, but I faked a smile and continued talking.

"Fredericksburg, but I spent a lot of time in Mason. I practically grew up on a cattle ranch."

"Cows. How fun," Jill said with an eye roll.

What in the world did Jase ever see in this girl?

Reaching deep down inside, I dug out my inner Meagan. "What about you, Jill?"

She snapped her head over and contemplated if she wanted to answer me. "What about me?"

"Did you grow up in Llano?"

Squaring off her shoulders, she said, "I did. I grew up around horses . . . although cows sound like a ton of fun. Too bad you won't be able to keep up with those racehorses Jase plays around with."

She did not. Wow. This girl is a bitch.

Shay smiled. "Do you ride, Taylor?"

With a nod, I replied. "I do. I've been around horses my whole life."

Glancing over to where Jase was, I saw him down another beer. I knew he had been working a lot lately and was wanting to cut loose and have some fun, but I was stunned by how much he was drinking.

Jill sighed and said, "I'm going to find better company. Excuse me."

My mouth dropped as I watched her walk away. I felt like I was back in high school as I looked around with a stunned expression. *What is it with Jase's friends? They are so immature.* "Ignore her, Taylor. She's just pissed that you're here with Jase. I'm sure she was hoping to get her claws into him again."

"It's okay. She does realize we are all adults here though, right?" I asked as I watched her walk over to where Jase was.

Shay chuckled. "I think she is still stuck in high school. Watch her, though. With the way Jase is knocking them back, I wouldn't be surprised if she was planning on something."

My head turned to Shay. "Like?"

I couldn't help but notice how she was looking at Jill with a disgusted look. "Let's just say she has a way of trying to make something seem like it is something it isn't."

Swiveling around to look at me, she smiled and said, "I think I'll go find my fiancé before he finds trouble. See ya later."

"See ya," I said as I made my way over to Jase. Jill kept laughing and putting her hand on his stomach. Anger began to build in my veins. When he took a step away from her, my body relaxed a bit.

Here I thought Rick was going to be the problem and it was Jill.

"Hey," I said as I kissed Jase on the cheek.

"Hey, sweetness. Having fun?"

His eyes were blurred and I knew he had probably had more to drink then he should. I knew in college Jase would let loose and drink. I'd seen him a few times at parties. But why he was doing it now, I was unsure. Maybe because he was with his friends and that's what they did? All I knew was I wasn't pleased he was getting drunk.

"Maybe you should slow down on the beer," I said with a grin.

Jase held up the beer bottle and looked at it. "Jesus Christ, lay off of him. It's not like you're married to him. If he wants to drink let him drink."

I curled my lip and peered at Jill. "Maybe you've had too many as well or do you make it a habit to hang on men who are taken."

"Oh shit," Jase mumbled. "You know what, you're right, Tay. I've had too much to drink. Let's head to the cabin. My head is pounding."

I didn't even bother to look back at the little bitch this time. I was seething mad. "Which cabin is ours?" I asked.

"Ten. I'm not feeling so great."

"Wonder why? Oh wait, it's probably the twelve pack of beer you drank."

"Fuck, my head is killing me."

Making my way up the steps to the cabin, I opened the door and turned on the light. It was cuter than I thought it would be. "It's cute in here."

Jase pushed past me and ran into the bathroom.

When he started throwing up, I rushed in there. Grabbing a wash cloth, I ran it under hot water and handed it to him. "Did you drink anything else besides beer?"

He slowly nodded. "Rick gave me a couple shots. I should have known better. I haven't had a thing to eat all day since breakfast."

Not wanting to nag him about it, I rewet the washcloth. "How's your head?"

He stood and stumbled. "Shit, I'm more drunk than I thought."

Wrapping my arm around his waist, I led him out of the bathroom and over to the bed where he collapsed.

"Fuuuck. My head."

Sighing, I closed my eyes. He was only going to get worse unless I had something to give to him.

"Jase? Baby, I'm going to take your truck and run to HEB. Get some water and Advil. Do you want anything else?"

"Hamburger. I want a hamburger."

Smiling, I kissed him on the cheek. "I'll grab one on my way back to the cabin from the pit."

He mumbled something about my sexy ass and telling Rick off. I guess that explained why Rick had stayed away from me for the last few hours.

"I need your keys, Jase."

He flipped over on the bed and spread his legs open and gave me that crooked smile of his. "They're in my p-pocket . . . you needs to reach in there and get 'em."

"You're a terrible drunk, do you know that?"

Jerking his hips up, he wiggled his eyebrows. "Crawl on top of me, baby. I want you to fuck me."

"As tempting as that is, I'd be afraid you'd puke on me." Pulling his boots off, I dropped them on the floor.

"Damn . . . I feel so bad."

My heart broke for him. Even though a small part of me was glad he felt so bad. He should have never drank so much.

Reaching into his jeans, Jase smiled. "That's what . . . I'm talkin' . . ."

He started snoring before he finished his sentence. Leaning over, I kissed him on the lips. "I love you, Jase Morris."

Twenty-Five

Taylor

A PART OF me was glad we were away from everyone and in the cabin. I was having a miserable time. I got the feeling Jase must have been a very eligible bachelor in Llano, because I was not welcomed at all by the female members of his little group. Even Shay, who had a fiancé, seemed to dislike me.

Rick was now manning the grill when I walked up carrying four HEB bags.

With a smile, he asked, "How is he?"

"Drunk. He passed out before I left. He did however request a hamburger. Since he hasn't had anything to eat, I think that might be a good idea."

Rick chuckled and handed me a plate. Grabbing a bun, I put mustard on it only. Holding the plate up for Rick, he placed a burger on it.

"Thanks, Rick."

Turning to leave, Rick called out for me. "Hey, Taylor?"

"Yeah?" I asked as I stopped and turned to him.

"I'm really sorry if I made you feel uncomfortable around me."

I furrowed my brows. "Jase talked to you?"

"If you want to use the word talk . . . I'd say yell."

Glancing down to the ground, I replied, "I'm sorry. I asked him not to. I was going to talk to you myself. The last thing I want is to get between you and Jase. I know how long y'all have been friends."

"Nah, you had every right to say something. I actually knew I was hitting on you and a part of me was doing it because I was jealous."

"Jealous? Why?"

With a shrug, he looked away. "I don't know. Jase was happy, really happy and I knew how much he loved you. Guess a part of me wants what he has. But I am honestly happy for him. I swear."

I smiled weakly. "I should get back to him. Thanks for the burger."

Rick nodded and focused back on the task at hand. As I walked closer to the cabin, I noticed a group of women standing there talking with two guys. They were the same group Jill had been hanging with. I walked past them and one of them grabbed my arm. "Wait! Um . . . why don't you hang with us for a bit? I mean, with Jase passed out and all what fun is it in the cabin?"

I went to answer her when it dawned on me. "How did you know he was passed out?"

Her smile faded as she glanced up at the door to the cabin we were staying in.

My heart dropped. "Let go of me, now. Please."

The girl dropped her hand as I quickly made my way up the steps and pushed the door open.

Dropping the bags onto the floor, I gasped. Jill was naked and attempting to take off Jase's pants.

"What in the hell are you doing?"

Stumbling back, Jill tried to cover herself up. "Jase asked me to come in here."

My eyes drifted over to Jase who was sound asleep and in the same position he was when I left. "Is that so? He asked you to come in here and what?"

She quickly grabbed her dress and pulled it over her head. "Isn't it obvious? He wanted a quick fuck, but he passed out again."

A part of me panicked. What if Jase had woken up and asked Jill to come in here? My heart raced as her perfume suddenly became over-powering and turned my stomach.

"Please get out."

Lifting her chin, she smiled. "Fine. It's not my fault he isn't happy with what you're giving him and he had to seek it out on his own."

My patience had now run out. Walking up to her, I reached for her boots and grabbed her by the arm. Dragging her toward the door, I opened it and used all my might to push her out. I tossed her boots out and glared at her.

"Get out and stay the hell away from him."

The two guys and three girls standing outside started laughing. Stepping back into the cabin, I slammed the door shut. Turning, I leaned against it and tried to calm my breathing down.

Jase mumbled my name and rolled over. My hands came up to my mouth as I tried to contain my sobs while I sank to the floor.

My mind was racing. Pulling my knees to my chest, I buried my face in my arms and cried silently.

∽

HEARING WATER RUNNING, I opened my eyes and tried to adjust to the bright light. Stretching, I sat up and yawned. It was then everything from yesterday hit me again. My eyes landed on the empty bed.

"Hey, morning."

Jase's voice calmed my rapidly beating heart. Standing, I turned to see him in the little kitchen area holding a cup of coffee. He took a drink before setting it down and grabbing the Advil and popping some in his mouth, followed by water.

"How do you feel?" I asked.

He grimaced and took another drink of water. "Better than I should. I'm so sorry, Taylor. I ruined yesterday and last night. I'm not even sure why I was kicking them back. Being around my old friends I guess."

Wringing my hands together I tried to remember what I had told myself last night. Nothing happened. Jase didn't ask Jill to come in. I knew he would never hurt me like that. Shay's words of advice played over and over in my head last night after I had my mini breakdown.

"How much do you remember?"

He pushed out a frustrated breath and sat down at the small table. "I remember getting sick, you helping me fall into bed. You taking off my boots and me asking you to crawl on top of me . . . which honestly, I'm still hoping you'll do."

I couldn't help but giggle.

"Do you remember Jill being in here . . . trying to undress you?"

His eyes widened in horror. "What? What are you talking about? When?"

"I left for HEB and when I came back, one of her friends tried to keep me from coming into the cabin. When I walked in, she was naked and trying to take off your pants."

Jase quickly responded. "Taylor, I would never."

Holding up my hands to stop him talking, I smiled. "I know that. I won't say that last night I wasn't a bit upset walking in and seeing her trying to have sex with my boyfriend who was clearly passed out. I was very upset. But I trust you."

"I would have woken up and stopped her. You have to know that."

Placing my hands on his chest, I looked lovingly into his eyes. "I know you would have."

He closed his eyes and shook his head. "We shouldn't have even come. You didn't enjoy yourself at all. I could see it on your face all afternoon."

Reaching up on my toes, I gently kissed his lips. "It's okay. I am ready to go home though, I learned something important."

Lifting his eyebrows, he asked, "What's that?"

"I don't think I like your old high school friends and I'm certainly never going to a party where Jill will be."

Jase threw his head back and laughed. "Same goes for me."

Pushing my body into his, I flashed him a sexy smile. "Now, about me being on top."

Before I could say another word, Jase had me in his arms and was carrying me over to the bed. When he placed me on the ground, things turned frantic. We couldn't get undressed fast enough. Jase laid on the bed while I crawled on top of him. Positioning myself over him, I slowly sank down until he filled me completely.

We both moaned as I moved slowly at first, then faster. The feel of making love to him like this was heavenly. My orgasm hit me quickly as I called out his name. Jase lifted his hips and moaned as he poured himself into me. It was still fairly new for us to be having sex with no condom. We had both been so freaked out by the false pregnancy results that we had used a condom for a month after I started the pill.

The first time we didn't use one was the first time Jase came before me while having sex. Actually, it was the first he came as quick as he did. I couldn't blame him though. It felt amazing.

Collapsing down on to his chest, I fought for air while his dick continued to jump while inside me.

"That felt so good," he softly spoke.

Once my breathing was under control, I pushed up and smiled down at him. "It always feels so good."

He lifted his hips and wiggled his eyebrows. "Yeah, it does and if you give me a few minutes, I might be ready for round two."

I was about to agree when his cell phone started ringing. "Shit. That's my dad's ring."

Lifting myself off of him, I missed the feel of him immediately.

Jase jumped up and grabbed his jeans. Pulling his phone out.

"Hello? Shit, are you serious? Yep, I'll be there in about fifteen minutes. No, we're in Llano. Right. Will do."

I quickly headed to the bathroom and cleaned up when Jase came walking in. He took a towel, wet it and cleaned himself off. "Someone cut a hole in the fence. Probably trying to hog hunt. We've got about twenty-five head of cattle missing."

"Oh no!"

"Do you mind heading over to my folks place? I'm sure my mom is home but I need to get there right away."

"That's totally fine. I'll grab a book or something to read while I wait if your mom is busy."

Jase placed his hands on my shoulders. Capturing my eyes with his, he turned serious. "I would have woken up, Taylor."

My finger came up to his mouth. "Nothing happened. It's over and done. Just another lesson we both learned. No harm."

"No foul," he replied.

"Right. Now come on, let's get the hell out of here. I'm afraid if I see Jill I may want to knock her lights out.

Jase chuckled as we both quickly got dressed, gathered up our stuff, and headed to the ranch. Right before we pulled down the driveway, Jase stopped his truck.

"What's wrong?" I asked.

"There was something I wanted to talk to you about last night, but I obviously never got the chance to."

"Is it something that can wait until later or do we need to talk about it now?"

Jase licked his lips as he looked about nervously. "I was wondering if you would go with me to see Drew . . . I mean Gunner tomorrow. He was going to ask me some questions about the house and well . . . I see you as part of my future, Taylor. And that means we need to talk about things like where you want to live and where I want to live. Things like that."

Warmth radiated through my body as my smile grew bigger. Knowing Jase wanted me to be a part of something so big in his life made my stomach flutter. I loved that he was thinking of our future in the same way I was. "I see you as part of my future too, Jase."

His hand slipped behind my neck as I unbuckled my seat belt and let him pull me closer to him. When his lips crashed against mine, he made a low growling sound from the back of his throat. My insides quivered while he kissed me more passionately.

When we finally pulled away from one another, we rested our foreheads together.

"I want so badly to do things the right way. To sweep you off your feet, Tay. But I have to ask you right now before I burst. I swear to you I'll make it up to you and ask again, but I have to ask now."

A tear slowly made its way down my cheek as I held my breath.

"Will you marry me, Taylor?"

A sob slipped from my lips as I pulled back and looked into his beautiful blue eyes. My tears spilled out as Jase reached up and wiped them away.

"Yes! Yes! Yes! A million and one times yes!"

I'd never seen Jase smile so big before. "You have no idea how happy I am right now!"

"You?" I said with a giggle. "I'm pretty sure I have an idea."

"Buckle up, I need to get going."

Doing as he asked, I quickly buckled up. My heart was beating rapidly and I couldn't contain my smile.

Jase asked me to marry him.

Marry him!

When he reached for my hand, butterflies danced around like mad. *I wonder if I'll ever tire of his touch? Never.*

Pulling up, Jase parked and jumped out of his truck. He ran over to my side, opened the door and pulled me out. Holding me in his arms, my feet dangled while he kissed me again.

"Don't say anything to my mom!"

Nodding. "I won't."

"I've got to run."

Running back around the truck, Jase jumped in and rolled the passenger side window down.

"I love you!"

"Wait!" I called. "Is your mom expecting me? Do I just walk in?"

He flashed his dimples and nodded. "Just walk in, sweetness."

Putting the truck in drive, he started to take off slowly. "I love you too! Be careful!"

"Always!" he shouted and took off. I stood there like a silly girl who had just received her first kiss. Watching his truck until I couldn't see it anymore, I wrapped my arms around my body and started running in place as I let out a squeal of delight.

"My . . . that must have been some kiss."

I spun on my heels and looked at Whitley. "Oh . . . um . . . well." I let out a soft chuckle. There was no way I could hide how happy I felt. My cheeks actually hurt from smiling so big.

Whitley walked down the front porch steps toward me. "That smile is the most brilliant smile I think I've ever seen."

Covering my cheeks with my hands, I could feel my face on fire.

Stopping right in front of me, she tilted her head and examined me. My hands moved to my mouth where I tried like hell not to smile.

The back of my throat ached as I attempted to hold it in. There were no words I could say. If I tried to talk I was surely going to laugh or cry.

"Oh my word," Whitley whispered.

Wrapping her arm around my shoulders, she guided me up the stairs and into the house. She took my hand and pulled me quickly into the kitchen where she motioned for me to sit down. Whitley stood back and regarded me carefully before turning and getting two wine glasses down.

I'd never in my life experienced being this happy before. There could not have been any better way for Jase to ask me that than right at that moment. Straight from his heart.

Whitley poured wine into each glass and handed me one while she sat down and watched me carefully.

Taking a deep breath, I took a drink and set the glass down.

"Now . . . breathe in and slowly let it out."

I did what she said.

With a wide grin, she lifted her brows and waited for me to talk.

"Sorry about that. Jase and I have just had a really wonderful day."

"That's obvious and I'm glad to see he makes you happy, Taylor. I hope you know how happy you make him."

Nodding my head, I bit the inside of my cheek.

"You seem to be glowing. I take it something . . . magical happened today."

Chewing on my thumbnail, I grinned. "Every day is magical with Jase."

"Every mother wants to hear a woman talk about her son that way."

I closed my eyes and sighed. "Oh, Whitley. You and Layton did an amazing job because Jase makes me feel so alive."

Feeling my face heat, I shook my head and looked away. "I'm sorry, I shouldn't be talking about your own son that way."

Whitley reached for my hands. "Yes! You should."

The excitement of the last few minutes grew more. Thinking about Jase asking me to marry him, I placed my hand on my stomach to calm the butterflies. "He says the sweetest things to me," I gushed.

Scrunching her nose, she grinned. "Oh, he got that from his daddy.

Layton has a way of making me feel so loved and special."

"Yes!" I replied.

She chuckled and then winked as she said, "But he also has a way of bringing out another side of me that is . . . only for him."

Feeling my face warm, I whispered, "Yes."

It was as if a memory swept through her mind as she fell back against the chair and smiled even bigger. "I have so many wonderful memories with that man."

"You both seem to be so in love still. My parents are the same way. The way my father looks at my mother gives me chills. I see Layton look at you the same way."

"And I see Jase look at you that way." She leaned forward and took my hands in hers. "Taylor, there are going to be ups and downs. More ups in the beginning for sure, but life is going to test your love for one another as well as your patience and trust. You'll come across people who are jealous of what the two of you share and they will do whatever they can to try and rip it apart."

I instantly thought of Jill and the stunt she had pulled.

"Don't let them. The key is communicating. If you're upset or angry about something, you have to talk to each other. The worse mistake you could ever make is holding it in because you think it will get better. Don't hold things in . . . talk about it."

I wasn't sure what came over me, but it was as if I was bubbling with excitement and I had to tell someone right that very second.

"Jase just asked me to marry him!" Slamming my hands over my mouth, my eyes widened.

Whitley gasped. "I knew it! I could tell the moment I saw you jumping all around!"

Dropping my hands, I said, "I wasn't supposed to say anything."

"Don't worry, sweetheart. You're secret is safe with me. I won't tell a soul until the two of you are ready."

Moving my feet as if I was running in place, I let out another squeal. "I'm engaged!"

We both jumped up and grabbed hands as we jumped all around until we hugged. I knew in that moment Whitley was going to be so much more to me than just a mother-in-law. I already felt like I could tell her anything. I had just gained someone amazing in my life.

The day couldn't get any better . . . that was until Whitley pushed me back at arm's length and said, "Welcome to the family, Taylor."

Twenty-Six

Jase

ROUNDING UP THE last cow, I led her back onto our property as my father whistled for Reed and Walker to bring them on up while we worked on repairing the fence.

I grabbed the fence pulls and headed over to where my father was working.

"So, are you going to tell me why you can't wipe that shit-eating grin off your face?"

Thinking back to Taylor saying yes, my damn stomach fluttered like a pansy ass.

I had no clue why I did it, but I blurted it out. "I asked Taylor to marry me and she said yes."

My father stopped what he was doing and looked up at me. All I could see was his blue eyes set off from the black cowboy hat he was wearing. When a smile slowly moved across his face and his hand reached out for mine, I let myself breathe.

"Well, congratulations are in order then."

Nodding and feeling like a damn schoolboy who just got his first kiss, I replied, "Thanks, Dad."

"Oh hell," he said as he pulled me into his arms. He slapped me three times on the back and said, "Your mother is going to be a crying mess when she finds out."

I couldn't help but chuckle. "I feel like I'm about to be a crying mess."

"And that's okay if you do. Love does crazy things to us. I once washed with women's fragrance soap then kicked one of my best friend's asses all before a huge business meeting."

Furrowing my brows, I asked, "Why?"

He shrugged and said, "Because of love. Your mother had me in knots in the beginning. Half the time I didn't know which way was up and which way was down. Shit . . . she still does."

Letting out a gruff laugh, I agreed. "Sounds familiar."

"Did you make it special for her?"

Looking away, I sighed. "Nope. I kind of blurted it out in the truck at the end of our driveway. It's weird, Dad. It was like I had to ask her right that second or I was going to explode."

"Sometimes it's the spur of the moment things we do that they love the most. There have been times when I had every intention of planning the most elaborate romantic evening ever, only to have it fall apart and I have to take her on a moonlight picnic. It never fails . . . she falls apart in a crying mess and proclaims me to be the most romantic man in the world."

My mouth fell open. "Holy fuck, Dad. I'd hate to see what an elaborate romantic evening would be because I'd have never thought about a moonlight picnic."

He smiled and winked. "You can use it, son. I don't mind."

Laughing, I clipped the fence pullers onto the fence.

"I just want to make her happy."

My father attached the clips as he looked up at me. "It's not that hard. Make sure you always make her feel special. Even if she is sick as a dog and her nose is all red from blowing it all day and her hair looks a mess and she's talking like Fran Drescher . . . tell her she's beautiful."

Looking at him with a confused expression, I asked, "Who's Fran Drescher?"

He rolled his eyes and twisted the clip. "Never mind. The point is, never lose an opportunity to let her know how special she is to you. Remind her every day that you love her more than life itself. Surprise her with little things like a single rose." He stood up, took off his hat and wiped the sweat away with his shirt sleeve. "Better yet, pay attention when she says she likes something. Your mother once went on and on about this book she loved so much. With the help of Courtney, I contacted the author and got her a signed book."

He wiggled his eyebrows and said, "Nine months later Liza was born."

I made a gagging motion and held up my hand. "TMI, Dad. Way too much."

"The bottom line, Jase, is treat her like a princess. Be the reason she smiles . . . not cries. And most of all, be faithful to her."

We finished the fence repairs in silence as I let everything he said sink in. I tossed the tools into the back of the ranch truck as my father climbed in. Walking up to his door, I cleared my throat.

"Um . . . don't say anything yet about me asking Taylor to marry me. I'm not sure when she'll want to tell everyone."

"Sure. Your secret is safe with me."

With a slap on his shoulder, I flashed him a smile. "Thanks, Dad. For the advice and for listening."

"Anytime, Jase. I'm always here if you need me. For anything."

Taking a step back, I shut the door and watched him drive off.

Making my way back to the truck, I sent Taylor a text.

Me: Finished and heading back.

Taylor: Okay! Talking with your mom! We're having fun making fudge so take your time.

My heart felt full and content as I read her text again. I couldn't wait for my mother to find out that Taylor and I were getting married. The look on her face would be priceless.

WALKER AND I fed the herd while my father and Reed went over some information Ryder had sent them regarding converting fully over to organic. I was meeting Nate in two days in Austin to fly out and tour an organic cattle ranch in Wyoming. Since I'd be handling most of the cattle ranch and Walker focused on the breeding of the horses, it only made sense that I would be the one to go.

"All right, dude. I'm heading home to my wife and son. You got this?" Walker asked.

"Yeah, I'll finish up, you go on. Taylor is back at the house with my mom so no worries."

Walker tipped his hat and headed out of the barn. "Tell Liza I said hey."

He held up his hand and waved. "Will do."

"And give my nephew a high five!"

Calling over his shoulder, he said, "Got it!"

After finishing everything up, I checked in on Bell. She was a new mare I had bought for Taylor who was expecting a foal in the next week or so. Taylor was beyond excited.

"Hey there, pretty girl," I said as Bell walked up to me for a hand full of oats.

I ran my hand down her neck and smiled. "You're going to be a good girl for my Taylor, aren't you girl?"

Bobbing her head, she nudged me for more oats. With a chuckle, I shook my head. "Oh no. You've had enough, girl. Sleep tight."

As I made my way from the barn to the house, I thought about Taylor. I wanted to see her. The urge to hold her in my arms and kiss her was almost overwhelming. I had asked her to marry me and then I dropped her off to spend half the day with my mother. She was probably dying to tell one of the girls our news.

Walking up to my father and Reed, I stopped short of them to allow them to finish up their conversation. Reed turned and gave me a smirk. My eyes quickly moved to my father.

"You told him."

Reed grabbed a hold me and brought me in for a bro hug, slapping the living hell out of my back in the process.

"Damn. It wasn't that long ago you were following us around

claiming to be the best cowboy in the land. And now look at you. Engaged."

Grinning, I shook his hand and glared at my father. "Remind me to never tell you a secret again."

"I couldn't help it. I'm excited."

With a roll of my eyes, I walked past them both. "Well, neither one of you say a word to Mom and Courtney. I want Taylor to be the one to tell everyone."

"My lips are sealed," my father said behind me as Reed laughed his ass off.

"I've heard that before, Dad."

Walking through the back door, I stepped into the kitchen. Courtney and my mother both turned and looked at me. The smile on their faces instantly told me Taylor spilled the beans.

Peeking over at Taylor, she had her lips pressed together in an attempt to hide her smile. Her cheeks were flushed and her eyes were filled with joy. Adrenaline rushed through my body at the idea that I was the one who made her that happy.

My father's words replayed in my head.

Be the reason she smiles . . . not cries.

Reed and my father walked in behind me and I held my breath to see which side would break first.

"You get the fence fixed?" my mother coolly asked.

Reaching for the tea she held for him, he grinned. "Yep. All fixed and all cattle are accounted for."

"Good."

Slipping my arm around Taylor's waist, I leaned in and whispered, "You told them didn't you?"

"I couldn't help it! It was like your mother knew and I broke. The next thing I knew Courtney was here and we were wedding planning!"

With a slight smile, I placed my lips next to her ear. "I want to celebrate."

Her breath hitched as she peeked up at me. "Ring shopping?"

"No. Love making."

She bit on her lip and my dick jumped in my pants. "I like the sound of that better."

With an evil smile, my father asked, "What have you beautiful ladies been up to?"

Shrugging, my mother replied, "Nothing. Making fudge and talking girl stuff."

When he looked at me I shook my head.

"I can't take it!" Courtney shouted. "I have to tell!"

"Oh no," Taylor gasped as my mother turned to Courtney with a horrified look.

"Jase asked Taylor to marry him!"

All eyes landed on Reed. Placing her hands on her hips, my mother glared at him. "Reed Moore. How could you blurt that out and steal the kid's happy news away from them?"

Pointing to Courtney, Reed replied, "She was about to spill the beans first."

"I can't believe you stole my thunder," Courtney gasped.

My mother turned to Courtney. "Your thunder? Court, if you weren't my best friend I'd slap you."

"That might be fun to see," my father said wiggling his eyebrows.

"Oh, brother. Can the four of you just stop," I said walking in between them all. I shot a dirty look to each of them. "All I can say is when the next big news happens . . . and that won't be for a while mind you, but—" Pointing my finger to them each, I widened my eyes, "You can be assured none of you will find out our next big news when it happens."

"A baby!" my mother said covering her mouth. "Jase Morris, you would never hide something like that from me."

With a glimpse over at Taylor, I grinned as she tried her best not to laugh. "Yes. Yes I would, Mom. You have all shown yourselves as sucky secret keepers."

"Us?" my father said with a roar of laughter.

My mother gasped. "You and Taylor are the ones who suck at it! You both spilled the beans within an hour of asking her."

"I'd worry about Courtney. She was the first to cave," Reed said as he sat down and took a drink of tea.

"Whatever. Come give me a hug, Jase. I've already tackle hugged Taylor," Courtney said.

Walking up to Courtney, I did as she asked. She and Reed had been like my second parents. I was glad they were able to share this day with Taylor and I. We spent the next hour talking to my parents about possibly getting married by the large tank on our ranch. I'd taken Taylor there a few times and she loved it.

Finally putting an end to the early wedding plans, I dragged Taylor away from everyone.

"Time for us to go." Taylor jumped up and took my hand as we headed out.

"Jase Morris! You can't always be taking her away like this!"

Without even bothering to look back, I lifted my hand and called out, "See y'all later!"

The sooner we got back to her place the better.

Twenty-Seven

Taylor

I WANDERED AROUND in the boutique while my mother went on and on about some new hair product she found. My mother's beautiful red hair was something I always loved. When I was little and needed to get to her right away, she was the easiest mom to find . . . I just looked for her hair. When Meagan dyed her hair brown I was stunned. But then again, Meagan looks amazing as a brunette or a red head.

Sighing, I glanced around. I hated shopping with a passion. I wanted to tell my mother over the phone about the engagement, but Jase and I decided to wait until I picked out a ring and then we would make it official . . . that is if his parents could keep it to themselves.

"Taylor, you seem a million miles away."

Trying to force a smile, I nodded. "Nah, I think I'm just tired."

"Are you still liking your job?"

That was one thing I did love talking about. My job!

"Yes!" I replied with excitement in my voice. "It's so different and something new every day, I swear. You wouldn't think so with it just being horses, but there is so much that goes into taking care of them on every level. It's been really great being able to help the business save money."

She tilted her head and looked at me adoringly. "You sound so happy. So much more than when you were working for Granddad."

"Ugh," I mumbled. "How has Daddy worked for him for so long? No wonder y'all moved so far out."

Giggling, she shook her head and said, "Oh you have no idea, Taylor. None at all."

"What do you mean?"

"Let's just say when your father and I were first married, I wasn't your grandmother's biggest fan."

I pulled my head back in shock. "Really? But y'all get along so well."

"Yeah well, that story needs a good bottle of wine and chocolate."

With a chuckle, I shook my head and held up a shirt.

"Something else is on your mind though . . . I see it in your eyes."

I wasn't sure what was wrong. I felt guilty not telling her about the wedding, but I was more an edge with Jase leaving in two days.

"It's probably just me feeling sad because Jase is leaving for Wyoming in a few days."

"Oh? What for? Did you tell me this and I forgot?"

"I think I told you. He's going with Nate Montgomery to look at a cattle ranch that is all organic. It is one of the top ranches in the country. Nate and Ryder, his brother, helped them convert over the ranch like they are Jase's family ranch."

My mother nodded. "Interesting. You wouldn't think there would be that much to it but I guess you have to be certified and all of that."

"Yeah, it's crazy insane."

"He'll be fine, sweetheart. Don't worry."

Feeling the tears build, my eyes caught my mothers. "Oh, Taylor, come on let's go find a place to sit down."

I felt like a fool for over reacting the way I was. Once we got outside, my mother guided us over to a bench where we sat down. Quickly wiping my tears away, I let out a muffled laugh. "I'm not sure why I'm so emotional."

Pushing a loose piece of hair behind my ear, she gave me a look of understanding. People walked by us like they didn't even notice us sitting there. I could smell the wine from all the people walking by holding their stupid samples of wine. I hated that my simple little country town had been turned into a mini wine capital.

Blowing out a breath, I dropped my head back and moaned. "Oh gosh, Mom. What is wrong with me?"

"Nothing. You're newly in love and the idea of being separated for any length of time sucks."

I chewed on the corner of my lip. "He's going in a private plane."

"So?"

My shoulders sagged. "Nate is flying it."

She looked at me like I had grown two heads. "Is that a problem?"

"No. Well, I don't know. Why can't they just fly in a normal plane and drive to the ranch? Just because this rancher has his own landing strip and Nate wants flying hours . . . ugh."

I buried my face in my hands. I could feel my chest tightening as I struggled for air.

My mother pulled my hands away from my face and held them. "Is that why you're so on edge? You're worried about him flying up there?"

I couldn't hold the secret in any longer. "That's part of it, but I've been keeping a secret from you."

Her eyes widened. "Oh. Okay . . . well let me get myself ready for this."

She licked her lips and then pressed them together as she closed her eyes. Was she saying a prayer?

Oh. God. She thinks I'm pregnant!

"I'm not pregnant, Mom."

Her body slumped over as she sighed. "Thank God! Your father would beat Jase's ass."

Trying not to giggle, I shook my head. "Well . . . he still might, if I know, Daddy."

Her eyes lit up and she smiled from ear to ear.

"Jase asked me to marry him."

She yelped as she slammed her hands over her mouth. Then her hands dropped and she started crying.

"My baby is getting married!"

I quickly glanced around to see who was witnessing her

breakdown. A few older ladies smiled and gave me a polite nod. "Okay, Mom . . . maybe we should grab lunch."

She jumped up. "Lunch? We have to start thinking about the dress! Let's go."

And just like that, I created a monster I was positive I wouldn't be able to contain.

"Where are we going?"

Looking over her shoulder, she laughed. "Home, of course. We need to make a game plan!"

Rolling my eyes, I moaned. Maybe this was the perfect distraction I needed. My mother on a mission.

Yay. Me.

ONCE I WAS safely in my car, I dragged in a deep breath and let it out slowly. "Holy hell. I'm not going to make it."

My phone rang in my purse as I quickly dug it out. Seeing Jase's name, I smiled.

"Hey."

"Hi there, beautiful. How was your day with your mom?"

Dropping my head back, I moaned. "I caved."

Jase laughed. "Was she happy?"

"So happy that I just spent the last two hours mapping out a detailed plan on what wedding dress shops we were going to visit. Of course, it all depends on what time of year the wedding is."

"Why?"

"I asked the same thing! I did tell her it would be by the lake on your family's ranch. She loved the idea."

Jase chuckled again. "Hey, can you meet me where we decided to have the house built? Gunner is wanting to finalize a few things so we can get started building the house."

My stomach fluttered. "I can't believe we're building a house together."

"You don't think we're moving too fast, do you?"

Staring straight ahead, I smiled. "It feels right."

"So right. But you know I can sell this land and we can build any-where you want. It doesn't have to be here in Llano."

My chest expanded as Jase spoke. He was so caring of my feelings about everything. It made me love him even more. "No. I want to live where you grew up. The idea of raising our kids in your backyard makes me happy."

"You're sure?"

"I've never been so sure of anything in my life."

Jase cleared his throat. "The way you love me leaves me breathless."

With a chortle, I shook my head and started my car. "I feel the same. I'm leaving my parents' house now. I'll head straight to the land and meet you there."

"Sounds good. Be careful driving, sweetness."

"Will do. See ya in about forty minutes."

When I drove down the dirt road we had made coming out to the land, I couldn't contain the excitement building. Jase and I were building a house. We were getting married.

I reached over and pinched myself.

"Still not dreaming."

Pulling in behind Jase, I quickly jumped out of my car and made my way over to the site we had picked to build our two-story house. I wasn't sure what Gunner needed. I thought we had signed off on the plans last week.

My eyes danced between the little table that was set up and Jase who stood there holding a box.

"Wh-what's going on?" I asked as I walked up and saw the picnic basket on the table.

"I thought maybe you'd like to have a picnic."

My entire body tingled. "Jase! This is so wonderful!"

His face beamed with pride as he pulled the chair out for me to sit down. "But first . . . you need to open your gift."

"What's the gift for?"

"No reason other than I love you."

My heartbeat quickened. *I'm living in a fairytale.* "You're spoiling me!" I said with a slight giggle.

He set the box down on the table. Before I had a chance to open it, the lid popped open and the cutest boxer puppy tried to jump out. There was a pink bow tied around her neck and she barked as soon as she saw me.

"It's a puppy!" Jumping up, I swept her up into my arms.

"It's a girl," Jase said.

Holding her up, I looked at her adorable white and black face. "She's beautiful." Turning to Jase, I reached up on my tippy toes and kissed him. "I love her already!"

"Sit down and let her run around."

I did exactly what he said. "Oh my sweet little girl. What should I name you?"

Jase sat down next to me as the puppy jumped all over both of us.

"Bella! I'm going to name her Bella!"

"I think that is the perfect name for her."

Bella ran up and jumped on me and that's when I saw it. My breath hitched as I grabbed onto my new puppy to keep her still.

"Oh my gosh. Jase!"

Reaching over, Jase untied the bow and took the ring off. He took my hand in his as tears rolled down my cheeks.

"I want to dance every dance with you for the rest of our lives. Every breath I take is for you, Taylor."

A loud sob escaped from my lips as he slipped the ring onto my finger. It was a beautiful princess-cut diamond flanked by smaller diamonds. It was breathtaking.

"This ring was given to me by my father. It was his mother's."

Knowing how much that meant, I cried harder as I got on my knees and threw myself into Jase's arms. "It's stunning! I love it and I love you so much."

Pulling back, his hands cradled my face. "I'm sorry I made you wait so long."

Narrowing my eyes, I looked at him confused. "Some people would think we were rushing this."

He looked down at the ground and shook his head. "If I hadn't been so stupid, I would have made you mine a long time ago."

My arms wrapped around his neck. "None of that matters. All that matters is we're together and everything is amazingly perfect."

Bella barked, causing Jase and I to laugh. "I think your baby girl wants some attention."

After playing with Bella and wearing her out, we ate the sandwiches Jase had made and snuck off to the truck while Bella was sleeping in the little doggy playpen Jase had set up.

The anticipation of what was to come had my lower stomach pulling. Jase picked me up and pushed me against his truck.

Moving my panties out of the way, he pushed himself into me as I dropped my head back.

There was nothing I loved more than Jase buried deep inside me as he whispered my name against my lips.

This was beyond perfect.

It was heaven.

Twenty-Eight

Jase

BELLA RAN AROUND as Taylor sat on the edge of the bed watching my every move.

"I'll only be gone for a few days, sweetness. You won't even know I'm gone."

She pouted and pulled her knees up to her chest. My heart was aching. As much as I wanted to go . . . I didn't want to go. "You could come, you know."

Chewing on her lip, she contemplated it again. "I can't ask for time off. Even though it's Scott, I still can't do that. I feel like I'm still too new."

"It's only for four days."

Her legs dropped to the ground. Standing, she walked up to me. "I want to, but honestly the small plane scares me."

I tried not to laugh, but it was cute how worried she was. "It's not that small. It's a private jet yes, but that damn thing is huge."

"Are you sure Nate is okay to fly it?"

"Yep. Plus, there will be another pilot. He was a navy fighter pilot, baby. If I'm not safe with him then I'm really fucked."

Frowning, she snapped back, "Don't say that, Jase."

My arms wrapped around her while I pulled her closer to me. "Everything is going to be okay."

Her eyes searched my face. "Promise?"

I kissed the tip of her nose. "I promise." Slapping her ass, I stepped back. "We better head out so we make it to the airport in time."

"Meagan's coming with us, if that's okay."

Glancing over my shoulder, I smiled. "Of course it is. I'll put Bella in her crate."

Right as we were putting my luggage in the trunk of Taylor's car, Meagan pulled up. "Wait! I want to see, Bella!"

Dashing into the house, Meagan gave Bella a few quick hugs and put her back into her crate. "All right. Let's get the show on the road. I've got some shopping to do while in Austin."

Taylor's mouth dropped. "What? I don't want to go shopping, Meg."

With a quick shrug of her shoulders, she got into the backseat. "Too bad. I'm taking full advantage of no kids."

❦

WE STOOD IN the airport and kissed one last time.

"Have fun. Be careful and don't make any cows mad," Taylor said with her hands on my chest and tears pooling in her eyes.

"I'll be back before you even miss me."

Her lips trembled. "I should be going."

My hand slipped behind her neck as I pulled her lips to mine. I didn't care that people were walking by; all I cared about was her knowing how much I loved her.

Slightly pulling back, I spoke against her lips. "I won't be gone long."

"O-kay," she whispered between sobs.

"I've got to go."

Nodding, she took a step back and tried to give me a smile.

"Taylor?"

Her eyes brightened up as her breath caught. "Yes?"

"I love you."

Her body hit mine, knocking me back a couple of steps. "I love you too."

"Taylor, he'll only be gone a couple of days. You're starting to look desperate," Meagan said as she pulled on Taylor's arm.

With a chuckle, I kissed her quickly on the lips and quickly headed to where Nate would be waiting for me. I looked back to see Taylor watching me. She quickly wiped her tears away and smiled a brilliant smile. Lifting my hand, I waved while she waved back.

"Jase, how's it going?" Nate asked as he gave me a slap on the back.

"It's going good."

"We're out of Gate Two; let's head on down."

Thirty minutes later I was sitting in a jet with a flight attendant taking my drink order. I took a picture and texted it to Taylor, hoping it would calm her worrying down if she saw it was a bigger plane.

> Me: *Look. I have my own personal flight attendant.*

Less than a minute later, she responded.

> Taylor: *Wow! That's bigger than I thought. Are you sure Nate can fly it?*

> Me: *Yes, and if not William the fighter jet pilot is co-piloting. Stop worrying, baby. I'll call you when we land. Nate said it will be about a three hour flight.*

"Mr. Morris, we're getting ready to take off."

"Thanks!"

> Me: *Got to go, getting ready to take off. Love you!*

> Taylor: *I love you too!*

❦

TESS, MY OVERLY-ATTENTIVE flight attendant, offered me another drink.

Lifting my hand, I politely said, "No thanks. How much longer?"

"We're almost into Wyoming, so not too much longer."

We hit turbulence and Tess went flying up and off the floor. "Shit!" I shouted as I unbuckled to help her.

"I'm okay, Mr. Morris, I need you to buckle back up. Please! Now, sir."

Doing as she asked, I watched as she quickly made her way to the front of the plane.

We hit more turbulence, but this time I swore the plane rocked from side to side.

A feeling of dread washed over me as Taylor's words replayed in my mind about how worried she was. "Oh God. Please don't do this to me. Please don't do this to us."

Tess came rushing out. "A storm just developed in our flight path and William is now at the controls. We're going to try and . . ."

The plane jerked and Tess went flying again; this time she hit even harder against the ceiling of the plane.

"Tess!" I yelled out as the plane shook harder.

"Don't. Get. Out. Of. Your. Seat," she said as she crawled along the floor to her seat and buckled in.

Nate's voice came over the intercom. I could barely hear him as he shouted, "Jase, we've hit a storm that came out of—"

A loud bang rang out as the plane bounced again and Nate's voice disappeared. My heart was pounding so loudly it was drowning out the sound of the plane. Pulling my phone from my pocket, I pulled up the picture I took of Taylor and Bella this morning.

The plane rocked again and this time felt like it did a free fall for a few seconds. Tess gripped her seat, but still tried to give me a reassuring smile. *There is no way this is good. No way at all.*

Closing my eyes, I attempted to breathe normally while picturing Taylor's beautiful smile and her soft skin. *What I wouldn't do to have her in my arms right this second.*

Another bang caused me to jump and Tess to scream.

When I saw the tears streaming down her face, I had to keep from throwing up. The fear in her eyes was evident.

We were going to crash.

Tess covered her mouth and cried harder as she leaned forward and took the position for a crash landing.

Where in the fuck is he going to land the plane?

I looked around the plane as if searching for answers somehow. In that moment I closed my eyes and thanked God Taylor hadn't come with me. My heart had never ached like it did right then. The thought of never seeing her again tore me apart, but the idea of her never living out her dreams killed me.

The plane felt as if it was in a nose dive as my chest tightened and I pulled up my message to Taylor and typed out a quick text.

Me: *I'll love you forever, Taylor.*

The noise grew louder and the oxygen masked dropped from the ceiling. Tess yelled for me to put it on while she did the same. Out of the corner of my eye, I saw Nate trying to make his way over to me.

"We've been hit by lightning and we've lost all power."

"Holy fuck," I mumbled under my breath.

"The plane is equipped with a drag chute. William is having to glide it in and also find a flat area to land!" Nate shouted.

Jesus. Taylor.

Tess lifted her oxygen mask and yelled, "Mr. Montgomery! *Please* sit down and buckle up! Put your oxygen mask on right away!"

I couldn't think straight as the plane dropped again, causing my heart to accelerate even faster.

Nate quickly did what he was told as he took the seat across from me. Grabbing the oxygen mask, he fought to get it on as the plane bounced all over the damn place.

Shit started flying everywhere.

I caught Nate's eyes and they said everything. Lifting his mask, he yelled, "William's . . . trying to get us . . . into Wyoming. To find . . . a place to land." He shook his head. "I'm sorry, Jase."

I tried not to let Nate see the fear in my eyes as I snapped my head forward.

I was never going to see Taylor again.

This was it.

Our whole future flashed before my eyes as I tried like hell to take in air. My chest felt as if someone had set a hundred pound weight on it.

I brought my phone up and looked at the picture of Taylor while leaning back over.

Tears stung my eyes as I finally let them fall.

"I'm sorry, Taylor. I'm so sorry."

Twenty-Nine

Taylor

"MEG, PLEASE. I don't want to be in this store another second. The smell is making me sick! Plus, I have to get back to Bella."

"I thought Colt was letting her out?"

I rolled my eyes. "Ugh. I'm going outside."

Meagan had begged me to stop at some stupid bath bomb store. My nose and eyes were burning. I got that she was excited to get away for the afternoon and be on her own, but why at my expense?

Pulling my phone out, I looked at the time. Jase should be landing soon. My chest felt tight as the weirdest feeling came over me.

Meagan came out the door with a huge smile on her face holding up four bags. Not being able to hold it in, I laughed. "Holy crap. Did you buy enough for a year's worth?"

She pinched her eyebrows together and looked at the bags. "I bought some for all the girls. Including you. It will do you good to sit in a hot bath and relax."

We started toward the car and I couldn't shake the weird feeling I had. Pushing it away, I tried to focus on Meagan going on and on about the sexy lingerie she bought for Grayson.

"He's going to come just looking at me. I swear we haven't had hot crazy sex in months. We are so overdue. Mom and Dad are watching the twins tomorrow night and I plan on being fucked six ways to Sunday."

Snarling my lip, I made a gagging sound. "Gross. The image alone makes me want to hurl."

Meagan bumped me with her shoulder and wiggled her eyebrows. "Don't tell me you haven't let that hotter-than-hot fiancé of yours have his wicked way with you."

The heat instantly hit my cheeks as Meagan gasped. "Oh. My. God. My sweet little innocent sister is not so innocent anymore."

Deciding to give her a taste of her medicine, I replied, "No, she is far from innocent."

Meagan stopped walking. Glancing over my shoulder, I winked.

"Holy shit! Tay, what have you let that horny bastard do to you?"

I threw my head back and laughed. "So now he's a horny bastard?"

"Well, yeah. I mean he's doing the nasty with my baby sister."

She walked up next to me as we walked into the parking garage. Before we got to the car, my phone went off.

Grabbing it, I smiled and showed Meagan the text from Jase.

Jase: *I'll love you forever, Taylor.*

Pushing her finger into her mouth, she made a gagging sound. "He must have landed."

I hit his number. "That's weird. It went straight to voicemail."

"Maybe he sent that before he took off and it just came through."

Staring down at my phone, I chewed on my lip. "Yeah. Maybe."

❧

WHEN WE PULLED up to my place, Colt and Scott were sitting on the porch. An uneasy feeling quickly swept over my body.

Something was wrong.

"A welcome party!" Meagan said as she jumped out of the car and reached in the backseat for her damn bath bombs that stunk up my car.

I checked my phone again and still nothing from Jase. Calling again, it went to voicemail. My heart started pounding as I sat in the car with my hands trembling.

"Something's wrong. He should have landed over an hour ago."

My body went numb. I forced myself to get out of the car. I stopped dead in my tracks when Layton came walking out of the cabin.

Please don't do this to me. Do not do this to me!

The thought of something happening to Jase hit me right in the chest as I felt my heart drop.

The look in Layton's eyes told me everything I had feared was about to come true.

Meagan dropped her bags and quickly came back over to my side. "Taylor, baby, breathe for me."

I hadn't even been aware that I wasn't breathing. "Wh-what's happened? I had a feeling something happened."

My eyes burned as I fought to hold my tears back. When Colt walked to the other side of me, I felt my legs go weak.

This is just a dream. It has to be a dream.

Layton walked up and stopped just in front of me.

"Taylor, sweetheart. I . . . I need to tell you something."

Shaking my head frantically, I mumbled, "No. Please don't, Layton." My chin trembled as I repeated my plea. "Please don't."

His eyes filled with tears while he cleared this throat. "Ryder called. He was meeting Nate and Jase in Wyoming and . . . their plane didn't land on schedule. The Denver airport said an unexpected storm popped up."

"No," I whispered as I let my body go while Colt held on to me. My body felt cold. I could hear Layton talking . . . yet at the same time it felt as if I was drifting away.

"They lost them on radar as they were coming out of the Rockies and into Wyoming. A search plane is already on the way to where they first lost them."

A search plane.

My head started to hurt. It felt as if someone was taking a hammer to it and hitting it as hard as they could. "Layton . . . please . . . no."

"Sweetheart, let's not give up hope, but . . ."

My eyes caught Whitley standing behind Layton. She had been

crying.

Everything went numb. Nothing in this world mattered if I didn't have Jase to live it with.

"But there is a chance the plane . . . the plane might have . . ."

I shook my head frantically as sobs racked my body and my legs gave completely out. Meagan and Colt went to the ground with me. Meagan wrapped me in her arms as I started screaming out Jase's name.

It's a dream. That's all this was.

A horrible, awful nightmare.

Thirty

Taylor

I SAT ON Jase's bed and stared out at the setting sun. It had been four days since he left me standing in the airport watching him leave. Four days of them searching for their plane only to find nothing.

Don't give up hope.

That's all everyone kept saying to me. If they didn't find them today, they were moving the search area more into Wyoming.

I glanced down at my phone. The last text from Jase was pulled up as I read it again.

I'll love you forever, Taylor.

When had he sent that to me? Before the plane took off? During the flight? After they—

Swallowing hard, I looked back out the window. My mother, Courtney, and Whitley tried talking softly, but I could still hear them. They thought I was sleeping, but I hadn't slept more than two hours since Layton told me the plane went missing.

"She won't leave his room, Amanda. I'm starting to worry," Whitley said.

"Has she slept today at all?"

I heard Whitley sniffle. "No. And she was at the barn last night when the horse Jase bought her birthed the foal."

"She wouldn't leave even with Walker and Layton begging her to," Courtney added. "I'd give anything to take her hurt away."

Falling back onto the bed, I closed my eyes.

Jase's piercing blue eyes invaded my mind. Every time he made love to me, his eyes spoke of how much he loved me. Blazing with nothing but love. I focused on them while I tuned everything else out.

My body ached. Not nearly as much as my heart did. I couldn't cry anymore . . . it was as if I had cried ten rivers. I had nothing left.

The knock on the door caused me to roll over. Opening my eyes, I looked at the sun as it touched the horizon.

"Taylor? Sweetheart, are you sleeping?" my mother asked softly.

"No."

She sat on the bed and rested her hand on my shoulder. "Ryder called. They're moving the search area further into Wyoming. There is a good chance the pilot was able to navigate them to a flatter area to land."

"If they had landed, someone would have found them by now," I numbly said.

"Maybe, but that area is vastly uninhabited."

I had overheard Layton and my father talking last night. Layton had had one too many drinks and the truth was spilling from his lips. He didn't know I heard every word he said. I had just walked back in from the barn when I heard the two of them talking in his office.

"Even if they had landed safely, why haven't we heard anything? All they keep talking about is how the plane was equipped with an emergency beacon. Why in the hell has it not gone off?" Layton said.

"Layton, don't give up hope. Maybe they couldn't get out right away to get help."

"This is my fault. I should have been the one going. I sent my son who had his whole future ahead of him. I've robbed him and Taylor of a life together."

Leaning over, Layton cried. It was then I turned and headed up to Jase's room. Taking a T-shirt out of his drawer, I slipped it on and crawled under the sheets where I laid staring out into the darkness.

My mother's voice pulled me from my thoughts. "Taylor, I'm worried about you."

"I'm fine," I mumbled.

She stood and looked down at me. I could almost feel her eyes penetrating me. "You're not fine. You haven't eaten or slept in days. You've hardly left this room. You need to get some fresh air and eat. Libby and Luke are here. Everyone has been coming in shifts to help Layton and Whitley and to check on you."

"I know, Mom. They all keep coming in here and saying the same damn thing."

I sat up and faced her. "Don't give up hope? Well, I'm sorry if I can't be perky and happy while I wait for them to tell me the only man I ever loved . . . the only man I ever wanted to spend my life with is dead!"

She covered her mouth to hold back her own sobs. Dropping her hands, she went to talk but I held up my hands.

"Don't! Please don't say something you think will make it better, Mom. Please." I fiercely wiped my tears away as I looked out the window and then back at her. "That's the whole thing though . . . I know everyone is starting to think he's gone." My chin trembled as I tried to keep talking. "He doesn't feel gone, Mom. Wouldn't I . . . wouldn't I feel it if he was . . . gone?"

Horror filled her eyes as she looked at me with pity. "Oh sweetheart, I wish I could answer that for you."

I buried my face in my hands and screamed as she wrapped me in her arms. "I can't live without him. I don't want to live without him," I cried out while she pulled me closer to her.

It was then I felt more arms around me. Dropping my hands, I saw Libby.

"Libby," I barely said while my mother stepped away and Libby held me in her arms as I cried.

Her hand moved lightly across my back as she softly repeated the one thing no one had told me I could do.

"Taylor, let it out. Just cry and let it out."

My emotions were beginning to mix together. I wasn't sure if I was angry or sad. My throat and my chest ached. Looking at her, I shook my head. "He promised me, Libby. He promised me!" I shouted.

Standing, I began to pace across the room. "He was my everything and he's gone. How am I supposed to go? I can't go on! Damn it, I don't want to go on without him." Tears began to stream down my face as Libby wiped hers away. "He's gone and I feel so lost." A sob escaped from my lips as Libby stood up. Holding my hand up to stop her, I shook my head. "I don't know who to be angry with! If one more person tells me everything will be fine, I'm going to punch them!"

"Grace. We can use Grace for that," Libby said.

My eyes widened in surprise as I let Libby's words sink in. "I think Meagan would be the better choice. She used to steal my make-up all the time."

Libby cracked a small grin. "It's okay to be angry."

My lips trembled. "I don't know what I am, Lib. All I know is I feel so lost without him."

Libby took me in her arms as we sank back to the bed.

I wasn't sure how long Libby had stayed in Jase's room with me. We sat on his bed in silence as I stared out into the darkness.

"Mireya really wants to see you, Taylor. Can you come downstairs and see her?"

With a slack expression, I nodded and slowly stood up. My feet felt so heavy as I followed Libby downstairs.

Mireya was sitting next to Layton and Walker on the couch watching a movie. She was such a little flirt and I couldn't help but smile when I saw her sitting between them.

When she turned and looked at me, I could see the confusion on her face.

She jumped up and called out, "Tay Tay!"

I forced a smile and dropped down to catch her in a hug. "Hey, princess. Are you watching a movie?"

She nodded her head. "Yep. With Wayton and Walker. I gonna marry Walker!"

My eyes snapped up to Luke who moaned. "I'm not ready for this at all."

With a chuckle, I turned back to Mireya. "Oh, sweetheart, I hate to tell you this, but Walker has a wife."

Mireya peeked over at Liza and blushed. "Tay Tay, I love you!"

When her little arms wrapped around my neck something happened. The sadness was still there and weighed heavy on my heart, but something else was there as well.

Something I hadn't seen until I looked into the eyes of my best friend's daughter.

Hope.

Thirty-One

Taylor

A FEW HOURS later, Luke buckled a sleeping Mireya into her car seat while I kissed Libby goodbye. Trey had already fallen asleep a couple hours earlier and was safely tucked into his car seat.

Turning to Luke, I hugged him and kissed his cheek. "Thank you for bringing the kids. They were exactly what I needed."

"We love you, Taylor and there isn't a damn thing we wouldn't do for you."

I nodded. "I know."

"Let me know if you need anything, okay?" Libby said as she got into the truck.

"I will."

With a barely-there smile, she took my hand in hers. "I love you, Tay."

Stumbling on my words, I tried to grin. "Love you too."

I watched them pull off and drive away and tried to ignore the heaviness in my chest.

Jumping when I felt hands on my shoulders, I turned to see

Whitley. "It's late, why don't we have a cup of tea and then try and get some sleep?"

Not having the energy to argue, I agreed. My parents were staying in one of the guest rooms, but they had excused themselves right before Luke and Libby left.

Walking into the kitchen, I couldn't help but think of when I blurted out to Whitley that Jase had asked me to marry him.

I glanced down at my engagement ring and dropped down onto a chair. "Bella?" I asked, looking at her.

She smiled and said, "Colt and Lauren have her."

I shook my head. "I just abandoned her."

"Nonsense. She's been fine. If you'd like for them to bring her here, you're more than welcome to have her."

"I'd like that if you're sure you don't mind."

Her eyes were filled with love as she replied, "Of course not, sweetheart. This house has always been filled with dogs except for the last few years. Honestly, I've missed having a four-legged friend. I hope you don't mind, but I've asked Lauren to bring you a few changes of clothes and some other items, like your toothbrush and such."

Looking down, it was then I noticed I was completely dressed in Jase's cloths. An old pair of sweets and one of his high school football shirts.

"You can wear them, Taylor. But I thought you might like some of your own as well."

Whitley set a cup of hot tea down in front of me while she waited for her own to brew.

"I'll never love anyone like I love him," I said as I looked directly into her eyes. "And as much as my heart feels broken, I don't feel like he is gone."

A single tear slowly rolled down her cheek. "I feel the same way. He'll always be with us."

I wanted to clarify with her what I meant, but she looked so tired.

When she got her tea, she sat down across from me. I wasn't sure what came over me, but I had to say what I felt.

"I don't think he's dead."

Her eyes lit up.

"Wouldn't we feel it if he was? I've felt so empty these last few days. But when I saw Mireya, something happened. It was as if a light switched on and I started thinking clearly. My mother told me I was tired and needed sleep, but that's not it. I feel it in the depths of my soul that he isn't gone."

She covered her mouth as she closed her eyes. It took a few moments before she dropped her hand and opened her eyes. With a smile, she simply said, "You just said what I've been wanting to shout from the roof-tops."

I reached my hand out for hers. "I'm not giving up hope until they find the plane and tell me he's gone. Until then, I'll be on my knees praying for him to come back to me." Pressing my trembling lips together, I whispered, "He has to come back to me."

Thirty-Two

Jase

Five days earlier

"IS EVERYONE OKAY?" Tess yelled out.

"Yes . . . I'm . . . okay . . . I think," I said as I tried to adjust my eyes. The plane looked like it was filled with smoke or dust.

"Mr. Montgomery? Are you okay?"

Nate moaned and then let out a string of cuss words. "I think my leg might be broken."

Glancing over to Nate, we both shook our heads. "William landed the plane safely . . . somehow," I said as I got out of my seat and made my way up front to check on him.

"William, are you okay?"

"Yeah, my ankle is stuck and I can't get it out. If you can pull that back some, I think I can get it out."

I pulled where he pointed and it moved just enough for him to pull his leg out.

"Is it broke?" I asked while helping him out of the seat.

He shook his head. "No . . . I don't think so, but it's not normal either."

Looking out the front window all I saw was sand. "Where the hell are we?"

William followed my stare. "I'm guessing near or in the Red Desert in Wyoming. I need to work on trying to get the radio working at the very least. We lost power when the lightning hit us . . . twice. It fried everything."

He looked at me and frowned. "Including the emergency beacon."

"Fuck."

"Yeah, which means when they realize we've gone missing they're going to be looking in the wrong area."

Pulling my head back in confusion, I asked, "Why?"

"They'll assume we crashed in the area will be where they lost radar. We need to somehow let them know we made it a lot farther from where they think we should be."

Gripping his shoulder, I smiled. "How in the hell did you fly this plane with no power?"

"It wasn't easy, I'll tell ya that. The sand though at least made for a lighter impact. How are Tess and Nate?"

"Nate thinks he broke his lower leg, Tess seems to be okay, but we should all let our adrenaline settle and then assess how we feel."

William agreed. "We also need to start looking at food and water. Who knows how many days this plane will be our home. I'm going to guess no one has a cell signal?"

"No."

"Let's turn off the phones and save the batteries."

"Mine's already off, but I'll let Tess and Nate know to do the same."

After things settled, we discovered Nate had indeed fractured his lower leg. We were able to put it in a splint and find something to act like crutches so he could get around.

While Tess was helping Nate, she gasped and held onto her wrist.

"Let me see it."

"It's fine," she softly said. Her eyes said something different.

"Tess, your wrist is probably broken with the way it is swelling. You probably did it when you hit the ceiling of the plane."

With a slight nod, she replied, "I thought so, but I was holding out hope."

"Let's make sure to count out the pain med's to ration between the three of you. William isn't sure if his ankle is just badly sprained or if it is broken."

She gave me a weak smile as I reached down for a bandage and began wrapping her wrist.

After making sure Nate and Tess were okay, I walked up to William. Bending down, I handed him the screwdriver he was blindly reaching for. "Tess and I found a few cases of bottled water along with some peanuts and bags of chips. Plus, I have some protein bars in my luggage we can divide up."

He nodded. "Good."

"How's it going?" I asked.

Letting out a frustrated sigh, he shook his head. "The whole electrical system is fried."

"Did you get any kind of a distress call out?"

"No. That's the thing, that storm literally came out of nowhere and by the time I got the controls and was about to raise our altitude, we got struck by the lightning."

Pushing my hand though my hair, I looked out over the vast desert. "Do you think I should leave and try to find help?"

"No. We stick together and all stay in one place."

"How long before they spread their search area out?"

William looked up at me and then glanced over to Tess. With a frown, he motioned for me to get close to him. "Depends. I'd say it would take four to five days for them to get through the process of elimination. Then start gridding it out on where they think we might be. The problem is I glided down and we are a long ways off course."

Closing my eyes, I mumbled. "Fuck." Looking out into the vast area of nothing, I mindlessly said, "Taylor is probably freaking out."

"Girlfriend?"

With a weak smile, I replied, "Fiancée."

His eyes turned sad. "My wife is eight months pregnant and does not need this kind of stress."

"Damn, dude." Frowning, I placed my hand on his shoulder. "We're getting out of here. Let me know what I can do to help fix this shit and call for help."

With a wide grin, he glanced at Tess. "Let's just hope Tess stays as positive. She looks scared to death."

Turning over my shoulder, I watched as she helped Nate sit back in a seat. "Don't worry about her. I'm sure Nate and I can keep her spirits up."

I went to stand and William grabbed my arm. "Jase, even if you think we aren't going to make it and I'm not saying that, but even if you doubt, don't do that to Taylor."

Looking at him with a confused expression, it dawned on me what he was saying. "Oh, hell no. I would never do anything to hurt Taylor. I think all Tess needs is a little attention . . . nothing grand and nothing that would lead her on."

"Good. You had me worried there for a second with your comment about keeping her spirits up. I couldn't help but notice how flirty she was with you before we took off."

With a gruff chuckle, I headed over toward Tess and Nate.

After giving Nate an update on what William was doing, I told them both to turn off their cell phones. Tess asked if I could find something to build a fire with outside and she'd make coffee.

As we both walked outside, I really took Tess in. She was pretty. Older than me, probably closer to thirty. It was then I noticed the wedding band on her hand. *I wonder how her husband would like to know how much she flirts?*

"How long have you been married?" I asked as I headed over toward an area that had some brush. Beyond that about a mile was the tree line.

"Six years."

"Wow! Kids?"

She let out a dry laugh. "God, no. He wants them, but he also wants a lot of other women and a divorce, so . . ."

"Damn, I'm sorry to hear that."

With a shrug, she blew out a breath and pointed straight ahead. "Looks like the tree line is a good walk away. Should we grab something to put the wood in so we can carry it back? I would think we could be here at least a week while they expand the search areas."

It was then I saw her in a totally different light. She was far from weak, and not on the verge of breaking down like I had thought earlier. Up in the plane we were all scared. Even with a broken wrist, she was ready to pitch in her weight.

"That's a great idea, Tess. Let's head back and find something."

If we all stayed positive and rationed out what little food and water we had . . . we had a fighting chance.

I promise I'll be home soon, Taylor. I promise.

Thirty-Three

Taylor

THE COOL MORNING breeze felt good hitting my face. Last night was the first night I'd slept over four hours. I was beginning to feel the effects of lack of sleep, but I didn't care. When I was awake, I could think about Jase. Pray God would keep him safe.

"Tay? You feel like company?"

Turning my head and looking up, I smiled at Meagan and Grace. "I'm not much company, but feel free to join me."

They both sat on either side of me, each taking my hand and holding it.

"Whitley invited everyone over for lunch. I guess they're having Coopers cater it. You know how much I love Coopers."

With a weak grin, I turned to Grace who stared straight ahead. "Yes. I know how much you love it, Grace."

The next thing I knew, the back screen door flew open and Mireya ran by holding something. "I take it Libby and Luke are here?"

Meagan squeezed my hand. "Hell, the whole gang is here. Whitley may think twice before inviting us all over again."

I tried to chuckle, but couldn't.

Grace cleared her throat. I felt her eyes burning into me as she pondered what to say or ask. "Have you um . . . have you heard from Ryder?"

"Yes. The area where the plane was last on radar was pretty rugged. He said something about the plane having some kind of chute it can deploy and help glide it down. They're hoping they used it and were able to find a safe area to land."

"So, it's still a search and rescue?"

My body went numb as those words hit me. I didn't want to lose hope, but as each hour went on my heart ached even more. "For now."

"They're going to find them, Tay. You have to feel it in your heart that he's okay."

Swallowing hard, I felt a tear escape from my eye as I wiped it away. "Sometimes I do, but then I'm so overcome with grief sometimes I don't know what to think. It hits me so hard that I'm almost positive he's . . . he's . . ."

"Don't say it. Until they change it to recovery, or until we know something else, we keep going on that they will find them."

Turning to Grace, I could see how strongly she believed the words she was saying to me.

"I'm trying, Grace. But I'm so tired and my brain doesn't know what to think anymore."

We heard a puppy bark. All three of us turned to see Mireya playing with Bella.

"Bella," I whispered as I broke down crying. Meagan quickly dropped to her knees in front of me.

"Baby, it's okay to cry. Shit, it's okay to be angry."

Nodding my head, I pressed my lips together. "I am angry. I'm mad at myself for not going with him." Meagan shook her head as tears slipped down her face.

"I'm angry at Jase. I'm so angry that he left me. He promised me it would all be okay. He swore to me he would never hurt me again."

Grace joined Meagan as she looked up at me. "You can be angry, but don't be angry at Jase. If he had the choice you know he would never hurt you. It was an accident, Taylor. Something out of his control."

My hands came up as I buried my face in them. "I know! Oh God I know that and I hate myself for being angry. My emotions are everywhere and I just want to scream."

"Sounds like to me . . . you need to take a walk."

Dropping my hands, I jumped up when I heard her voice. "Grams!" She held her arms out as I gently hugged her.

"I'm not going to break, child. Give me a proper hug and then let's go for a walk."

Chuckling, I nodded as I hugged her then wrapped my arm with hers. We slowly started down the stairs and toward the barn.

"I'm not as young as I once was . . . but I still walk a mile a day, you know."

My heart felt lighter instantly. There was something about Grams that had always soothed me. "Grams, did you ever lose hope when times got hard?"

She made a tsking sound and then nodded. "Everyone loses hope at times. It's all a part of life."

"I knew things were too good to be true. It was as if I was waiting for the rug to be pulled out from underneath us."

"Nonsense. Don't ever think that way again. God doesn't give you happiness just so he can yank it away. He may throw a few heartaches in there, some anger, some confusion, stubborn men who will always be stubborn."

Giggling, I knew she was talking about Gramps. "But, sweetheart, he doesn't take happiness away from us."

Sniffling, I fought to keep my tears at bay. "I don't feel very happy right now."

"No. I'm sure you don't. You probably feel helpless and maybe even giving up hope that . . . oh fiddle sticks . . . what is your beau's name?"

Smiling wide, I answered, "Jase."

"That's right!" she said as she snapped her fingers. "Jase."

We stopped outside the barn and sat on a bench. Looking back at the house, I saw everyone making their way outside. I'd heard Whitley mention something about heating the pool. Both Baylie and Mireya were running on the tanning ledge as Bella jumped in and out of the pool.

"The whole crew is here. Everyone except, Jase," I whispered.

Grams placed her hand on my leg. I watched as everyone set up food on the outside tables. Grayson kissed my sister as he placed the twins in a portable playpen.

"Jase would love to see this. Everyone together."

My chest ached as the scene played out in front of me. Everyone was sad, but going on with their lives and all I wanted to do was curl up in a ball and dream of what my future with Jase would have been like.

"If God doesn't want us to be unhappy . . . why did he take Jase from me?"

She remained silent for a few moments. "Think how unhappy you would have been if you hadn't loved him at all."

My head snapped over to look at her. Her blue eyes sparkled and held my stare. Winking she broke our connection when she glanced back over to everyone. "'Tis better to have loved and lost than to never have loved at all. My momma used to say that to me all the time."

Closing my eyes, I tried to understand it but maybe I was just selfish.

I wanted Jase with me.

I wanted to have kids and grow old with him.

I wanted our dreams to come true together.

The only thing I could understand now was how sad I was.

I shook my head and chewed on the corner of my lip. "No. No I'm not going to just sit here and believe I should be happy with the memories we made." My chin trembled as I watched Mireya and Bella playing. "He's coming back to me, Grams. He promised."

She took my hand and held it. "Then that's what you hold on to, Taylor. That feeling right there. Grip it and hold on to it tightly."

෴

I TRIED DESPERATELY to not withdraw back into myself while everyone sat around both inside and out. Not being able to help myself, I pictured what my wedding would have been like. Most likely exactly like this. Everyone I loved surrounding me in celebration.

Then it hit me. Everyone I loved was surrounding me now. It might not have been to celebrate my wedding, but it was to show me how much they loved me and Jase. My mother and Whitley played hostess to everyone and kept busy making sure everyone had something to drink or they got enough food to eat. They were keeping their minds busy.

I stood and made my way over to Mireya. "You wore Bella out!"

Mireya giggled. "Want to play hide and seek?"

Her eyes lit up as she jumped up. Her bouncy curls going every-where. "Yes!"

Alex brought Bayli over to us as I called out, "Who wants to play hide and seek?"

Layton carried Nickolas in his arms and walked up. "Count us in."

Smiling, I reached up on my toes and kissed him on the cheek. His blue eyes reminded me of Jase as my heart dropped. When he smiled back, I knew no matter what happened, I was going to be okay. Surrounded by people who loved me and cared about me, I knew I would be okay.

"Not it!" Alex called out as Bayli jumped in excitement.

"Not it!" Layton cried out and took off running while Nickolas laughed.

My hands landed on my hips as I gave everyone an evil smile. "Fine. I'll be it. Home base is . . ." Spinning around, I saw Bella. "Bella!"

"Oh lord, that puppy doesn't stay still for nothing," Grace said.

"A moving home base. I like it," Walker replied with a wink in my direction.

I closed my eyes and started counting. Everyone could be heard taking off in all different directions.

This was exactly what I needed if I couldn't have Jase.

My family and friends.

Thirty-Four

Jase

Present day

NATE REACHED OUT and took the two Advil and a bottled water. "How's it looking?" I asked.

Rolling his eyes, he said, "Swollen. I swear I have new respect for Ava now."

I couldn't help but laugh. "Yeah, that had to have sucked with a broken leg and ankle."

"Fuck that. I will tell you what I'm grateful for."

Lifting my eyebrows, I asked, "What?"

"I'm grateful for the person who packed that damn first aid kit and had the sense to put so much aspirin and Advil in it."

With a light chuckle, I looked away. I didn't have the heart to tell him there were only a few pills left. Between the three of them, we were running low.

Next thing I heard was William yelling. "Holy shit! Holy fucking shit! I'm so stupid. So. Fucking. Stupid."

Nate sighed. "Damn. I thought for sure Tess would be the first to lose her shit and flip out."

"Hey!" Tess said smacking the back of Nate's head. "You asshole."

The two of them had been at each other's throats the last two days. It might not have been obvious to them, but I could tell they were attracted to one another.

Standing, I took in a deep breath and quickly forced it out as I worked up the nerve to go see what William was going off about.

"I'll go see what's going on."

Before I could take a step, William came hobbling toward us. "Your cell phone batteries! Has everyone kept their phones off?"

I nodded and then looked at Nate and Tess. "Yep. Mine's been off the whole time," Tess answered.

Nate nodded. "Same here."

The smile that spread across William's face was the first sign of hope we had had in the last five days.

"I don't know what in the hell I was thinking trying to mess with the radio. The emergency beacon is what we need to get working."

Tess jumped up. "Yes!"

"Using our batteries from our phones, I can wire them together in a series to get enough juice to get the beacon going."

My heart raced. "Are you sure?"

"Well, I'm not a hundred percent certain it will work, but it's worth a try. Why I didn't think of it before now is beyond me."

I turned to Nate and Tess. "Where are your phones?"

Nate reached into the seat pocket and pulled his out. "Here's mine."

Tess rushed to where she had her luggage. Reaching into her purse, she pulled out her phone and handed it to me. I could see the hope in both their eyes and I was positive mine reflected the same thing.

"Let's do this," I said as I followed William to the little work station he had set up.

After a couple of hours of watching him, I stood up and walked out for some fresh air and to look around. It was beautiful here. Freezing at night, but beautiful.

Closing my eyes, I tried to think positive thoughts. I prayed every night that God would send Taylor some kind of sign that I was still alive. William prayed every night for his wife and unborn daughter. The more he talked about them, the more I had the desire to tell Taylor the second she was in my arms I wanted to have a baby.

When I opened my eyes, I turned to see Tess standing next to me. "He's driving me crazy. I actually feel like I want to put a pillow over his head and hold it there."

Letting out a chuckle, I shook my head. "I think he likes you."

Her head jerked back as she let out a gruff laugh. "Really? If that's his idea of liking a woman, I'd hate to see what he's like when he doesn't like them."

"Awe, come on, Tess. Nate's a good guy. You're not the least bit attracted to him? I mean, I know you're married and all, but you did say you filed for a divorce right before our fun little trip to the desert."

She snarled her lip at me. "No, I am not attracted to him at all."

Lifting my brow, I tilted my head and stared at her. "Really? Not at all."

Crossing her arms over her chest, she said, "Nope."

"You know, he told me he thought you looked cute in his sweat-pants and sweatshirt."

Her upper lip twitched as she forced herself not to smile. "He's delirious from the pain of his broken leg."

"Uh-huh. And your excuse?"

Giving me a scowl, she asked, "My excuse for what?"

"Jase! Tess!" William called out.

We both turned and rushed back to the plane.

Nate was standing next to William with a huge grin across his face. "It's working! He got the damn thing to work!"

Tess turned to me and hugged me before turning and doing the same to Nate and William. "You did it! I knew you would!" she cried out in glee.

Reaching my hand over, I shook William's. "Good job, dude."

He glanced down at it and nodded. "Let's hope they pick it up before our batteries die out."

My body rushed with adrenaline. We were going home. I could feel it deep in my bones.

"I promised Taylor I was coming back to her. And if it I have to start walking out of the fucking desert to find a way out, we will be going home."

William's eyes pooled with tears. He looked away and softly said, "I'll be home soon, baby."

❧

IT HAD BEEN five hours since the emergency beacon had started. Nate and Tess were asleep as William and I sat there watching the damn thing. Waiting for the batteries to go dead and the thing to stop working.

There was no doubt in my mind we were thinking the same thing. Where was the search team?

"I swear it feels colder tonight than any night we've been here," William mindlessly said.

Wrapping the blanket around me, I agreed. "I'm going to add more wood to the fire. If they do fly over this area, they'll at least see the fire going."

"Need help?"

Motioning with my hand for him to stay seated, I shook my head. "Nah. Stay off your ankle. It looks worse today than it has all week."

"Hurts like a mother fucker too."

I walked out and over to the fire. Earlier that day I had hiked back over to the tree line to get more wood.

Grabbing a hand full of sticks, I threw them into the fire. Glancing up, I got lost in the vast amount of stars that lit up the black sky. If I didn't hate this place so much, I would totally be lost in the beauty of it.

After warming myself up, I decided to head back into the plane, but stopped when I heard something.

Not moving at all, I stood perfectly still.

A plane. That's a fucking plane I hear!

I quickly ran back to the plane and grabbed two flash lights. "What's wrong?" William asked.

"It's a plane. I hear a plane!"

He stood and grabbed the stick he had been using as a cane. Reaching for another flashlight, he followed me outside.

Seeing the lights from the plane, I pointed and yelled out, "Over there. It's over there!"

"I have a laser pointer!" Tess screamed as she pointed it up toward the plane.

We probably looked like crazy fools as we all jumped and screamed. Nate had made his way over to me and took the other flashlight out of my hand and started waving it back and forth.

My heart was racing and all I could think about was seeing Taylor. Her smile that lit up my entire world. Those stunning green eyes that I saw every time I closed my eyes.

"Down here!" Tess cried out.

Tears were streaming down her face as we quickly looked at each other and then back up to the plane.

Flashing the light on and off, Nate yelled, "We're here!"

Each one of us was yelling. A mixture of emotions being let out. Hope that we would be seen. Fear we wouldn't. And dreams of being back in our loved ones' arms.

Tess screamed louder, causing the other three of us to do the same. Of course they couldn't hear us, but it was the first sign of anyone since we had crashed here six days ago. Hell almost seven days ago.

"Oh my God! They're turning around!" Tess yelled out as she jumped.

When we saw the plane drop in altitude, we stopped carrying on like crazy fools.

"Please see us," Tess whispered.

The plane flew so low as it went over us, there was no way they hadn't see us.

"They see us!" William cried out. We all turned and looked at each other. It was in that moment that we truly knew we were going to be okay. My heart didn't ache quite as much as it did earlier. Tears flowed freely from each of us as we formed a huddle and celebrated.

I'm going to see Taylor again. My sweet, beautiful, Taylor.

"Stop grabbing my ass, Nate!" Tess cried out as William and I both laughed.

Dropping my head back, I let out a long sigh of relief as I looked at the brightest star in the sky. "Thank you, God."

Thirty-Five

Taylor

MY MIND DRIFTED to the last kiss Jase had given me at the airport. Running my fingers along my lips, I looked out at the night sky. Was Jase looking up at it as well? God I hoped so.

The door to Jase's bedroom flew open and Layton came rushing in. "The beacon!"

I jumped up and turned on the light. "What?"

He walked up to me, wrapped me in his arms and spun me around before putting me back down.

"Ryder just called. They picked up the beacon signal a few hours ago. It was nowhere near where they were searching."

"Where is it?"

"In Wyoming at the edge of the Red Desert and the foothills. Ryder went with them in the plane to the location. He didn't call because he didn't want to get our hopes up."

My breath hitched as I felt my heart pounding throughout my entire body. Tears streamed out of my eyes. For the first time in days I had such a strong feeling of willingness to believe that all would be okay. A strange sense of calm came over me.

"Please tell me," I whispered.

"They found them, Taylor. All four of them are alive."

An unexpected release of tension had my body collapsing into Layton as I sobbed in relief.

The pain in my chest replaced with a lightness I couldn't describe. "I knew it! I knew he wasn't gone!" I cried as I buried my face into his chest.

"I've booked three tickets on the first flight out from Austin in the morning."

Pulling back, I looked up at him as he looked at me with so much love and happiness. Wiping my tears away, he kissed my forehead.

"Where is he?"

"They took them to Rock Springs to a hospital there. Looks like everyone is okay, but Nate has a fractured leg, William sprained his ankle and Tess broke her hand."

My stomach felt sick. "Jase?"

"From what Ryder said, it was a good size cut on his forehead and that's it."

My shoulders sank in relief.

"In the morning they are flying them to Cheyenne. That's where we'll meet them."

"Why hasn't he called?"

Layton grinned. It was at that moment my cell phone rang.

"He wanted you to be told first before he called."

I quickly raced over to the side table and grabbed my phone.

"Jase!" I practically screamed.

"Damn . . . it's so good to hear your voice, Taylor."

My body shook as I cried. "Thank God! Thank you, God!" I cried out as I sank down on the bed. Layton sat next to me and it was then I noticed Whitley.

"I'm so sorry, Taylor. If I could go back and never get on that plane I would."

I shook my head. "It doesn't matter. None of that matters. You're alive and I get to see you tomorrow."

"Ryder said Dad booked three tickets and y'all were meeting us in

Cheyenne." Grinning, I looked at Layton. "Yes. Hold on, your dad and mom are here."

I handed the phone to Layton. Whitley sat on the other side of me and wrapped her arms around me. For the first time in seven days, I felt like I could breathe without it hurting my heart. Leaning closer to me, she whispered, "He's coming home. Our Jase is coming home."

⁂

WHEN THE PLANE touched down on the runway in Cheyenne, I breathed a sigh of relief. Peeking over at Whitley, her knee bounced up and down. I knew the moment my eyes landed on Jase I'd want to be in his arms. Whitley had to feel the same way.

Talking it over with Layton, I told him I thought they needed to see Jase first and then I would see him. Reaching her hand across the aisle, she winked. "It won't be long now."

"I know. My heart is pounding so hard in my chest."

Her eyes filled with tears. "Are you sure you don't want to see him first?"

Pressing my lips together, I smiled and nodded my head. "I know the moment I see him I won't want to let him go."

With a wink, she replied, "Fair enough."

Layton had hired a car to pick us up at the airport and take us to the Marriott where Jase and the others were staying.

When the car pulled up to the front of the hotel, my stomach was rolling and my breathing had sped up. I was both nervous and excited to see him.

The valet opened the door and helped Whitley and then me out of the car.

Layton walked around and gave me a reassuring smile. "Are you okay, sweetheart?"

I couldn't find my voice so I nodded. "Would you rather go to our room and wait or just wait in the lobby?"

My eyes drifted over to the bar. "I think I'm going to get a drink to calm my nerves down. I'll be at the bar, so you can just text me."

Whitley walked up and kissed me on the cheek. "I know your

chomping at the bit to see him. We'll make it quick."

"O-okay," I stuttered.

Layton took my hand and squeezed it before kissing my forehead and heading straight to the elevator. I was praying they wouldn't check into their hotel room. Just knowing that Jase was in the same building was driving me insane.

"What was I thinking saying they could go up first and alone?" I mumbled under my breath as I made my way over to the bar.

"What can I get you, pretty little lady?"

I smiled at the older bartender and said, "Something strong to calm my nerves."

"I've got just the thing."

He turned around and opened up the small refrigerator. When I saw him pull out a small container of milk, I chuckled.

Pouring a small glass, he put it in front of me. "Trust me . . . booze doesn't help at all."

With a wide grin, I took the milk and said, "Thank you."

"That there will do the trick. You in town for work?"

"No. It's more of a reunion type thing."

He lifted his eyebrows. "Well, I hope it goes well for you."

Finishing off the milk, I set it down and replied. "I have a feeling it's going to go very well."

We talked small talk for the next few minutes until another customer came in. I was glad to have had his company though to take my mind off of everything.

Glancing at my phone, it had been almost fifteen minutes since Layton and Whitley headed up to Jase's room.

Closing my eyes, I took in a calming breath before looking over my shoulder at the elevator.

My phone buzzed causing me to jump. Reaching for it, my hands shook while I opened up Layton's text.

Layton: We just left. He's anxious to see you.

Me: I'm on my way.

I pulled out some money and left it on the bar. Lifting my hand, I said, "Thank you so much for the milk!"

With a chuckle, the bartender smiled. "Good luck!"

Stepping onto the elevator, I hit the button for the seventh floor. My mouth was dry and my pulse was racing. I wasn't sure what I wanted to do first. Kiss him, or look over his entire body and make sure he was okay.

The doors opened and I stepped out of the elevator as my pulse sped up. Glancing up to the room numbers, I turned to the left and quickly made my way to Jase's room. Scared what I might find when I saw him, I was also beyond excited. My mind raced with the same question . . . was he really okay? I planned on checking out every inch of his body.

Stopping at the door, I covered my mouth and got my emotions in check. This was it. Finally, I was going to be in his arms again. I wasn't sure what my hesitation was for. The moment I saw him I knew I was going to cry as the flood of different emotions I had experienced the last week was released. It was as if I could feel his presence right in front of me.

My hand lifted to knock when the door opened and he stood before me looking as handsome as ever.

"Thank you, God," I whispered as I threw myself into his body.

Sobs racked over my body while he wrapped his arms around me and held me close to him. The feeling of being lost was completely washed away by the sound of his voice.

"Oh, Taylor. Baby, I missed you so much."

I buried my face into his body. "I was so scared."

He set me down and cupped my face with his hands. Those beautiful blue eyes of his searched my face while his thumbs wiped my tears away. "I was too, sweetness. But I never gave up hope and I knew I would see you again."

My lips trembled and I prayed like hell this wasn't a dream. "Kiss me," I pleaded.

When his lips touched mine, my body exploded. *It is real and he is here*. We were finally together.

Relief, passion, love, all of it raced through my veins as our kiss deepened. I'd never felt so at peace or so safe in my entire life. This is where I belonged. In the arms of the man I loved more than life itself. Slowly getting lost in a way I had dreamed of for over a week.

Jase moaned into my mouth, causing a warmth to flow slowly through my entire body. Reaching down, he lifted me in his arms and carried me over to the bed, gently placing my feet on the ground.

His lips moved across my neck as my body trembled with anticipation.

"Taylor," he whispered while he ever so slowly undressed me. It was like he was taking in every motion he did. Every brush of his fingers against my body built up the pool in my lower stomach.

He took a step back and undressed himself while I took in his perfect body. My eyes quickly scanned everywhere until they landed on his forehead while my heart dropped.

"It doesn't hurt, sweetness. I promise."

Tears flooded my eyes.

"No . . . don't cry. Please don't cry."

Cupping my face with his hands, he lightly brushed his lips across mine. "I thought about your smile every second of the day. The feel of your lips against mine and the way you crinkle up your nose when you're about to laugh."

My lips pressed together while I stared up into his eyes.

"Jase," was all I could manage to get off my lips.

Moving his body closer to me, I bumped into the bed. No words needed to be spoken as I lay down.

I was soon looking into those bright blue eyes that were filled with nothing but love as Jase gently pushed into me while whispering my name.

His lips moved ever so slowly up my neck and to the base of my ear. "Taylor, I love you."

My body trembled as I held onto him tighter. "I love you . . . I love you so much."

∽

I TRAILED MY finger lazily around his chest as we laid next to each other in the bed.

"Every time I tried to sleep I saw your beautiful face and dreamed you were in my arms," Jase softly said. I could hear how tired he was in his voice.

Lifting my head, I looked deeply into his eyes. "I'm in your arms now and that's all that matters."

His lips brushed over mine, causing the butterfly effect again. Would it ever get old? God I hoped not.

"I don't want to waste another second being without you, Taylor. I want to give you all my love every single day and night. I want to make all of your dreams come true. Every breath I breathe is for you and only you. I want to be the reason behind your smile."

I sat up and looked down at him. "Do you have any idea how happy you make me?"

His face curved into a smile that took my breath away.

"I think you should show me. In the shower."

I secretly wished Layton and Whitley weren't here so we could spend the rest of the day and night locked away in the hotel room.

After the shower, we got dressed and sat on the sofa in the hotel room and talked. He told me about how William had landed the plane and how they finally got the emergency beacon to work.

"Nate broke his femur? That really sucks that he had to go so long like that."

Jase chuckled. "Yeah, he was grumpy at times and poor Tess took the brunt of most of his asshole-ness."

"Oh no. Poor girl."

He rolled his eyes. "Trust me. She took it, but she was also good at dishing it out."

"And she broke her wrist?"

"Yeah when we hit turbulence she got tossed up and slammed into the roof of the plane. It was terrible. Luckily William only had a really bad sprained ankle."

My finger drew circles on his chest as I blew out a breath. "Thank God y'all are all okay. I can't even begin to tell you how devastated I was."

Jase kissed the top of my head. "I'm so sorry I got on that plane."

Resting my chin on his chest, I looked up at him. "It doesn't matter.

All that matters is we're together now."

"How's Bella?"

Chuckling, I smiled. "Well, Lauren and Mireya have both fallen in love with our puppy. I thought Lauren was going to break down in tears when I asked Libby if they wanted to watch her."

His laughter rumbled through his chest. It was a sound I would forever cherish and never take for granted again.

"Did Lauren watch Bella a lot?"

"Yeah. I um . . . I kind of got lost in myself for a few days. I spent most of the time in your room. Colt and Lauren picked up Bella and I kind of forgot about her for a couple of days. "

His face softened while he ran his finger down the side of my face. "Mom told me. She said you were dressed in my clothes."

"Well in my defense, I didn't have any clothes with me at first."

"Uh-huh. I kind of like the idea of you in my clothes."

Pushing myself up, I crawled on top of him and rubbed against him. "That can be arranged."

It didn't take long before we were completely and utterly lost within one another. I couldn't even tell where I ended and he began.

Perfect way to end the worst week of my life.

Thirty-Six

Jase

SITTING ACROSS THE table from my parents, I tried to focus on what the conversation was. My mind kept going back to the smell of Taylor's hair hanging in my face as she made love to me.

Her hand rested on my leg and I couldn't help but notice how she had not stopped touching me since we left the hotel room. It was as if she was afraid I would disappear on her.

"Jase, are you tired, sweetheart?"

My eyes turned to my mother. "I'm ready to get home, to be honest."

"First thing tomorrow morning you'll be on a plane and headed back home."

The thought of being on another plane had my stomach in knots. Taylor squeezed my hand and gave me the sweetest grin ever.

"Did Nate make it to Montana okay?" my father asked.

"Yeah, he sent me a text a few hours ago. He was glad to be home and planned on staying there for a few weeks. His family was relieved, as I'm sure you can relate."

My mother picked up her glass of wine and said, "Well, I don't blame him one bit for wanting to spend some time with his family. It had to have been terrifying for all of you."

With a nod, I forced a grin. "William's wife is expecting their first child in about a month."

With a gasp, Mom said, "That poor girl. She must have been so scared. I can't even imagine."

Taylor's eyes looked so sad. "Are they both okay? I would be so worried news like that would throw her into labor."

"That's all William worried about, but luckily they are both okay."

Clearing his throat, my father stood and looked down at my mother. "I know I'm exhausted. How about we let Jase and Taylor finish the wine and you and I call it a night."

His hand went out for hers as she stood and took it. Making her way over to me, she kissed me on the cheek and whispered, "I love you, Jase. I'm so glad you're back with us."

"Me too, Mom. More than you know."

She kissed Taylor and gave us both a gentle smile. "Good night you two. Try to get some sleep, Jase."

Taylor's face blushed as she looked away. We had been late getting to dinner when our second shower took longer than expected. "I'm pretty sure once my head hits the pillow I'll be fast asleep."

My father nodded as he said, "We'll all meet in the lobby at six then head to the airport."

"Sounds good," I said as I laced my fingers with Taylor's.

"Night y'all."

"Good night, Dad. Night, Mom."

We watched as they both headed out of the restaurant. "They were so worried about you."

Turning to look at her, I couldn't believe how damn lucky I was to have someone like Taylor.

"It was really nice of you to let my parents see me first."

She focused back on me and grinned. "Well, don't think I'm that great of a person because the whole time I was wishing we didn't have to have dinner with them."

I chuckled and shook my head.

"Plus, I knew the moment we saw each other we would get lost in one another and that would mean they would be waiting even longer."

This time I laughed harder. "That's true. I didn't think about it that way."

"I did," she said as she took a sip of wine and wiggled her eyebrows.

After splitting a piece of peach cobbler, we headed back up to the room.

"Want to watch a movie?" I asked as Taylor slipped one of my T-shirts she brought from home over her head.

I couldn't help but grin at the sight before me. She slipped under the covers and snuggled up against my side.

"Sure. If you're up for one."

Searching the movies, I picked a chick flick thinking she would like that. When she relaxed more into me I finally felt like everything was going to be okay.

"God, this feels so good," I said, kissing the top of her head.

She draped her arm over me and replied, "Mmm . . . it sure does."

It didn't take long for my eyes to grow heavy. The last thing I remembered was Taylor turning off the lights and climbing back into bed. Pulling her closer to me, I breathed in a deep breath then slowly blew it out.

The feel of Taylor up against my body was something I had always longed for . . . more over the last week. It was a feeling I would never again take for granted.

Slowly I drifted off to sleep and heard Taylor whisper, "Thank you for bringing him back to me."

❧

THE SECOND I walked into my parents' house I was overcome with the amount of people there. Everyone came up and started hugging or slapping me on the back. Taylor never left my side.

"It's damn good to have you back, dude," Walker said pulling me in for a quick hug.

I let out a huff of air and replied, "It's damn good to be back. Everything okay here on the home front?"

"A few cows might have missed your pretty-boy face but other than that all is well."

"Ha. You're funny."

After my fair share of hugs and congratulations on being home, I pulled Taylor off to the side.

"How about we sneak away?"

Her mouth dropped open. "What? Everyone is here for you. You can't leave."

"Why not? No one seems to even notice I'm still here."

She narrowed her eyes and bit down on her lip. "Where would we go?"

"Our spot. I want to sit in the very location we plan on building our house."

Her smile grew bigger. Taking my hand in hers, she whispered, "Lead the way, Mr. Morris."

We took two steps and came to a stop. "Now, did I ever tell you kids about the time I jumped up on a bull to impress my Emma?"

Taylor giggled as Garrett stood there looking between us. The man did not look, nor did he act like he was ninety-eight years old.

"Um . . . I don't think so, Gramps," Taylor said.

Garrett turned to me and winked. "Oh, you're in for a doozy of a story, son. Grab us some iced tea and I'll meet you right here."

Garrett walked back into the dining room and sat down in a chair. "Do we have to?" I asked as Taylor's eyes widened in surprise.

"Yes! Jase Morris, go get some tea for Gramps. I'm excited to hear about his bull riding days!"

Moaning internally, I walked into the kitchen. Gunner and Jeff were talking to my father.

Jeff let out a laugh and said, "You look like someone just rained on your parade, son."

Rolling my eyes, I poured a glass of tea for Gramps. "You could say that."

"What happened?" my father asked.

Glancing over my shoulder to make sure we were alone, I turned back to them. "I finally talked Taylor into sneaking off with me and Garrett stopped us. Said he wanted to tell us a story about him bull riding."

Jeff and Gunner looked at each other and busted out laughing. My father and I looked at them like they were crazy.

Gunner was holding his side while Jeff was bent over trying to catch his breath from laughing so hard.

"Did I miss something?" I asked my father with a confused look.

He chuckled and took a drink of his beer. "If you did, I missed it too."

Once they finally got themselves under control, Jeff let out a sigh and wiped at his eyes. "Oh man. Shit, I must have needed a good laugh."

Gunner looked at me and shook his head. "When we were your age, Jase, my grandfather I swore had some kind of detection system. If you were close to having any kind of . . . relations . . ." he said lifting his eyebrows. "You could almost plan on Gramps walking in and stopping it."

Jeff blew out a breath and smiled as if remembering something. "I had to have extra locks put on our house because Garrett had walked in and called out Ari or mine's names one to many times."

My father and I both laughed. "And it wasn't just us. He did it with everyone." Gunner turned to Jeff. "He even banged on the hotel door at Heather and Josh's wedding when Ellie and I snuck away for some . . . alone time."

With another round of laughter, Jeff shook his head and lifted his hands up. "Sorry. Sorry, it's just funny as hell to know the old man still has it in him."

Taylor came walking into the kitchen looking flustered. "I need water."

"Why? What's wrong?" I asked as I quickly poured her a glass.

"Sweetheart, are you okay? You look like you've seen a ghost," Amanda said as she walked up to Taylor.

Ari walked up to Jeff and smiled. "What's with the grin from ear to ear?"

"Garrett stopped Taylor and Jase from sneaking away."

Amanda and Ari both laughed. "Old man still has it," Grace said as Amanda tried not to laugh harder.

Taylor frantically shook her head. "Oh God, don't say that. Then that means she still has it too . . . oh shit."

Amanda faced Taylor again. "What? What's wrong?"

When Taylors beautiful green eyes shot over and pierced mine, my heart dropped to my stomach.

"Nothing. It's nothing. I think all the stress from last week hit me all at once. I'm not feeling very well. Jase? Would you mind if we left?"

Turning to Layton, Taylor said, "I know everyone is here and I hate taking him away."

Kissing her on the top of the head, he replied, "No I don't mind. No one will mind. Y'all get home and get a good night's sleep and I'm sure you'll feel better tomorrow."

Grace and Amanda glimpsed at one another before Amanda grinned and said, "Sweetheart, y'all take off. Don't worry about anyone else they will all understand."

"Go out the back door so you can slip away without Garrett catching you," Grace said with a wicked smile.

The idea of being alone with Taylor was too strong of an urge to pass up. Walking up to her, I reached for her hand and pulled her with me.

"You heard them. Let's go, Taylor."

Jeff and Gunner busted out laughing as we walked past them.

Once we got outside, I spun around and pressed my lips to hers. "Don't think about anything but me kissing every inch of your body."

Her eyes searched my face. "Emma said I was pregnant. Did I ever tell you how incredibly accurate that woman is with that kind of stuff?"

I chuckled and leaned my forehead against hers. "You're on the pill, Taylor. Everything is fine as long as you kept taking them last week."

She nodded slightly. "I did."

"Then don't worry. Come on . . . let's go home. Colt said they left Bella in her crate at the house. I'm dying to see her and smell her puppy breath."

"Sounds good," she replied weakly as I wrapped my arm around her and led her to the truck.

Peeking over my shoulder, I softly said, "Hurry . . . I think I hear Garrett!"

Thirty-Seven

Taylor

June

"WHAT DO YOU think?" Jase asked as I gazed at our house.

Bella ran around me barking. All she was interested in was playing fetch. "I think it's amazing and I cannot believe it will be done in three weeks."

Jase picked up the tennis ball and absentmindedly threw it. Bella took off running after it . . . buying us a few moments of peace.

He reached for my hand and led me toward the house. "The only thing really left to do is some inside stuff."

"I guess I need to give Gunner some paint color choices."

"Yep."

Letting out a frustrated moan, I dropped my head and closed my eyes. "That reminds me. I have to go with my mom next Tuesday for the final fitting of my dress."

"Fun times."

"No. Not really. If you thought wedding dress shopping with her was hell . . . try doing the fitting. She keeps telling the seamstress how to do her job."

He chuckled and reached down to pick me up. Bella got super excited and jumped as Jase carried me inside. He did it every single time we walked into the house.

Trying to hide my smile, I said, "You know. You can't always carry me in like this."

With a stunned expression he replied, "Why can't I?"

I hit his chest playfully. "Are you going to put me down?"

"If I must."

He slowly let me down as my body slid against his. "I used to ask myself if I was dreaming during moments like this."

His eyes searched mine while my heart raced with the intensity of his stare. "Not anymore?"

With a tilt of my head, I smiled. It felt as if heat radiated through my body as it warmed and tingled. "No. I've come to learn that you make me so incredibly happy that all I needed to do was get used to the feeling of being so loved."

"I do love you, Taylor. More than you could ever imagine."

Reaching up on my tippy toes, I softly kissed his lips. "The same goes for me. My love for you grows more and more each day."

With one more kiss, we made our way around the house. Making notes of what still needed to be done and picking out colors. Soon we would be moving into the house as Mr. and Mrs. Jase Morris. The thought alone had my heart skipping with joy.

"Damn, baby. There is a lot happening in the next few weeks. The house finishing up . . . the wedding."

My teeth sunk into my lip and I raised my eyebrows. "The honeymoon."

"The honeymoon. What excites you the most about that?"

Lifting my eyes in thought, I replied, "Let's see. Being back in Paris, where it all started. Staying in our hotel room for as long as we want. Romantic walks through the city. What about you?"

His crooked smile had my stomach fluttering. "I'm going to be all yours for one whole week."

"Mmm . . . that will be nice. What else?"

His finger came up to my face while he traced my jawline. "My fingertips tracing the goose bumps that always pop out when we first get undressed and I touch you."

Swallowing hard, my pulse began to pick up. "That's true . . . your touch excites me."

With a raise of his eyebrow, he nodded. "I hope it always will."

"Keep going," I said breathlessly.

"Close your eyes."

I did as he asked and gripped onto his shirt.

"Picture a room filled with candles burning."

"O-okay."

"I'm going to relearn every curve of your body. Move my lips across your soft skin until you beg me to make love to you. But I won't just yet."

My lips parted open. "Why not?"

"Because I don't want to take for granted that the most beautiful woman in the world is lying next to me in bed and she is mine. Forever and always mine. So, I'll go slow with every touch and kiss. I'm whisper against your lips how much I love you and want you. I want to love you, Taylor, like it's our last time together."

The ground felt as if it was moving as my knees grew weak and my lower stomach pulled with desire. "Jase," I whispered.

When his lips pressed against mine, I wrapped my arms around his neck and kissed him back with as much passion as I could. Things were quickly heating up. His hand moved up my shirt. Moaning into his mouth, I moved my hand over his hard hard-on and squeezed it.

"Jesus H. Christ. That is the last thing I want to see. Ugh. Noah, help me back outside 'cause I think I'm about to puke!"

Jase smiled against my lips. Giggling, I stepped back to see my very pregnant best friend standing there with a snarled lip.

"Hello to you too, Grace."

Noah waved off Grace. "Don't mind her; she woke up on the wrong side of the bed this morning."

I quickly walked up and took Hope out of Noah's arms. "Hi, sweet baby girl. You're getting so big! I can't believe in a few months she'll be one!"

Grace ran her hand over Hope's back. "I know. Makes me so sad she is growing up so fast."

Jase and Noah shook hands and started talking about baseball. Rolling my eyes, I turned back to Grace.

"How are you feeling?"

With a wink, she let out a short chuckle. "I'm okay. Just uncomfortable and I still have a month and a half to go. Wait until you see Alex!"

Alex was due with her second child the beginning of July.

"My gosh, why is it so hot?" Grace remarked while trying to fan herself.

With a shrug, I replied, "Cause it's Texas in June."

"And you had to plan a wedding outside. Did you not take into account your three best friends were knocked up?"

Attempting to keep my smile hidden, I spun Hope around while she laughed. "How terribly inconsiderate of me."

"I know, right?" Grace bit back.

"Do you want to go outside and talk about the landscaping?"

Her eyes lit up. If there was one thing Grace loved more than her husband and daughter, it was plants and trees and dirt.

"Yes!"

By the time we walked outside, Alex and Will pulled up.

I watched as Will ran around the front of his truck to the passenger side. "She is in a mood . . . fair warning!"

With a soft moan, I leaned closer to Hope's ear and said, "Great, we have to deal with two of them."

"What did you say?" Grace asked with a scowl.

"Nothing. Nothing at all."

Alex came waddling over. Not walking. She was actually waddling. I tried . . . I really did. But when Jase walked up next to me and asked, "Why in the hell is she walking like a duck?" I lost it.

Grace turned and hit Jase across the head. "Asshole. She's a few weeks away from pushing out a kid. How would you walk?"

"Um . . . probably not like—"

Noah stood in front of Jase. "Dude! Don't do it. Trust me on this one. Just close your mouth and don't utter another word unless asked."

"But . . ."

Holding up his hand, Noah exclaimed. "Do you value your life? Do you want to walk down the aisle with two good legs?"

Jase snapped his eyes over to Grace who was glowering at him. "Two good legs would be nice."

"Good answer, dickhead," Grace said as she made her way over to Alex. I couldn't help but giggle when Noah smiled.

"Dude, if she calls you names it means she likes you."

Jase's eyebrows furrowed. "She called me dickhead."

"It's okay. She's called me that at least six times today."

I handed Hope back to Noah and kissed Jase. "Pregnancy hormones, baby. She didn't mean it."

Noah cleared his throat and made a face.

Turning, I made my way over to Alex and hugged her. "How are you feeling?"

"Like a beached whale. But let's get this landscaping planned."

I dropped down and pulled Bayli in for a hug.

"Auntie Tay Tay!" she called out. Kissing her on the cheek I picked her up and held her.

Peeking at Alex I couldn't help but notice how miserable she looked. "Alex, sweetie, we can do this after we move in."

"Nope. I don't want to wait because what if Grace and I both go into labor at once? Then it will be even longer. I'd rather get it figured out now."

"Early labor? I'm all for it. If this baby kicks me one more time in the bladder, I'm pretty sure I'm going to just start peeing."

I scrunched up my nose and looked down at her before lifting my eyes to her as I let Bayli back down.

"Let's do this!" Alex called out as she waddled toward the house while holding Bayli's hand.

As I watched two of my best friends walking away from me I couldn't get the feeling of envy out of my system. I knew I wanted to wait for a baby but something had just washed over me and I found myself longing for one. I glanced back over to Jase. He was watching me intently. With a smile, I quickly caught up to Alex and Grace.

I could feel Jase's stare and I prayed like hell he hadn't seen my moment of weakness.

Thirty-Eight

Jase

I COULDN'T PULL my eyes off of Taylor. I saw it in her eyes as she watched Alex and Grace walking off.

She wanted a baby.

"Jase, are you even listening to me?"

Turning back to Will, I laughed. "Yeah. Um . . . you said your dad would have the wedding present for Taylor ready in time. She's going to love the desk for her office."

Will glanced over to Noah and then back to me. "It's gotten to you, hasn't it?"

With a confused expression, I asked, "What's gotten to me?"

"The pregnancy bug."

I pulled my head back and laughed. "What in the fuck? No. Shit, y'all let me get through building a house and getting married before you have me with a kid."

Noah threw his head back and laughed. "Oh man. Jase, do you really think you can fool us? We've stood right where you're standing now. I'd know that look anywhere. You're thinking baby."

"Am not," I shot back.

Noah turned to Will and raised his eyebrow as if exchanging some kind of secret. Will looked me over carefully. "Oh, yeah. I'm telling you . . . it's in the water in Mason."

My head snapped over as I looked at Taylor. She had her hand on Alex's stomach. It felt like someone hit me in the chest with a post when I saw the tear roll down her cheek. She quickly wiped it away, but I saw it in her eyes. In that moment I knew what I wanted.

"Oh fuck," I whispered. "I've got the baby bug."

Will and Noah both chuckled as Noah put his hand on my shoulder. Turning to look at them both, I couldn't help but mirror their smiles.

Noah squeezed and shook his head as he said, "It's a helluva good life."

Will turned and looked at Alex. "It sure the hell is. I wouldn't trade it for the world."

Peeking back over to the girls, all three of them were laughing. I nodded. "And it only gets better."

◦✎

I PACED BACK and forth, wringing my hands together.

"You're going to wear yourself out before the honeymoon night."

My stomach was a mess. My nerves shot.

Turning to Walker, I flashed him a dirty look. "I'm nervous, asshole."

He chuckled and punched me lightly on the arm. "I've been there, Jase. I know how you're feeling. But think about your life before Taylor."

I shook my head. "I can't. I wasn't alive before her."

He lifted his brow and grinned wider. "And it only gets better from this point on."

I blew out a quick breath. After all the years of staring at Taylor from afar and dreaming of being with her, pulling her in and pushing her away, we finally found ourselves where we were meant to be. *I'm the luckiest son-of-a-bitch in the world. I'm marrying the love of my life. My best friend.* "I can't believe the day is finally here. That's what has me so freaked out. Like if I dare to dream this is really happening, I'll wake up."

"Trust me . . . it's happening."

"Do you think Taylor's nervous?"

He laughed and nodded his head. "Yes."

I started pacing again. "I need to see her."

"You will soon," he said as he adjusted his tie.

I shook my head. "No. I need to see her now."

Spinning around to face me, Walker's mouth dropped. "Now? Jase you can't see her before the wedding."

The knock at the door had us both looking over at it. Luke, Grayson, and Noah walked in. I'd asked Rick to be in the wedding, but he had taken a new job that relocated him to Oregon and he couldn't get the time off. It seemed strange at first that we were both moving on with our lives. I was happy for him though. Even happier he found someone he was serious about.

"I need backup." Walker said.

Noah chuckled. "Why?"

Jerking his thumb toward me, Walker said, "He wants to go see Taylor. Now."

Noah's smile faded.

"Oh, hell no. Do you know how mad the girls would be if they knew we helped you sneak in a quickie!" Luke said.

Shaking my head, I replied. "I don't want sex! I mean . . . that might help." Holding up my hands, I motioned for myself to stop thinking like that. "No. No, that's not what I want right now. I just need to talk to Taylor. It will be five minutes, no more."

I glanced around the room at all four of them. We had all become really close in the last few months. It almost was like we had known each other our whole lives.

"Hell, I'm down for sneaking you in to a secret pre marriage meeting," Grayson said standing tall and proud. "We're going to be brother in-laws. We need to stick together."

I pointed to Grayson. "See! Gray gets me!"

Walker moaned. "Shit. I guess that means I'm in."

Fist pumping, I turned to Noah. "Hey, my wife is already pissed at me because she's nine months pregnant. I have nothing to lose."

Luke sighed and dropped his head. "Libby is going to kill me if she finds out . . . but I'm in. Brotherhood all the way."

Will and Colt walked in and I couldn't help but smile and say, "The gangs all here. Let's plan this shit out!"

"Oh hell. We just walked in on something," Colt mumbled.

*

WALKER AND I waited in the barn for Taylor.

"What if she doesn't come?" I asked.

Walker looked at his watch. "Considering she'll be right in the middle of getting ready, I'd be surprised if she comes."

"Do Colt and Will have everything under control?"

Walker looked at his phone. "Yep. Amanda and your mom are currently heading over to see the made up mistake with the tents. They told them they were placed in the wrong location. Once they get there they'll see they are in the right spot."

Smiling, I replied, "Perfect."

"Don't get your hopes up. We still have to get her away from the other girls and the makeup and hair lady."

"I have faith, Walker. I have a faith."

"Glad you do," he mumbled.

Luke came walking in with Taylor and my heart dropped. "Look who I found all alone in the house."

Taylor smiled a brilliant smile as she walked up to me. "What in the world are you boys up to? There is so much chaos going on right now, I thought for sure Grace was about to go into labor."

Luke laughed. "I told her Alex was having contractions. That cleared out Taylor's room quick."

Taylor focused on Luke. "Yes. Everyone started heading out of the room and Luke held me back. Once everyone was out of the room, we went down the back stairs where Noah and Gray were distracting everyone."

I had to know. "How were they distracting them?"

Rolling her eyes, Taylor said, "Gray said something about you knowing some football player who was currently pulling up out front to surprise you."

I nodded my head. "Nice."

Walker slapped my back and said, "You have five minutes tops before we have to get you both back to the house."

"Thanks. That's all I need."

Luke laughed. "Poor, Tay. Look what you have to look forward to."

Taylor smacked him on the chest and told him to leave.

Making her way over to me, she pressed her lips together and gazed up at me through her lashes. "Everything okay?"

"Everything is more than okay, but I had to talk to you about something."

"It couldn't wait until after the wedding?"

I shook my head. "Nope. Last night when we walked through the finished house and I saw how happy you were, I wanted to make you even happier."

With the sweetest smile ever, her green eyes lit up as she replied, "Jase, I am the happiest I've ever been. There is nothing else for you to do except marry me."

Taking a hold of her hands, I brought them to my lips and kissed the back of each. "There is something else. I didn't want to wait until tonight or our honeymoon because I need you to know I've changed my mind on something and you have to know before we get married."

Her smile faded some.

"Nothing bad, I swear sweetness."

Relaxing her face a bit, a look of confusion swept over it. "O-okay . . . what is it?"

I swallowed hard and glanced down. Closing my eyes, I took in a few deep breaths. Putting my attention back on her, I smiled and said, "I want to have a baby."

Widening her eyes in surprise, she asked, "Wh-what?"

"I mean, I don't want to focus everything on that . . . I just want to stop *not trying* to have a baby and see what happens."

Her eyes built with tears while her lips trembled. "Really?"

"If you're not ready though, I'll wait."

She blinked and the tears were set free. Reaching up, I wiped them away. "Please tell me they're happy tears, Tay."

Throwing herself into my arms, she cried harder. "Very happy tears, Jase! Very happy!"

"I knew it!" Libby called out as Jase and I broke apart and turned to her. Meagan stood next her with her hands on her hips.

"You horny little bastard. You just had to see my sister before the wedding, didn't you? And you have her crying!"

Meagan walked up and got in my face. "You are so dead."

Taylor took my hand in hers and squeezed and I knew that was the farthest thing I was.

"You're wrong, future sister-in-law. I'm so alive, I want to shout it from the rooftops!"

Thirty-Nine

Taylor

I STOOD IN the mirror and took in the sight before me.

"You're lucky that little stunt you and Jase pulled didn't set us back," Lauren said as she pushed the last pin in to hold on my veil.

Liza smiled and shook her head. "My goodness. Taylor you're the most beautiful bride I've ever seen. Wait until Jase sees you . . . again."

Giggling, my mother huffed as I turned to her. "Don't be upset, Mom. It was important."

"Nothing is that important to go to the lengths that boy did."

Whitley agreed. "He could have simply asked to talk to you. We wouldn't have denied him that."

Amanda turned to Whitley. "My heart is still pounding thinking the tents were all set up wrong."

Hiding my smile, I looked back at myself. My wedding dress was perfect. The strapless sweetheart neckline showed off my cleavage just like my mother said it would. The silver accent belt around my waist was beautiful and added the perfect touch to the lace and satin dress. Lifting my gown, I smiled at the brand new cowboy boots the girls bought me. They each signed the bottom of the boots and I cried like a baby at my wedding shower when I opened them.

My mother walked up to me and softly said, "Taylor, it's time, sweetheart."

Turning around, I looked around the room at the people closet to me. My mother and Whitley stood near the door and both looked beautiful.

Slowly moving my eyes around the room, I took in each of my best friends, all dressed in beautiful soft pink dresses finished off with cowboy boots.

Meagan. My beautiful sister and my best friend. I learned from her how to be strong.

Grace. The spit and fire of the group who looked beautiful with her hands resting on her ever-so-big pregnant belly.

Alex. The sensible one in our group. Her smile alone lit up the room never mind the fact that she was due in a week and was still her bubbly self.

Libby. Sweet beautiful Libby who had the biggest heart of all. There wasn't anything she wouldn't do for any of us.

Lauren. The ever so happy and always positive best friend. She looked so beautiful as she stood there with her hands rubbing her unborn child. Lauren was the first to drop everything and come to your aide. I loved seeing how happy her eyes were.

Liza. The newest addition to my best friend circle. Anytime I needed advice, she was the first to offer it. She never left my side when Jase's plane went down and I'll never forget that.

Mireya and Bayli stood in front of their mothers dressed in beautiful little white gowns as they clutched onto their flower girl baskets.

Tears filled my eyes as I realized how blessed I was.

"I think we should get going now. Brad is waiting outside the door," Jessie, said. She not only catered the reception, but she was also the wedding planner.

I stood there as each person gave me a kiss on the cheek. When I was finally alone, I took in a deep breath and blew it out as I tried to calm my nerves.

The door opened and my father walked in. Tears pooled in his eyes as he closed his eyes and shook his head before looking back at me. "My goodness. You are breathtaking."

Blushing, I replied, "Thank you, Daddy."

Walking up to me he took my hands in his. "I thought your mother was the most beautiful bride. You and your sister Meagan have proved me wrong. The three of you are . . . simply . . . flawless."

"Daddy," I whispered. "Don't make me cry or Lauren and Meagan will have to do my makeup again."

"Right," he said with a nod. "I want you to know how happy I am for you, Taylor. I see the way Jase looks at you and he loves you so very much."

"I love him."

"I guess it's time," he said while he slowly blew out a breath.

"I guess so," I answered.

He handed me my bouquet of white roses Alex made. They were wrapped in the same color fabric as the bridesmaids gowns.

I took my father's arm and let him walk me down the stairs and to the car. The wedding was taking place at the lake on Layton and Whitley's ranch.

My heart was beating so hard in my chest, I felt like it was rocking the car. We were the last to pull up. I looked out the window to see the girls walking down the aisle. I couldn't help but smile when my eyes landed on Jase. He looked so handsome dressed in a black tux. The windows to the limo were tinted and no one could see me inside.

My father bumped my shoulder. "You ready?"

"I've never been more ready for anything in my entire life."

He got out and walked around to my door. A group of people gathered around and somewhat blocked the view of me as my father helped me out, adjusted my dress and held his arm out for me. When I slipped it around his, they stepped aside and Jessie ushered Bayli and Mireya down the aisle as everyone gushed about how cute the girls were as they skipped down the aisle literally throwing pink rose petals everywhere.

The music changed and the wedding march started while I locked eyes with Jase.

His smile was so big, I couldn't help but giggle.

"I'd say he was happy by that grin across his face," my father whispered.

"He looks so handsome," I whispered.

I tried to pull my eyes off of him to look at our guests, but I was mesmerized.

It felt like forever by the time we made it up to the altar. My father lifted my veil and kissed my cheek as he placed my hand in Jase's.

"Take care of my little girl."

Jase nodded. "I will, sir. I promise."

Walking up to the altar, Jase and I faced one another. "You're so beautiful, I feel like I can't breathe looking at you."

My face warmed as I squeezed his hand. "Thank you. You look so handsome, I couldn't take my eyes off of you."

The pastor cleared his throat and began the ceremony.

The whole thing was a blur. Jase and I stared at each other almost the entire time. When he finally announced us husband and wife, Jase cupped my face with his hands and smiled. He slowly pressed his lips to mine as everyone yelled out and clapped. Pulling back slightly from me, Jase winked.

Turning to face everyone, Jase held up our hands as if we had just won a race. We started down the aisle and off to the side where a few quick photos would be snapped before we headed to the reception.

Stopping, he pulled me closer to him and kissed me once more. "Do you know what makes me the happiest man in the world?"

Lifting my mouth up in a smile, I asked, "What?"

The back of his hand moved softly down my face. "Loving you."

"You have no idea how much I love you," I softly spoke.

"I think I do. Now kiss me before they start making us pose."

And kiss I did. Luke cleared his throat as he walked by and said, "The photographer isn't waiting patiently for the two of you to stop sucking face. Save it for later."

We spent the next thirty minutes taking beautiful pictures as well as silly ones with our best friends and family.

Nothing would ruin this day.

It was perfect.

Beyond perfect.

Forty

Jase

I WATCHED TAYLOR move from person to person wearing that beautiful smile of hers.

Lifting my beer to my lips, I slowly shook my head.

She's my wife. Taylor was officially mine for the rest of our lives.

"You look happy sitting here staring at your wife."

Lifting my gaze up, I smiled at my father. "I like hearing that."

"I remember thinking the same thing when someone first called your mother my wife. I'm pretty sure my chest puffed up with pride."

I chuckled and took another drink. "It feels like it took us forever to get to this day, yet, it feels like I just asked her out on our first official date. I blinked and here I am."

My father took a seat next to me. "And the rest of your life you'll feel like that. The day we brought you home from the hospital feels like yesterday. Watching you and your sister grow has been such a blessing, but at the same time makes me so sad."

I smiled as I looked at my father. "I pray I'm as good of a father as you are, Dad."

His eyes filled with tears. "You will be, Jase. You will be."

"Can I get everyone's attention please," Jessie said as we both stood. Taylor turned to me and scrunched her nose up with the cutest smile.

Leaning in closer, my father said, "I believe it's the bride and groom's time to dance."

With a nod, I set my beer down and made my way over to Taylor. Wrapping my arm around her waist, I pulled her into my side.

"The bride and groom are about to dance. Now, they picked out a song, but Jase has a bit of a surprise for Taylor."

Sucking in a breath, Taylor turned to me. "What did you do?"

"Nothing big. I just wanted it to be a little more special."

Noah walked out carrying a guitar.

"Oh my goodness," Taylor said as she covered her mouth to hold back her sobs.

Noah walked up to the mic and smiled. "When Jase asked me to sing this song for the first dance, I quickly said no. Then my very pregnant . . . and beautiful . . . wife, Grace, persuaded me into singing it."

The crowd laughed and most turned to Grace, who grinned from ear to ear.

"So, it's my pleasure to sing the first song that Jase and Taylor will dance to as Mr. and Mrs. Morris. Y'all come on up here."

Taking Taylor's hand in mine, I led her to the middle of the dance floor and pulled her body next to mine. Noah began playing the cords to the song 'Yours' as Taylor buried her face in my chest.

I softly sang along as we glided over the makeshift dance floor. Taylor pulled her head back and looked up at me. Her green eyes danced with happiness. Leaning down, I gently kissed her tears away.

"Thank you for loving me like you do."

She pressed her lips together to keep from crying.

"You are my life. My entire world, Taylor. Forever."

Her face beamed bright. "A forever love."

Noah finished singing as I pressed my lips to hers.

When I pulled back to look at her, we both smiled. "Nothing could make this day any better," she said with such love in her eyes.

"Oh, holy hell."

We both turned to look at Grace who was standing next to Noah, gripping his arm for dear life.

Taylor quickly walked up to Grace. "What's wrong?"

"Contraction. Strong one."

Noah's face dropped. "What?"

"Mom!" Colt called out as Ellie turned quickly to look at him. "Lauren's water just broke!"

"Wait! Why are they going into labor? I'm due first!" Alex yelled out.

Taylor and I looked at each other and laughed.

Leaning her body against me, Taylor giggled, "We're totally going to have the best wedding story out of everyone."

We stood there as everyone began scattering around. Jeff and Ari were helping Noah get Grace while Ellie, Gunner, Scott, and Jessie were all surrounding Lauren.

Alex huffed, going on and on about how unfair it was and for Will to get her something spicy.

Taylor spun around and flashed me the biggest most beautiful smile I'd ever seen.

"Best day ever! We're married and babies are coming!" she exclaimed.

"I have a feeling this is just the start of even more best days."

Her eyes turned dark as she lifted her brows. "And more babies."

The happiness inside of me, I swear, was about to burst as I looked into the eyes of the woman I had loved for so long.

Pulling her to me, I slipped my hand behind her neck and brought her lips up to mine. "Lots of babies if I can help it."

The End.

Epilogue

Taylor

One Year Later

JASE WALKED UP next to me and handed me iced tea. Bella was sound asleep at my feet, trying her best to ignore Annie playing in the front yard.

"Oh gosh, thank you. It's so hot out here and our little girl does not want to come in."

Jase grinned that crooked smile as he gazed out into the front yard.

"She's stubborn. Like her mother."

Rolling my eyes, I replied, "Hardly. She's exactly like you. Look at her. She's so excited she can't sit still."

With a chuckle, Jase stepped off the porch and reached down for our four-month old german shorthair pointer. "Don't listen to her, Annie. You can sit still, can't you, girl?"

Annie licked Jase's face while he laughed. "She's gonna make the best bird dog ever. Isn't she? Yes, she is."

I tried like hell to keep from laughing, but failed.

"What? She is! Once she is trained."

"Where are you going to find time to train her? You're so busy now."

My heart rate had increased to a rapid pulse. I prayed Jase wouldn't notice my breathing had picked up. He was so in tune with my body, it was unreal.

"Nah, I'm never too busy for time with my three favorite girls."

I stood and placed my hands on my hips. "Did you really just put me in the same category as the dogs?"

With a smile that instantly had my panties wet, he walked up the steps and kissed me softly on the lips. "Hell no. You'll always be my number one girl."

Lifting a brow, I asked, "Promise?"

"Don't you know by now, sweetness, loving you is my favorite thing in the world."

Jase headed into the house and put one very worn out Annie into her crate as Bella observed. He walked into the kitchen and glanced down at the envelope on the kitchen island. "What's that?"

My eyes quickly landed on the envelope. Heat radiated through my chest

Lord, please let him be excited about this. Please.

"Results from a test."

Jase glanced over his shoulder and furrowed his brows. "A test? Did you take an online test I didn't know about?"

My head felt like it was spinning. When I missed my period last month I kept it to myself. I had just stopped taking my birth control pills the month before. Jase and I talked about starting a family after the wedding, but decided we wanted to wait and spend more time together and wait a bit more. When I told Meagan I thought I might already be pregnant so soon after stopping the pill, she laughed and mumbled, "Damn Mason water."

Smiling, I placed my hand over my stomach. I was beyond the moon knowing I was carrying our child.

"Taylor? Baby is everything okay? You look . . . flush."

I pulled my lip in and bit down while I let my eyes drift back down to the envelope.

My eyes lifted to his. I could see them sparkle as he watched me carefully. He pushed off the counter, never once taking his eyes from mine. I swore the blue was changing colors. They seemed to get . . . brighter.

I swallowed hard while I watched him open the envelope.

This moment was going to be etched into my mind forever, so I carefully watched his face.

Pulling the piece of paper out, his eyes widened in shock.

"This is . . . oh my God."

My lips pressed together in an attempt not to start crying. My stomach fluttered when I saw the smile spread over his face.

"A baby."

I wanted to make him smile like that for the rest of our lives every chance I got.

He dropped his hands to his sides. "Taylor. You're pregnant!"

Nodding my head quickly, he rushed over to me and picked me up while I wrapped my arms around his neck. He spun me around and yelled out in excitement as Bella started barking.

When he finally put me down, his eyes searched my face before he pressed his lips to mine. His kisses still pulled out so much emotion from me. He would almost render me helpless after each one.

Slowly pulling back to look at me, he grinned so big I couldn't help but smile. "I think we should celebrate."

My stomach clenched. "I like the sound of that."

"A picnic!"

My smile faltered for one second, before I flashed it again. "A picnic?"

"Yep. Tonight under the stars."

My heart jumped to my throat. Jase was such a romantic. "I love that idea!"

Lifting his hand he pushed a piece of hair behind my ear. "Do you remember our first date in the back of my truck?"

"Yes."

He closed his eyes and smiled. His face was beautiful and for a moment, it felt like the ground moved. When he opened them again, my heart dropped at the site of the tears pooling in those beautiful baby blues.

"I held you in my arms right here in this spot as I looked up at a falling star."

I became aware of every single sound. My breaths . . . Jase's . . . the sound of the wind blowing the wind chimes outside, and even the woodpecker searching for his lunch.

My hands rested on his broad chest as I found the words to speak. "What did you wish for?"

I'll never forget the look in his eyes as he slowly shook his head and gazed down at me with so much love I could feel it in the room.

"For a little girl." He dropped his hand and slid it behind my back, pulling me in closer to him. "But don't worry sweetness, you'll always be my number one girl."

Laughing, I reached up on my toes and kissed the man I loved.

"I love you, Jase Morris."

He wiggled his eyebrows. "And I love you, Taylor Morris. Now come on."

Reaching for my hand, he laced his fingers in mine and pulled me to our bedroom. "I'm making love to you until the sun goes down and the stars come out."

I reached up and pinched myself.

Nope. Not dreaming.

Bonus Epilogue

Layton

Six Years Later

WHITLEY SAT IN my lap as we watched the kids playing in the pool. I couldn't help but think what a lucky man I was to have the woman I loved in my arms and my family surrounding me.

Liza splashed around in the pool with her daughter, Corinne.

"I'd give anything to have an ounce of that energy," Courtney said with a chuckle.

Agreeing with her, Reed wrapped his arms around Courtney while we all gazed out over the beautiful site in front of us. Nothing made me happier than all of us being together like this.

"I cannot believe how fast they are growing up," Whitley said with a sigh.

My stomach felt like a rock. I'd give anything to freeze time.

"Dad!" Nickolas yelled. "Can I teach Lacy how to cannonball?"

Walker stood at the edge of the pool. "You mean like this?" He jumped and tucked his legs in and hit the water hard. Splashing everyone around the pool.

"Walker Moore! You got my Kindle wet!" Ava yelled out.

Courtney and Reed were so happy to have Ava and Ryder in town. They had been here almost two weeks and would be leaving tomorrow to head back up to Montana, and I knew it was killing both of them to have them so far away. I couldn't imagine having Liza and Jase in another state.

Walker laughed his ass off as he climbed out of the pool and shook his hair, wetting Ava again. She tried to get up but had a harder time than normal. I couldn't help but chuckle.

"Damn, that girl is so much like you, Court, it's unreal," I said.

"You have no idea," Reed injected while Courtney shot him a dirty look.

Walker walked up to Ryder and lightly slapped him on the shoulder. "I hope you're ready for baby number two."

Beaming with pride, Ryder replied, "You better believe I am."

Looking between Ava and Ryder, he poked more fun. "I would bet the ranch it's a girl."

Ryder's smile dropped as he looked down at his daughter sleeping. When it was naptime, little Kate would drop wherever she was and sleep. Today it was on the lounge chair next to her daddy.

Reed had taken her for a horseback ride this morning. She had been beyond the moon happy she was having a date with her granddaddy.

Reed laughed. "Leave him alone, Walker."

Holding his hands up, Walker shrugged. "I'm just saying, I think with three girls in the house, Ryder might feel outnumbered."

Ava set her Kindle down and stared at Ryder. "Is that true? Do you wish it wasn't a girl?"

Ryder went to answer, but quickly closed his mouth. "Wait. What do you mean do I wish it wasn't a girl?"

Whitley quickly stood up and took Courtney's hand in hers. "Don't freak out yet, Court. Stay calm."

"I'm trying. I will . . . stay calm. How could she keep that kind of a secret from me?"

Ava smiled and waved her hand like she was trying to brush off what she just said. "I mean . . . um . . . well, I um . . ."

She looked at her father who said, "Don't look at me, princess. I can't pull the foot from your mouth."

Ryder skillfully maneuvered around Kate so he didn't wake her. "Ava, how do you know?"

Ava's eyes quickly began looking around at everyone. Liza and Corinne had moved over to the other side of the pool closest to Ava and were now waiting anxiously for her to spill the beans.

My chest felt as if it would burst. I loved having my family together and for knowing Ava's slip up was going to make Courtney beyond the moon happy. I hoped it eased the pain of them leaving tomorrow.

Chewing on her thumb, Ryder reached his hands down for hers and pulled her up. He placed his hand on her round seven-month belly. "You little sneak. You got the doctor to tell you, didn't you? And worse yet, you've been hiding it!"

Squeezing her eyes shut, she nodded her head.

"I'm so sorry, but when I went in the other day the doctor asked again if we wanted to know. I said no, we had agreed to be surprised, but then I asked him to write it down and seal it in an envelope and the moment I got in the car I tore it open! I don't know what came over me!"

Ryder laughed and pressed his lips to Ava's. Courtney instantly started crying as she turned and jumped into Reed's arms. "Another girl!"

Liza started clapping in the pool along with Corinne. "Aunt Ava is having a baby!" Corinne yelled out as everyone laughed.

Glancing over to my precious Kate, she was still fast asleep sucking her thumb.

"She's having another little girl, Corinne! We have another girl in the family!" Liza cried out.

"Oh no. Not another girl!" Nicholas moaned as Walker picked him up and threw him into the pool.

"Will she be starting school with me?" Corinne asked.

Ava laughed and looked down into the pool. "She will have to wait a few years like Kate did."

Ryder cupped Ava's face with his hands and smiled. I glanced up and saw Reed's reaction. I knew it made him happy to see how much Ryder loved Ava. Just like it did for me when I witnessed Walker's love for my daughter and their two kids.

Nickolas walked up and stood next to Ryder and Ava. He was dripping with water from just climbing out of the pool. He puffed his chest out and I couldn't help but smile. Damn how I loved that boy. He had already started asking his daddy if he could start working on the ranch. My heart ached for a moment. I'd have given anything for my parents and Mike to be here.

"Don't worry, Uncle Ryder and Aunt Ava. My dad told me since I'm older it's my job to protect the girls. If anyone hurts them, I'll kick their ass!"

Corinne gasped and turned to Liza. "He said a bad word, Mommy! Nickolas said a bad word."

Everyone looked at Walker as he took a few steps back.

Ava turned to Reed. "He's your son, so this is your fault."

Narrowing his eyes at her, he asked with a confused expression, "My fault? "How in the hell is this my fault?"

Corinne gasped again. "Grandpa!" Shaking her head, Corinne looked at Courtney. "Grammy, you better spank Grandpa for saying that bad word."

Courtney sighed. "Oh, sweet little girl, if I did that Grandpa would like it too much."

Liza and Ava both covered their mouths in an attempt not to laugh, but it was too late. Everyone started laughing. Even Nickolas and Corinne who had no idea why we were all laughing.

Standing up, I smacked my beautiful wife on the ass and pulled her in for a kiss. Moving my lips to her ear, I took in a deep breath and let her heavenly scent settle in. "I think that sounds like something I might like as well. Oh the wicked plans I have for you tonight after everyone leaves."

Whitley hit me on the chest and pulled back. Our blue eyes each burning with desire. "How in the world can you make my stomach dip all these years later with something like that, Layton Morris?"

"Sorry we're late!" Jase called out.

Turning, I grinned when I saw my son carrying his daughter, Emma, on his shoulders. Taylor held onto Mason's hand as they made their way over to us.

"How was the party?" Courtney asked, holding her arms out for Mason. He quickly ran and jumped into her arms. "Grammy! Emma lost her tooth!"

Whitley gasped next to me as we all looked at Emma smiling with a huge smile on her face.

Jase peeked up and laughed as he said, "And tell Grandpa how much the crazy tooth fairy left you."

Emma's face lit up. "A hundred dollars!"

Everyone looked at Taylor.

"Thank God my child is sleeping and didn't hear that," Ava said with a chuckle.

Taylor chewed on her lip as she peeked over to Walker and Liza. Both Corinne and Nickolas had their mouths dropped open.

"She thought it was a ten!"

Corinne turned to Walker. "Daddy! Is she going to leave me a hundred dollars?"

"Yeah, Dad! Is she?" Nickolas asked.

Walker rubbed his hand on both their heads. "No y'all, she is not. Emma's tooth fairy was one in training and probably got put in timeout for leaving such a large amount."

Walker looked at Taylor who blushed and said, "Oh trust me. She did."

Jase laughed as he leaned over and kissed Taylor on the cheek. "I love you."

I sat back down and watched the whole scene play out in front of me. I imagined what it would be like to slow life down and do this every weekend.

My eyes soon found hers. Smiling, I couldn't help but notice the tightness in my chest as Whitley smiled at me. She made her way over to me, reaching up and kissing me softly on the lips.

"Tell me what you're thinking right this very second."

With another quick scan of everyone, I placed my hand on the side of her face as she leaned into it. "How I'm the luckiest man in the world. Thank you for giving me all of this. Thank you for never giving up on me."

Her eyes filled with tears. "Never. I love you, Layton."

My lips pressed to hers as we heard Emma and Nickolas yell out.

"Oh gross! Grandpa and Grandma are kissing!"

Laughing, I kissed Whitley's nose and looked up. "Who wants to see Grandpa do a cannonball?"

Bonus Epilogue

Gunner

Earlier that same day

WALKING UP FROM the barn, I stopped and took in the sight before me. My heart was filled with so much love and happiness, I needed a moment to stop and catch my breath.

Looking up, I smiled. "Gramps, you would have loved this."

Focusing my attention back on everyone, I took it all in as I slowly let my eyes scan across the yard as twelve little ones gathered around a piñata. It was something we did every year on Gramps' birthday. Today he would have been a hundred and five. My chest ached any time I thought about him and Grams.

Taking a deep breath in, I slowly blew it out.

"You okay?"

Turning, I smiled at the beautiful blue-eyed beauty in front of me. "Yeah. Thinking about Gramps and Grams."

Ellie walked up to me and flashed me that same smile that melted my heart still to this day. She was a far cry from the young girl with the sprained wrist who sat next to me and watched Cars. She was so much more. She was my everything.

"I miss them too, Gunner. But do you now what makes it easier for me?"

I grinned and nodded my head. I couldn't bring myself to say it out loud and Ellie knew that. "They somehow knew it was time and they went together, Gunner. Let that comfort you that they're together forever."

Grams and Gramps were found laying together in bed five years ago. Their fingers laced together. A love like theirs would only allow them to go together. There would be no way one could survive without the other.

Pulling in a deep breath, I smiled.

"Look at this crazy group we have."

Ellie giggled and rested her head on my shoulder.

"We're blessed."

"Hell yeah we are."

My heart felt full as I looked to each one of them.

Mireya. Libby and Luke's first and the first grandbaby of the bunch born. Next to her was her younger brother, Trey. He was spit and fire like his granddad, Jeff. Trey was trying to push Mireya out of line and she was having none of it. I couldn't help but smile as I watched Luke take Libby's hand in his and kiss the back of it.

Then we had my sweet Bayli. Not yet a young lady, but itching to be one. She stood in heels that clearly belonged to Alex. Joshua Drew was next to her yelling for her to help him on his turn. She was a wonderful big sister to Joshua. I was pretty sure Ellie secretly hoped they fought like cats and dogs like Alex and Colt had.

Alex and Will were sitting at a table totally lost in one another. The way Will looked at my daughter made me smile. It was clear how much he loved her. My chest felt tight knowing my daughter had followed her own dreams and had accomplished so much.

The twins were standing a bit off to the side. Arabella was attempting to braid Charlotte's hair as well as Grayson's.

"Oh my. Meagan is going to be brushing out knots tonight in Charlotte's hair," Ellie said with a chuckle.

I grinned. "I doubt she'll mind. I got to give props to Gray. That has to hurt with the way Arabella is putting all those little ponytails in his hair."

Ellie laughed and agreed.

Jacob attempted to try and sit on his sister Hope's shoulders while Grace started laughing.

"Jacob Bennet! You're going to fall and break your arm!" Grace called out.

"No I won't, Momma. Hope promised to break my fall if I fell."

Grace frowned and shook her head. "Don't count on it, Buddy," she replied as Noah wrapped his arms around his wife and kissed her cheek.

The sight before me was something I found myself longing to see more and more. It warmed my heart when we were able to have everyone over.

"Grandpa!" Anissa yelled running as fast as her little legs would take her. I bent down and scooped her up in my arms. She was the spitting image of Lauren with her blonde hair and the bluest of blue eyes. "Hey, sweetheart. Everything okay?"

Nodding, she rested her head on me, causing that overwhelming sense of love to hit me hard . . . right in the chest.

"Oh, how we have our granddaddy wrapped around our little finger."

I nodded. "And that's okay. She is perfectly fine in my arms."

Ellie winked and looked back over to everyone. "Dear lord, look at Hunter."

I couldn't help but laugh as I watched Colt and Lauren's son running around in circles with a bag over his head. *Yep. That's my grandson.*

Shaking her head, Ellie said, "You wouldn't know Hunter is three years older than Anissa with the way he acts."

We both laughed harder when we saw Colt mimic his son. Lauren yelled for them to stop, prompting my son drop the bag, pick his wife up, and start running with her, eliciting cheers from all the kids.

Anissa lifted her head to see what was going on. Not seeming to care, she snuggled back onto my chest, which was perfectly fine by me. "She's going to fall asleep in your arms again."

"Then I'll just have to hold her while she sleeps."

Ellie's breathtaking smile had me catching my breath.

"Aunt Ellie!" Emma yelled while running up and hugging Ellie's legs.

Ellie gasped and said, "Why Emma Rose, look at your beautiful dress."

Emma twirled around and gave us a huge grin. She was missing her front tooth.

I bent over and looked at her mouth as she snapped it shut. "I dare say, did you drop a tooth somewhere, Emma?"

She tried hard not to laugh, but lost her battle and went into a giggling fit. Her precious little blue-green eyes lit up when she finally looked up at me. "It fell out, Uncle Gunner!"

"I'll say it did. Now where did you get that pretty dress?"

Emma blushed and looked away. Taylor and the girls teased me all the time over Emma's little crush on me.

"My mommy made it. For our weddin'."

Ellie covered her mouth with her hand to hide her smile. "Our wedding, huh?"

"Yep!" Emma said . . . doing another twirl in an attempt to win my heart.

"What if you get it dirty before the wedding?" I asked.

She frowned and lifted her eyes. Turning to look at Ellie, who lifted her shoulders, she glanced back at me. "Mommy will clean it."

"Emma! Emma!"

A look of horror washed over Emma's face. "Bye!" she yelled out as she took off running before her little brother Mason could find her. Taylor and Jase had their hands full with Emma and Mason, that was for sure.

"Oh lord, that little girl has it bad for you, Gunner Mathews. It's those blue eyes and that dimple of yours. Not to mention you're still rocking a body at fifty something."

My heart hammered in my chest as I looked at my wife. "As much as I love this craziness we call our family, my favorite thing in the world is to lay on our quilt under our tree while I get lost deep inside of you."

Ellie's mouth dropped open as she lifted her hands and covered our granddaughter's ears. "Drew Garrett Mathews. Don't you talk like that in front of her."

Wiggling my eyebrows, I leaned in to kiss her. Pulling back slightly, I stared into those blue eyes that still left me breathless.

Her eyes were filled with pure love as she softly spoke. "I love you, Gunner."

Lifting the corner of my mouth into a smile, I replied back, "I love you more."

Thank You

A HUGE THANK you to everyone who has had a part in this crazy thing called writing a book. You know who you are!

These three series have been some of my favorite books to write, and to be able to combine the three of them has been such a fun (and at times insane) process. It's a bittersweet ending to an amazing journey, and I'm so blessed you were along for the ride! Thank you!

Playlist

CONTAINS SPOILERS
Kacey Musgraves—"Keep It To Yourself"
Prologue

Adam Sanders—"Thunder"
Jase decides to move on and let Taylor go.

Dan + Shay—"I Heard Goodbye"
Taylor sees Jase dancing with Jill.

Just Bieber—"The Feeling"
Taylor telling Jase they were not going to have a
future together and asked him to leave her office.

Carrie Underwood—"I Told You So"
Taylor after Jase came to her office.

Austin Webb—"Getting Even"
Taylor and Jase running into each other at the barn.

Kelsea Ballerini—"Looking At The Stars"
Jase and Taylor in his spot.

Alessia Cara—"Here"
Taylor at the river party.

Chase Bryant—"Change Your Name"
Jase proposing to Taylor with Bella.

Alan Walker—"Faded"
Libby and Taylor in Jase's bedroom.

Cole Swindell—"You Should Be Here"
Taylor and Grams talking at the barn.

Keith Urban—"Your Everything"
Taylor and Jase in hotel in Nebraska after he is rescued.

Lady Antebellum—"Dancing Away With My Heart"
Jase and Taylor at their house they are building.

Russell Dickerson—"Yours"
Jase and Taylor's wedding song.

Rascal Flatts—"The Day Before You"
Jase finding out Taylor is pregnant.

Frankie Ballard—"Helluva Life"
Epilogues

LOVE READING ROMANCE?

Fall in love with
pıatkus

Entice

Temptation at your fingertips

An irresistible eBook-first list from
the pioneers of romantic fiction at
www.piatkusentice.co.uk

To receive the latest news,
reviews & competitions direct to your inbox,
sign up to our romance newsletter at
www.piatkusbooks.net/newsletters

Do you love historical fiction?

Want the chance to hear news about your favourite
authors (and the chance to win free books)?

Mary Balogh
Charlotte Betts
Jessica Blair
Frances Brody
Gaelen Foley
Elizabeth Hoyt
Eloisa James
Lisa Kleypas
Stephanie Laurens
Claire Lorrimer
Sarah MacLean
Amanda Quick
Julia Quinn

Then visit the Piatkus website and blog
www.piatkus.co.uk | www.piatkusbooks.net

And follow us on Facebook and Twitter
www.facebook.com/piatkusfiction | www.twitter.com/piatkusbooks

piatkus

Do you love fiction with a supernatural twist?

Want the chance to hear news about your favourite
authors (and the chance to win free books)?

Keri Arthur
Kristen Callihan
P.C. Cast
Christine Feehan
Jacquelyn Frank
Larissa Ione
Darynda Jones
Sherrilyn Kenyon
Jayne Ann Krentz and Jayne Castle
Lucy March
Martin Millar
Tim O'Rourke
Lindsey Piper
Christopher Rice
J.R. Ward
Laura Wright

Then visit the Piatkus website and blog
www.piatkus.co.uk | www.piatkusbooks.net

And follow us on Facebook and Twitter
www.facebook.com/piatkusfiction | www.twitter.com/piatkusbooks

piatkus